More praise for I KN

MW00465547

"Amy Neswald's stories are the creations of a storytelling Hippocrates: these are the very, very rare sort of super-artful fictions that reveal . . . and also *heal.* Vulnerability, pain, beauty that makes you cry— the author doesn't merely hypnotize, she shows us the way Home. A magnificent debut." —TOM PAINE
author of *Scar Vegas* and *A Boy's Book of Nervous Breakdowns*

"Amy Neswald writes with ferocious honesty about the bonds between us and the secrets we all keep. I love a book that delivers sentence by sentence, story by story, and *I Know You Love Me, Too* is that kind of collection. It transports with lushness and brilliance." —LEWIS ROBINSON
Water Dogs and *Officer Friendly*

"Amy Neswald's story collection seem to be more than a novel. It is a full-fledged portrait, told in miniature and broad strokes, and somehow simultaneously. She's not only created indelible characters, it feels as though she's created a new form. As a writer, especially when working through, in and around the bedlam of the past year, I drew real purpose from Amy's characters as they "revive their paints," as Tom Stoppard once wrote. The spiritual connection I feel with Amy's characters has revived my paints. And that's a feeling I heartily recommend." —RICK ELICE
Tony Award-winning playwright of *Jersey Boys*

I KNOW YOU LOVE ME, TOO

AMY

NESWALD

newamericanpress

I

KNOW

YOU

LOVE

ME,

TOO

n e w a m e r i c a n p r e s s
www.NewAmericanPress.com

© 2021 by Amy Neswald

All rights reserved. No part of this publication may be reproduced,
stored in a retrieval system, or transmitted, in any form or by any
means, electronic, mechanical, photocopying, recording, or otherwise,
without the prior written permission of the copyright holder.

Printed in the United States of America

ISBN 9781941561263

Book design by Alban Fischer

"Friday Harbor" was first published in the *Saranac Review*
and "Forty-six" first appeared in *The Rumpus*.

For ordering information, please contact:
Ingram Book Group
One Ingram Blvd.
La Vergne, TN 37086
(800) 937-8000
orders@ingrambook.com

For media and event inquiries, please visit:
https://www.newamericanpress.com

FOR MY SISTERS

CONTENTS

THINGS I NEVER TOLD YOU

Security is a kind of death, I think, and it can come to you in a storm
of royalty checks beside a kidney-shaped pool in Beverly Hills or
anywhere at all that is removed from the conditions that made you an
artist, if that's what you are or were intended to be.

—TENNESSEE WILLIAMS

*In the first painting that sold, a young girl sits cross-legged on a lawn.
In her lap, a crow arches its neck, one wing spread, the other tucked,
paralyzed, at its side. Its beak, a breathtaking point of yellow-orange
against a collage of greens and grays, stretches open past a yawn
and into a howl. The bird is textured, its feathers ribs of black, its
wings, opalescent, highlighted in blues. The girl is flat, unmoving—a
paper doll cut from a cut-out book. The sky and grass are painted
in strokes and mottled splashes as if viewed through a camera lens
spotted with rain. Far in the background is a house, its perspective
skewed, flattened. Its edges are sharp, and the house is glued, like the
girl, to a world in which it does not naturally belong.*

Things I Never Told You *sold before the gallery show opened to a
well-heeled Art Collector who unlocked the gates to Ingrid Dempsey's
success. It sold before the painting was even hung.*

The Art Collector is a round man with a round face and a round
body, a study in circles. The gallery owner allows him to take the
work to his downtown apartment, where he hangs it in his foyer
for three days before committing to it. At the show's opening, a
small red dot, a sticker, marks the wall below the painting's placard,

1

and the Art Collector hovers protectively by his new acquisition, warmly discussing its virtues with whomever pauses to listen.

Four more paintings sell. Within the month, ten pieces are taken. The gallery owner retains three more for her permanent collection. In certain circles, it's not a lot of money, but for Ingrid it's enough to float her humbly for a year or so. Enough to quit her day job. She can always find another when the time comes.

She moves her easel out of her apartment and into a small artist studio in Port Morris, replacing her commute on the A train with a bike. Weekday mornings, she pedals across the Macomb's Dam Bridge and drinks bodega coffee by the East River, a block from the oil drums.

The studio windows are old pane glass, rippled with age. The walls, crumbling brick. The pipes clank; the radiators hiss steam heat. She layers three sweaters and wears fingerless gloves, a scarf wrapped around her neck. A knit cap pushes down her braids. Rikers Island floats outside her studio windows, stoic and sickly gray against the backdrop of low-flying planes landing at LaGuardia. She briefly dated a man who'd spent three months in the box at Rikers. He told her he went in an overweight alcoholic with no will to live, and emerged a straight and sober Soto Buddhist, a changed man.

It's lonely in the Bronx that first winter. She's not sure how to live her new life, devoid of the struggle she's cut her teeth on since she was young. These days, she stares at a blank canvas for hours, afraid she's run out of things to say. Sometimes, she squeezes color on her palette and mixes it with her brush and leaves it there to dry itself out. She's grown comfortable bathing in the fear of failure; she's had a lifetime to do so. But now comes the fear of success, a beast she's flirted with but has never before confronted.

She romanticizes the days she worked in her bedroom by the fire escape. She romanticizes the days she didn't have to be anything. No one knew her and no one cared. She cut evenings short and called out sick from work and sometimes locked herself in her apartment for days because she needed to paint.

Now she has time, but her zeal has waned. Thursdays through Saturday evenings are taken up with gallery openings and meetings, and she is trapped into the business of treading the treacherous, fickle waters of success. She's been instructed by her agent and others to never say no. Sundays, she meets friends or interviewers or her half-sister Kate for brunch. Sometimes Kate brings Ingrid's young nephew Pierre. Ingrid and Pierre will draw on napkins and paper placemats until Kate wrests the crayon from his hand and tells him to eat. When she meets with journalists, they never fail to notice her paint-spattered hands and how tightly her fingers wind themselves around her coffee mug. A grip that could crush bone.

In the first winter of her success, she pours a finger's worth of whiskey in her coffee in the mornings before she revives her paints. After the sun sinks down, she nips from a flask Kate gave her as a joke, engraved with the doodles she drew for her sister when she was young and Ingrid was away at college. The Daring, Darling Dempsini Sisters, Violet and Lil, stand side by side in crude lines, one balanced on her hands, the other whooping with a three-fingered wave. When Ingrid blurs her eyes, the etchings almost move. The whiskey tastes medicinal and burns going down. She doesn't like the taste, but she carries the romantic notion it will keep her warm. She worries that she will one day become a caricature of herself.

She paints a stolen past, which tumbles towards her in postcards and letters and family photos rescued from her mother's dining room drawers after she died and left her house for Ingrid to disassemble and sell.

There are days, so many of them, when Ingrid worries she's worshiped false gods. It's not that she's not happy, she is elated when she walks through the city, possessed by a pregnant secret. The secret: success is scarier than failure. It arrived too late and she doesn't know how to care for it. At forty-eight, the first year of her success, she's two years older than her father was when he died. She wonders if she waited until she outlived him to outrun him as well.

Kate takes her dress shopping a week before the gallery opening when is Ingrid still working a boutique in Park Slope, not far from her sister's house. The dress she buys costs an entire paycheck. At the gallery opening, she wears her dead mother's heels.

She doesn't tell anyone, not even Kate, that she was trying on dresses when her phone rang and the gallery owner told her *Things I Never Told You* sold for six months' worth of Ingrid's rent-stabilized rent. Not that Ingrid would see all the money, but, still. She cried huddled on a wrought-iron chair next to the dressing room mirror. Tears tumbled without force or will. She cried until the dress she was wearing was stained with tears around its collar and a saleswoman tapped on the door and asked if she needed a different size.

Ingrid unzipped the dress and hung it, front facing back, hoping the tears would dry before the saleswoman swept in.

She never told Kate about the dress or the tear stains or the phone call. The wave of dizziness—the sense of looking over the edge of a tall building or sailing on a glass-bottomed boat. But Kate knew. Somehow. She knew. Later that day, they shared a bottle of wine in the middle of the afternoon. She tells Ingrid that she walked out the dressing room surrounded by a cloud. "In a daze," Kate says. "You floated. Two inches off the ground." Kate stares at Ingrid, draped half in shadow, half in sun. "Like you'd seen a ghost."

The thing that frustrates Ingrid most about *Things I Never Told You* is that she couldn't paint the art of noise. There'd been the crow's labored breath as it looked at eight-year-old Ingrid with a calmness that came with surrender. There'd been her mother screaming and her father shouting in the background, their words muted by the brick of the house drifting across the backyard. There'd been the whisper of her rocking on the lawn, the pliant grass brushing the fabric of her sundress, young Ingrid singing parts of a prayer—the lines she remembered from Sunday school. The sound of her father driving away. She'd drawn her finger gently between the crow's eyes. Nor could she paint how the dying crow suddenly grasped for air and clawed at the distant sky and spread both its wings. It tried to fly the moment before it died.

THRUST

For the longest time, Kate's favorite painting is *Thrust*.

The piece is large, a four-foot by three-foot masterpiece painted on canvas Ingrid stretched herself, an acrobatic feat of contortion performed in the crowded living room of Ingrid's New York City apartment. It is a self-portrait.

In Thrust, the artist, eight years old, sits dwarfed in a brick-red armchair with holes worn into its upholstery. Her spindly arms push against the chair and her delicate hands grip the sides like claws as she leans hard into the chair back. On her face is an expression of abject terror and disgust, her body thrust back as if the chair is poised for takeoff. The background is intentionally flat, the painted wallpaper faded and dizzying. On her lap, a baby's stubby arms and legs stretch towards her like a monster from the deep.

The painting is modeled off a grainy photo, 110 film, a snapshot taken by Ingrid's stepmother.

Ingrid's father leaves Ingrid's mother three months before the photograph. The baby is three months old when Ingrid meets her half-sister. Aside from two strained conversations, Ingrid and her father haven't spoken in those three months. When his Buick Century, a metallic blue barge, coasts to a stop outside the house, Ingrid's mother pushes her onto the slate path and points her to the street.

Kate, who drank three glasses of chardonnay at the opening and two at dinner, sways mesmerized by the painting. She searches the canvas for clues.

"You loved me a little bit." Her words are slurred. Kate squeezes her husband's arm in a begging manner. "She loves me just a little."

Young Ingrid stares at her father from the front seat of the Buick. The vinyl of the bench seat, ghost blue, is muted by the permanent grime, years of use. As she watches him, she draws a finger along the seat's stitching, yet another hue of blue. They drive in silence until Ingrid starts humming a song. Her father flips on the radio.

When her mother announced in shrill tones that Ingrid was spending the night at her father's new house, Ingrid planned to let him know that she still wakes up every morning at six to watch the deer graze from the kitchen window, but in the car, he is a stranger; she changes her mind. She vows never to tell him anything ever again.

Her father's new house is a ranch, a single-floor sprawl with rooms extending off of rooms. The first night, she gets lost in the maze while looking for the bathroom. For the rest of her life, Ingrid remembers the new toothbrush hanging by the bathroom sink, the chemical smell of her brand-new mattress, the starched bedsheets, still creased from their packaging. A spotless doll with gleaming blonde hair in stiff recline against the pillows.

It's the first time she meets her stepmother, an uneasy woman who kneels before Ingrid and looks her up and down and says, "She doesn't look like the picture you showed me."

Her father shrugs. "She grew."

She follows her stepmother quietly through the house, unclear as to whether she is a guest or if she lives there now. She knows enough at eight years old not to say she hates the writhing baby on her lap grabbing at her hair.

The creek in the backyard is a trickle of water and the red clay mud that lines its edges holds its shape until rain melts it back into the earth. Over the summer, Ingrid pretends she's an orphaned Indian, native to the land. She forms pinch pots and decorates them with river rocks. The initial year of joint custody, Ingrid prefers the woods to the company of her overwrought stepmother and the squalling infant, her new, unwanted sister. She doesn't like the baby's innocent admiration when they lock eyes. She doesn't like its unconditional, fawning love, its constant demand for Ingrid's attention. She doesn't like the little thing at all.

"In the real photo," Kate tells her husband Brad, "Ingrid is smiling at me. In the real photo, the chair is blue. Denim blue. My mother loves blue." The gallery assistant, a fey young man so skinny Ingrid wonders how his body holds his organs, sticks a red dot below another painting placard. "What do the dots mean?"

"It means the painting's been sold."

A woman in the milling crowd cranes to look at Ingrid. Ingrid turns away. She drinks red wine until her head aches.

The gallery owner, a swan of a Modigliani, laughs with the Boteroesque Art Collector. Ingrid senses them moving towards her and pushes away through the crowd to the employee bathroom in the basement of the gallery, where she sits on the toilet lid nestled between a mop and an open case of paper towels, dizzy from drinking and the changing landscape of her life. She's wished for change every morning since she was eight, and now, here it is, murky and bright, frighteningly foggy, curt, and cold. There's comfort in knowing desire and reality will never meet. Now she's pressed up against the brick walls that separates the two, no idea what's on the other side. She sits cross-legged on the closed toilet seat, her dress hiked above her knees, her mother's silver heels empty on the floor until her sister knocks on the door and offers to drive her home. In the dim light of the basement, Kate looks like *her* mother, but kinder, surer of herself. She has the confidence of someone who's paid her dues early in life and expects clear sailing from here on out.

Ingrid recalls her stepmother's careful smile the day they met, when they were strangers sharing pieces of the same man, Ingrid rendered speechless on account of her delicate beauty. Her ski-slope nose. Her breakable cheekbones. The fragile pink of her lips. Entranced by it. Until her stepmother speaks. "Does she talk?"

"She talks," her father says. "Ingrid, say something."

When she tries to sleep in her new bed the first time, the doll's hair scratches at her neck. The baby's wailing carries through the thin walls. She swears she'll never, ever call this place home or these people family. She won't let herself love them, no matter how they might woo her. She'll never let them love her.

Of course, they leave the pouting child be.

Kate and Brad drop Ingrid off outside her apartment building and idle as she fumbles for her keys. Inside, she pauses at the bookshelf in the lobby and examines herself in the warped lobby mirror. She looks tired. She kicks off her mother's old heels, hikes her dress up, and takes the stairs two at a time to the sixth floor. She considers knocking on her neighbor's door.

Her favorite place in the building is the roof, which overlooks the Hudson. Wrapped in a sweater, she sits there until morning.

THE PIANO PLAYER

The studio is frigid in the winter and sweltering in the summer. By July, the breeze off the water is thick with humidity; industrial fans chop the air. She leaves her studio door open for the cross-breeze and drinks gin and tonics or vodka lemonade when she thinks of it, summoning the ghost of Tennessee Williams. In the afternoon, she naps on the velvet brown couch her sister passed on to her and dreams in watery colors about the parts of her life that have slipped away. And though she's happy enough to be doing what she was born to do, a part of her wonders if her life before, which seemed terminal in the midst of it, had really been all that bad. There's a flatness to life when struggle is taken away. She's been cut out of one picture and pasted onto another.

Without a set schedule, she loses track of time. She forgets to eat, and her collarbone points past her shoulders. Bones knit together beneath her skin from her neck to the top of her ribs. She paints. Tenuous connections from her previous life fray. She frets that the moment she's wished for all her life will pull back out to sea. That the undertow will drag her under.

Rikers Island skims the surface of the water, a blot on the horizon. Ingrid imagines the inmates standing on chairs—are they allowed chairs?—to peer out of the high slit windows in their cells, craving color, seeing none.

In July, *The Piano Player*, comes to her. It'll be a portrait from memory of her great-aunt who, as a young woman, played piano for the silent movies. Her aunt had been a beauty back then, but when Ingrid is growing up, aunt Rose is as wide as the piano bench she sits upon, stacks of curled and yellowed sheet music piled in small towers beneath the piano legs. She wears cat-eyeglasses, and tented house dresses. The Yamaha lid is closed and is locked down by doilies, fake flowers, and china figurines. On either side of the closed piano keyboard are matching crystal ashtrays, seldom emptied, piled with ash and cigarette butts stained with lipstick, Cherries in the Snow. Her aunt speaks in a raspy feline whisper, words struggling to escape the weight of her chest. The corners of her mouth fold into her cheeks. She dies before Kate is born, and from that time on exists only in photographs and family lore. There was the way she gently brushed Ingrid's hair when she visited. There was the time she broke the swing under the porch by sitting on it. There's how her cancer was buried so deep in the valleys of her fat and flesh that the doctors couldn't find it, even though they knew it was there. But, before the weight of an unhappy life descended upon her, her beauty had traveled across continents. Ingrid is entranced by the transient fickleness of beauty, how a person can unravel it without much effort.

During the week, the artists who work at the studios are either successful enough to survive without day jobs or committed to art above all else. They're a reclusive, intense, and solitary bunch. The weekends are rowdier. The weekend artists play music. They show one another their work. They host illegal cookouts on the roof of the building, a habit Ingrid finds teasingly unfair to the incarcerated on the island in the middle of the river. She avoids working on weekends for these reasons, though every once in a while, an idea pulls her east and she bikes to the studio, despite herself.

She sketches her memory of Aunt Rose on a Saturday, curled up on the velvet couch. Down the hall, New Orleans jazz plays on a radio. The choir of trumpets and the husky singer's voice carries alongside the weekend artists' chatter. She closes her eyes and tries to remember the smells of her great-aunt's apartment. Must, boiled cabbage, stale candy ribbon, cigarettes, Clean Green.

The Piano Player, is considered a masterpiece of Ingrid Dempsey's early style, one of her most tragically enticing celebrations. Her aunt, oval upon oval upon oval, a rounded pyramid, reaches for the piano keys, a cigarette dangling from her lip, painted in Cherries in the Snow, a glimmer of faded beauty sublimely planted in every stroke.

As Ingrid channels her obese aunt, her succulent swirls of fat, the density of her eyelids, there's a quick rap on her open door. She summons her aunt's catlike grin.

The first word Adam says to her is, "Hey," in a half-whisper from the open studio door. "Sorry to bother you."

"Yes?" Ingrid allows herself to respond with luxurious ennui.

She's seen him before, of course, in passing. He's an abstract artist. His head bobs when he talks. His fists press into his front pockets. Somehow, there's always three days' worth of stubble on his chin. He's much, much younger than Ingrid. Decades younger and part of her is jealous that he, and others, have found their way to the studios, to their medium, to believing in themselves. At the same age, she languished in a string of retail jobs, wandering the woods.

"You're not usually here on weekends."

"No."

He rubs his hands against the legs of his jeans, scratches the back of his neck. "It's just that we're having a cookout on the roof later, if you want to join."

"I don't think so," she says. "I'm not staying. And I have nothing to bring."

"Okay." He shrugs. He hooks his thumbs over his belt. His head bobs harder, wider. "Doesn't matter. Bring yourself."

"I'll think about it." She means to dismiss him with a gentle nod, but he steps into her studio and kneels by a painting on the floor. "Don't judge unfinished work."

Around six, she wanders up to the roof. Someone's rigged speakers and slow jazz skims the East River. She wonders if the men at Rikers hear the music through their slat windows. Adam hands her a beer. She stays longer than she means to. Around midnight, he leans in to kiss her. She stops him with a hand to his chest.

"I'm a lot older than you."

He pauses, smiles. "Doesn't matter," he whispers and kisses her anyway.

✳

The thing Ingrid fears most happens. She has more blank canvases than painted ones. She's run out of things to say. She blames this on contentment.

For her birthday, Adam buys soggy blueberry muffins from the corner bodega. Instead of candles, he lights two cigarettes and pushes them into the muffin tops, the smoke peeling off in ribbons. She pours the last of the whiskey into their coffees. He presses against her at the window as a barge slogs by.

"I'm so much older than you," she says.

"Don't you get it?" he said. "I don't care."

A sister gallery in London is set to display her paintings. She's part of a group show in New York as well. She's used her influence to gain entry into the show for Adam's work. She feels good about that.

But the blank canvases haunt her. At night, she wraps herself around Adam, rests her head on his chest and wishes he were old enough, experienced enough, smart enough to see through her. But success is unchartered territory for both of them, and he's as lost as she. For weeks, she forces herself to paint the view outside her studio windows and the crumbling bricks inside. She waits for the ghosts that make her work famous in certain circles to return. She fears they've abandoned her, that in six months she'll be thrust back into the world of retail. Sink, swim, or tread water. The sun cuts its way across the facade of Rikers. Now, she realizes, the real work begins.

She doesn't tell her sister about Adam. She keeps her fears secret, too. Instead, when she meets Kate for coffee on Sundays, she tempers her quivering voice and lets the heat from her coffee mug run through her palms. She practices stillness. When Pierre's with them, she makes up stories to tell him. She memorizes the feeling of having outlived her father, dead for more than half her life, and masters the nuances of being half-connected to her half-sister, who knows a little less than half of the happenings in Ingrid's life.

The gallery owner insists this is the beginning, that Ingrid's voice, her palette, and her perspective are things the world, teetering on insanity, needs. But Ingrid wonders how long a beginning can be. Her window paintings, dreary, dull, repetitive, sky, water, Rikers Island, sometimes the red barge, don't feel like they're helping anyone step into another world. They are as carelessly lifeless as she is. A prisoner of a limited life set free. Afraid to move beyond the boundaries of her open cell. Left to fend for herself. Then she touches Adam's shoulder, or he takes her hand, and she feels like maybe everything will work out after all.

The Window Series is a departure from Ingrid Dempsey's previous, earthbound works, though reminiscent in them is the theme of separateness, of withdrawal. They're considered a celebration of otherness; the brackish waters of the East River are swirled with oily blues. Rikers in the distance, reimagined as a once-great kingdom, fallen into disrepair.

The Art Collector chooses a second Ingrid Dempsey piece from *The Windows Series* for his Hudson Valley home. He requests that Ingrid herself hang it. Though he only buys one of *The Windows* series, he's considering two more, by and by, to hang in broken rows. In this painting, Rikers is a floating rib of a city. Barges wrinkle time, abstract smears, oranges and reds, smash the palette of gray.

"I can't go." The thought of entertaining a stranger in his own house makes her nauseous. "They want me to be a dancing bear. I won't do it."

"We'll go together," Adam says. "You're the talent, I'm the muscle."

"I mean, really?"

"He admires you. We all do. Ingrid, you have no idea what you are, do you?"

"Oh, I have an idea," she said. "I've plenty of ideas about what I am."

The gallery ships the painting. Ingrid and Adam follow on the train.

They walk from the station through the town center, a quaint village with a vegetable stand, a café, and proud, stunted houses.

The Art Collector meets them at his door. His hands, ripe, ready fruit, swallow hers. His red sweater pulls the eye to the red in his face blotches of rosacea. His red wine looks purple in the glass.

"We finally meet, my dear." His voice is deceptively quiet, deceptively kind. "And who's this long, tall drink of water?"

"Adam Jones." Adam holds out his hand to shake.

"He's an artist, too."

"Hmmm? And what else? So handsome."

Adam blushes and hangs his head, bashful. Nervous laughter. Ingrid knows then that she'll never get tired of his laugh.

The Art Collector's husband, wiry and flat, stands just beyond the French doors, swirling a glass of white. "Ignore him. He's a flirt. Old man, be good."

"Well, art does not only exist in the abstract."

Adam's cheeks bloom further, beneath his three-day stubble. "Oh, now."

"Calm down, tiger."

The art collector says, "To me, art is a drug, better than heroin or whatever people are taking now. I find, when I purchase a painting, my life changes. Every time."

His melancholic husband nods ruefully. "Yes. We eat ramen for the rest of the year."

Rueful, Ingrid thinks.

The husband lights a joint he's been palming in his hand.

"Medical," the Art Collector says. "Medicinal. It keeps the weight on. John, where are your manners? Offer them some."

John squeezes another puff. "I'll get them the good stuff."

"It's a nasty habit, smoke." The Art Collector motions for the joint. "But it keeps you young."

"Young or mummified, sweet Stephen?" John leans back into the sofa, his wine refreshed, a fresh joint lit in the vee of his fingers.

The Art Collector exhales an endless stream of smoke. "We've been together for fourteen years. John's going to outlive us all."

"God help me. You'll haunt this place before you'd leave. I said 'til death do us part. We'll see how that works out."

"God help us all. But I do love this house."

Holding Ingrid's face in both his hands, Adam kisses the top of her brow. "I think we'll be fine here," he mutters in her ear.

She finds she likes it when he says "we."

"We'll hang the painting after dinner." The Art Collector leads them inside.

The house is smaller than she expected. The Art Collector's taste is impeccable and Ingrid tells him so. She recognizes his works from artists she's met. In the corners, on the tables, castings and sculptures: a bust of a one-eyed man, a gathering of sticks in a peeling birch pot, a vaguely organic, child-like ooze of clay dripping off a child's chair.

There's a baby grand in the living room, polished to a blinding black. Ingrid brushes her fingers along the keys. She leaves a fingerprint only Adam sees. She wipes at it with a corner of her shirt. A key plinks, sharp and resonant, and the sound lingers.

"Do you play?" The Art Collector spins around. The tenor of his voice wraps around the resounding softness. Ingrid wishes she knew how to paint that sound, the movement of sound.

"My stepmother used to. And my half-sister. She was good. Really good." Until Kate's mother called Ingrid when she was fresh out of college, figuring out life in the city. "Stop encouraging my daughter to be a musician," she'd said, "I don't want her to live like you." At the time, the telephone call felt like a slap, but Kate had done quite well without the yoke of artistry, hadn't she? She'd survived her fatherless adolescence and emerged far more functional than Ingrid. And still, somehow Ingrid feels like she's failed Kate. That feeling will never go away. "She didn't do anything with it."

"John is a concert pianist, some of the time. When he *feels* like it." The Art Collector rolls his eyes, but then smiles. "I love him. A little too much. Love is like that; it's hard to get the measurements just right."

While her little half-sister drills Chopin and hammers away at Joplin, Ingrid draws. It's the one thing she shares with her father. On weekends when Kate and her mother are away at whatever activity Kate is engaged in—dancing, singing, gymnastics, anything but art—Ingrid and her father sketch at the kitchen table. She watches him paint in his study. When they eat at the diner, both of them doodle faces on the paper placemats as Kate watches wistfully and Ingrid's step-mother frowns. Ingrid arranges leaking tubes of oils in his paint tray. She learns to love the smell. For the longest time, until she outlives him, she sticks with charcoal and ink before moving on to sculpture, pottery, collage, photography, leaving painting, the laying on of color, to him.

Until she met Adam, she moved through men in much the same way.

Dinner lasts past midnight, after which Adam teeters barefoot on the sofa, joking that, drunk and stoned, they'll need to either straighten the painting, or the sofa, the next morning.

"It's perfectly pitched," the Art Collector says. "Though I wouldn't mind watching you hang it for the rest of the night."

John bangs out a ragtime tune, then a ballad. The Art Collector hums along. "How can I not love this man." He sits on the bench as John plays, the two of them pulsing, the room pulsing. Everything pulsing. Ingrid is drunk.

At two, sleep made fitful by wine, Adam pulls Ingrid out of bed. They sneak through the kitchen and out to the backyard, where they watch for shooting stars and make love on the wooden floor of the gazebo.

"I think I love you."

"You don't love me," she says. "You love the me you think I am."

"I think you love me, too."

"Not at all," she whispers.

They leave on a slow train in the morning. Adam has a splinter in his thumb and they work on it, heads bowed, with the end of a ballpoint pen. As they roll backwards alongside the Hudson, she wishes she knew how to paint that moment, too, but the next morning, back in her studio, all that come to mind are crows, brick, and Rikers Island.

She'll dig through her photos soon. She'll look for something new.

NORMAL; REALITY *or* SOMETHING LIKE LOVE

It could've been any number of nights, but Ingrid knows it was at the Art Collector's house that she became pregnant. The stars. The hardwood. Crickets. Fireflies. The dampness of the grass when they tiptoed back inside. After the trip, she's chased by a melancholy she can't outrun.

She doesn't tell Adam. She doesn't tell anyone. There's no need to. She's forty-eight and ill-prepared to have a child. She doesn't need anyone to argue otherwise.

The night before her appointment to terminate the pregnancy, she wakes with cramps. Doubled over, she pulls herself to the bathroom. Adam, half-asleep, stumbles after her and hands her Advil. He rubs her neck until she sends him back to bed. It's early on into the pregnancy, four weeks at most. She's shown no signs, other than exhaustion. She doesn't let on the bleeding is anything other than her normal period. Adam wouldn't know enough to suspect otherwise. He's young. So young.

For weeks after, Ingrid is split in two by a mercurial sadness. Someone has sucker-punched her heart. True, she hadn't wanted the baby, but that the unnamed thing between them wasn't even viable destroys her. She lays a blank canvas, one he stretched for her, on her studio floor. She scores the fabric with a mat knife. She burns it with cigarette embers. She faces away from Rikers and paints without a plan. Without a stolen memory. She paints in broad strokes and confesses her confusion, her vulnerability, in vibrant reds and oranges. She releases the inherent sadness of her success.

She lets Adam love her.

There's something in the conversation she had with the Buddhist who'd spent time at Rikers that haunts her. He'd said he'd walked through fire two times in his life and both feared and relished the prospect of the third time, which he was sure would soon occur. It did.

They had three dates, but only spoke twice. Ingrid spent their third date in his hospital room. He'd had a motorcycle accident, followed by a stroke, and sat twisted in a chair while a physical therapist flexed and pointed his feet. She'd gone to the hospital because she needed to see, amazed at the brevity of their romance. She'd liked him.

"He's not aware of anything," the therapist said. "That we know of."

Her Aunt Rose once told her that the soul was made up of thousands of tiny birds that resided in the heart. They scattered when a trauma occurred. A person remained shattered if the birds lost their way home.

The Buddhist's entire flock was lost. But he smiled a lopsided smile, his head listing to the right, his muscles slack. He cooed as the therapist worked his toes.

Broken, but happy, she thought.

He didn't recognize her. She didn't think he would, but he faced her with such strange purity that she gasped for the love of it, the tragedy of it, the strangeness of their moment of connection. She wondered, *Did a bird just find its way home?*

A few weeks after the miscarriage, she still feels she's swimming against the tide. Adam knows her well enough to give her space. Her doctor calls her back for tests and then more tests on account of an abnormality. She mixes her oils thick and smears them on her canvas with a spatula. She carves the paint with a sculpting knife.

At the group show, Ingrid is giddy about two things: that her influence guaranteed Adam a spot in the show, and that there's an unheard message waiting for her from her doctor. She watches Adam from the middle of the room as he jokes with the Art Collector and his husband. Adam's painting, silvers and browns, a pirate's ship stranded on the moon, is luminous. He's grown so much. Ingrid thinks it's brilliant and hopes someone with money agrees.

Kate brushes her shoulder. "Brad couldn't make it. Stuck at work."

"Have you seen the painting?"

Normal; Reality *is an abstract, one of Ingrid Dempsey's first. Blood-red cuts oceanic blues in a violent swirl. There is an uncanny sense of motion, of flight, as a thick raking of black swoops to the corner of the canvas. There is a breathtaking point of yellow-orange, a beak. A crow.*

"It's so different . . . I don't understand," Kate gasps. She's taken, anyway.

Adam rests his hand on Ingrid's shoulder and kisses her above her ear. Kate's eyes widen, as if she's finally been let in on a secret.

"You must be Kate," Adam says.

"Who are you? Who's this? My sister never tells me anything. You never tell me anything. God." Kate turns back to the painting. "The red vibrates, the black, it's –"

"A song," Adam says.

"A prayer."

After her ovarian biopsy, Ingrid refuses painkillers. She takes only a local anesthetic. She wants to feel everything, the prodding and sharp sting where the surgical scissors snipped. She concentrates on the noises in the room, the rustling of scrubs, the hum of the air conditioner, the cars outside. She paints them in the dark canvas of her mind. At a moment of near quiet, while the doctor's out of the room, a swooping whisper brushes her face, the wings of a flying crow. Despite her discomfort, despite the pain, despite her worry that she isn't worried, she feels happy.

She'd wavered on the title of her piece. She'd settled for *Normal; Reality.* She wished she'd been brave enough to call it something like: *Love.*

TOLERANCE OF METAL, 1980

Hank first noticed the tear in the hinge of the mailbox on Thursday. August twenty-first. 1980. Eight months into the new decade. Four months since his father died. Six weeks since his mother's stroke. Ten days before the beginning of the school year. Autumn teased the edges of the maple leaves. The hinge had rusted and the tear cut across the edge of the box. It whined with a jagged, piercing, keening cry. To Hank, it sounded like a paper cut. Or a thought cut short.

He was waiting for *papers*. Divorce papers. From Deb. She no longer wished to be married. He stood at the edge of the drive of his parent's house, the house he'd grown up in, the house he'd moved back to, and watched the mail truck tool down the street. His father had died in May and his mother lived at the nursing home in the converted Victorian on the Post Road; his parents' bedroom still smelled of sick and he couldn't bring himself to sleep on their bed. Nor could he sleep in his boyhood room, where memories— those eight-legged monsters—skittered over the painted walls. Not childhood memories, either. He could've lived with those, but memories of nights in Korea. The sound of Mikey Dolan's laughter with his stomach torn open. Tom Gunn weeping for his mother. Hank's father tsking, then sighing, then yelling, telling him to let it go. As if he understood how the cold in the mountain shattered metal. Shattered bone. Froze souls. Froze smoke. Froze hauntingly delicate nothings.

No. He slept in the living room, his mother's balls of knitting yarn still piled in the wicker basket. The newspaper she'd been read-ing when the blood clot blocked her brain was splayed open on the living room floor. He kept his clothes folded in a large suitcase by the television.

The thing about moving back into the house he grew up in was the dirty fissure, the uneven weld between now and all the thens. There were the *young thens* when he'd been little and full of promise. There were *middle thens*, when he'd learned blacksmithing at his uncle's shop, the sparks sneaking down the collars of his shirts, no matter how covered up he was. A confetti of white scars, stars, mottled his neck and chest. He'd stopped working with fire after Korea. The heat reminded him too much of the burning cold of the mountains. The hammering of metal became gunshots. The furtive sparks and smell of scorched skin mingled with the memory of trench foot, the stink of gangrene, ugly, creeping rot. Bodies melting, inch by inch.

He missed his old house, where he and Deb lived. One town past, the *affordable* town. That was a small house with a small yard that contained the small memories they had made in eight years of marriage. Mundane memories. A failed attempt at adopting a dog. Autumn nights outside, smoking at the fire pit. A few too many beers at the kitchen table with Deb's friends from work. The nights that Hank woke up screaming from nightmares she stroked his back and whispered him to sleep. He liked how she whispered his name.

Over the summer, he visited his mother every day. At lunch, he spooned soft foods, potatoes and pudding, into her mouth, like she'd done for him when he was a baby, in that blessed time before memories and dreams. He didn't know if she recognized him, but she knew him, anyway. A sense of comfort. No more words. He loved her, despite her absence of self. Perhaps he loved her even more now that she was vulnerable and fading, her worry hushed into a whisper. There was nothing for her to worry about. It'd all finally happened and she seemed at peace.

Still, he was looking forward to the beginning of the school year when the students would filter in to his metal shop and bend sheet metal into boxes. Gusts of concentration as they measured the tolerance of metal, the clutching embrace of a bolt. The clank of the press brake, bending metal. The snarl of files gripping burrs. Jigsaws. Dremel drills. Unsteady hands. Every year on the first day of class, he held up his stumped thumb. The girls shivered and looked away. The boys stared and sometimes laughed as their own thumbs folded into their palms, hidden and hugged by their fingers.

A part of him feared that *the papers* had materialized in his school mailbox, that they were resting in the slot of his cubbyhole in the office, that someone would see the fine linen envelope with his wife's lawyer's address and know before he told them that the 'we' had become 'he'. Not that there was any shame in that.

Otherwise, he couldn't figure out *why* the papers were taking so long, since Deb told him *any day now* when he ran into her at the Stop & Shop. She'd caught up with him in the fruit aisle and stopped him with a gentle hand to his shoulder. Hank had been overwhelmed by the scent of oranges and the puckered fists of Mcintosh apples. Her voice echoed, hollow as a fading memory, a song in a dream. Too often lately his mind felt like an empty metal box, hard fabric folded around a cube of nothing. His platoon-mates had nicknamed him "Tin Man" in bootcamp. Even his name, Hank, had a metallic ring to it when certain people said it. But not Debbie. She spoke in muted tones, maroon and forest green. He loved how she said his name. But at school, it was different. Mrs. Traten in the principal's office, for instance. And one of the nurses at the nursing home. At the grocery, Deb's chin had puckered into a walnut when Hank simply nodded. He'd forgotten to ask how *the papers* would be delivered. Would he find them folded into the pages of a supermarket circular or would she swing by the house, or maybe even the high school, and interrupt his class with her knuckle tapping the glass window in the door? Would she push them across the table with one long, coral-colored nail? Or would a faceless stranger stop him in the street? He'd seen it done once that way on *Dallas* or *General Hospital* or some such show.

The collar of his shirt pressed against his Adam's apple and the afternoon had turned airless. Summer's last gasp. A single envelope lay on the floor of the mailbox. Two corners curled, two corners drooped. The envelope itself was saturated and spent in the New England humidity, as formless as a soaked sock.

No return address. He didn't recognize the looped curls of cursive. Nor did he know anyone in Bend, Oklahoma, where the letter had been postmarked with a round, fading stamp. He feared it contained depressing news, perhaps the death of one of his platoon buddies. But they'd returned from Korea decades ago. No one thought of anyone anymore, except for the dead who crept into dreams. On second look, he saw that the envelope was addressed to his father *Henry Day*. Perhaps it was from an old lover, thinking of him as she passed away. Perhaps it was from a secret sibling. Whoever sent the letter was not alone in being unaware of his father's death. There were still calls from credit card companies and charities soliciting donations. Bills still came for Henry Day.

Hank carried the letter in open palms back to the house like he might hold a dying moth. Or a bird. Or a butterfly.

He stared at the envelope a good long while as he drank cold coffee at the kitchen table. He allowed his finger to trace the curves and bends of his father's name and felt the slight grit where the pen had pressed hard into the paper, tore the fibers with its uncertain insistency. The address was written in black ballpoint and he imagined the person behind it, a woman unused to sending mail, middle-aged, deliberate and quiet and slow. He saw her biting her bottom lip as she wrote. It wasn't bad news in the envelope, he decided, but it wasn't good news, either. There was only the slightest chance that that which the envelope contained would change the course of his day: mother, garden, dying flower bed,

T.V. Guide, television. He supposed that he should go to the high school sooner or later to set up his classroom, sweep the floors, replace dull blades, dig out his patterns for the year, or perhaps cut new ones . . . Some teachers had already begun preparing for the new year. Some windows were already thrown open. Some pin boards decorated with photos of Mozambique and Kurt Vonnegut and plastic soda bottles bobbing in the ocean. By now, Mrs. Traten's office plants were climbing the shelves and brushing against her chicken bone ankles. Mr. Jonas was setting up easels in the drawing studio, sketching the trees outside the classroom windows. Rumor had it he occupied the classroom throughout the summer to use as his own private studio. Mr. Jonas was one of those understated types, quiet of voice, white beard that used to be ginger when Hank had been a student in that high school.

He supposed he should open his father's letter though there'd be no harm if he set it on fire or buried it unopened in the overgrown garden. He wiped butter off the butter knife and slid it into the seam of the envelope. His hand shook as he did. It still felt strange to open his father's mail.

The letter was folded in three on flimsy notebook paper, torn away from its coiled metal binding. A line of lopsided hearts framed the margins. *With LOVE all things are possible.* Hank wasn't sure about that. Hadn't he loved Deb? Hadn't she loved him? Hadn't they stood in front of family and friends in his parents' backyard— another crammed-in memory—and declared that love outwardly for all to hear—in sickness and in health? And hadn't his parents endured sixty years of marriage only to be separated at their most vulnerable, when love mattered most? It seemed to him that love had an expiration date. It went bad if it wasn't completely con-sumed. It soured or rotted or grew mold.

This letter has been sent to you for good luck.

God Dammit.

A chain letter.

He didn't have to send it on. He knew he didn't. It was addressed to his father. What was bad luck to a person who was already dead? His mother was sinking into the pillows of her nursing home bed, her skin retreating, her skull ripping through the shredded muscles of her face. Where the heck was luck when a person lay dying? Slowly dying, in excruciating increments.

Luck is the lock. Love is the THE KEY.

Should he turn his back on luck? He'd inherited the house with all its quirks in a town that out-priced him. There were renovations he wanted to complete by next summer. There were taxes he barely could afford and those would only go up—unless he got lucky. With a little luck, a side gig, a raise, maybe things could work. With a little luck, maybe Deb would change her mind. Or maybe he'd meet someone new. *Good luck*, Deb said at the Stop & Shop. She said it instead of goodbye. *Good luck* murmured like an apology just under her breath. A muffled muted sound. *Good luck.* He could barely hear himself think these days. Metal folded around nothing. A tin man had no heart, but he still felt pain.

The letter'd been started by Captain Curtis Bray of the Scottish Royal Army and had been around the world nine times, the letter declared. Hank tried to imagine the person who counted its revolutions. Watched it spool across the equator, choking the middle of the earth where the heart should be.

Still, it was Hank's dead father's responsibility to see the letter spread. And what falls on the father falls, eventually, on the child.

With LOVE all things are possible.

He found a pad of paper in his father's office, stacked beneath a chipped college mug stuffed with old drink stirrers, palm trees and mermaids. The envelopes were shoved in the desk's top drawer. There were no stamps in the drawers or the slots of his mother's secretary desk. Nor did he find any in the kitchen junk drawer. In his parents' dresser drawer, he unearthed two ballpoint pens with chewed-up caps, two dried-out felt tip markers, and his father's high school fountain pen. Back in his father's office, he filled the bladder of the pen with ink.

He considered driving to the high school to use the ditto machine, but Mrs. Traten might find the top sheet and trace it back to him. No. He'd hand write the ten clones that held hope hostage. After all, Frederick Harris of New Zealand received the letter and sent off his ten copies and won one hundred thousand dollars in the lottery, but Misty Stenapoulous threw the letter away and suffered a mental breakdown that left her in the hospital for six weeks. Betty Williams crashed her car when she forgot to mail the letters, but her husband found them and put them in the mail and met someone new. William Garland didn't send the letter on. He died.

Hank Day received the letter, which was addressed to his dead father and in the face of inertia and a ubiquitous sense of dread, a symptom of life, he decided that good luck was worth the cost of ten stamps and a hamburger and French fries from the Friendly's by his mother's nursing home. He picked up stamps at the post office, slid into a booth at Friendly's and prepared to write.

The Friendly's on Route 1 was forcefully red and aggressively cheery. Rows of booths stemmed from tracks that only the waitresses could walk down. They were dead-ends to the maze. They served square hamburgers on round buns. The place was quiet when he got there at two. One woman sat in a booth facing Hank's. She was pretty, he thought. His age, give or take. It was hard to tell, but her face was a little drawn, her hair pulled back in a barrette like the girls used to do in the sixties. She was talking to the waitress, high school aged. Hanks was sure the waitress had been in his class. He remembered thinking something about her. Maybe that she had good hands or a good eye. Maybe he thought that she'd one day build fine, beautiful things. The waitress breathed through her mouth, so many of them did. Her teeth were clamped together with tiny rubber bands, but her lips barely folded over her braces. The woman glanced up. Caught him staring. He tried to smile, but only one side of his lips curled up anymore. The other sometimes twitched and sometimes stretched sideways a tiny bit, but mostly it stayed frozen in place. Her eyes drooped to half-mast. She looked away. Hank flattened the letter and ironed it with the palm of his hand. He set out the writing pad. Uncapped his father's fountain pen.

The waitress wore a blue smock over her houndstooth jumper. Her hair was tied in a low ponytail. She hovered as Hank flipped through the menu, her pen poised over her pad. Her name tag was crooked on the lapel of her shirt. *Ingrid*. He remembered her. A quiet girl who stared out the window and understood the bendable nature of metal. Once, he'd seen her lay her cheek against the edge of the metal lockers in the school hallway and stay that way, lost in a dream until there was an indent from her temple down to the edge of her jaw.

"Hi, Mr. Day." Slight lisp.

Hank glanced up from the menu.

She smiled broadly, her metal braces catching her lip. "How's your summer? I tried to sign up for metal shop again, but they won't let girls take advanced."

Hank grunted, nodded, and sighed.

The woman in the booth thumbed through a magazine, licking the tip of her index finger before she turned each page. She smoked a cigarette and poked at her cold burger. She watched Ingrid. "Is that your mom? She looks like you."

"Yeah," Ingrid said. "I have a stepmom, too. They like to fight about who likes me less. Would you like a cup of clam chowder to start?"

This was the longest conversation he'd had with her. The longest he'd had with anyone since summer began. He didn't want her to leave. He re-opened the menu and glanced down the page. "Sounds good."

"You get a chain letter?" She set down a straw and soup spoon.

"I don't know who to send it to."

"People you don't like," she said. "Or maybe people you don't know." There was a darkness about her that Hank didn't remember. "Use a phone book. One from a different state."

"Good tip." He unwrapped the straw, but there was no cup to put it in. He laid it naked on the napkin.

"I'll bring you a Coke, too."

Low in the background, an Olivia Newton-John song played. He knew that song. Deb hummed it when she cleaned. Ingrid's mother slid from the booth and disappeared to the ladies' room. Hank's loneliness swirled into the swathe of the stark red walls and the eye burning lights. The chimes above the front door clinked, junk metal painted to look like brass. A family of three walked in.

The father wore glasses with heavy black frames. His forehead was wide and there was a frankness about him. The wife was slight, her face small and slightly pained, bothered. The daughter, however, was luminous. Fragile and kind, the type of child dolls were modeled after. She craned her neck and pulled against her mother's grip until she was free. She ran to a booth and slid in and waved at Ingrid, who'd arrived back at Hank's table, ready to take his order.

"Oh boy." Ingrid whispered just below her breath, a soft whistle of a sigh.

"I'd like a hamburger."

"Okay."

"Medium rare. Fries."

"Hold on." Ingrid hustled up one aisle and across to the next. She pointed her finger to the corner closest to the entrance. "You guys should sit over there." The little girl reached her arms over the barrier and cinched them around Ingrid's middle.

"Really, Ingrid," the woman said, "it's time for you to get a better job. At a clothing shop. Or an office. Learn skills you can use. There are food stains down your front."

"She's working," the man said. "She's my working girl." He was proud of her.

"Dad, please."

It happened so fast, the abrupt shift of Ingrid's mother's face as she emerged from the ladies' room. She stopped in her tracks, took one step back and slid into Hank's booth, right across from him. He hadn't even begun writing the letters, though the pen was uncapped and in his hands. Ink leaked from the nib of the pen onto the sides of his fingers. She rested her chin on her hand and grinned. Intently.

Was he supposed to say something? He wasn't sure. He shrugged instead. She tilted her head to the side. He cleared his throat and poised the pen just above the pad. When Ingrid brought the burger, the woman clutched her daughter's arm. "Cigarettes. Darling. Please." Her face was turned insistently away from both Ingrid and the family.

Ingrid crept to her mother's table and walked back with her pack, her lighter, and her purse.

"Thank god," her mother muttered. "Ashtray, Ingrid. Sweetie. Love."

With LOVE all things are possible.

Leaning in on both elbows, she bit the filter of her cigarette and waited for Hank to light it. Like in the movies, Hank thought. Like on T.V. For a moment he wondered if *the papers* would be slipped to him like a secret document below the table. He'd seen that once. On *Charlie's Angels*, maybe. Or maybe *Magnum, P.I.*

She blew smoke to the side. "Meredith," she said and held out her hand palm down. He took it and shook. Ingrid glanced at them from the register. "You're at the high school."

"Metal arts."

"I remember you."

Hank didn't believe her, but he blushed, anyway.

"Ingrid liked that class. She made a box or something. With a sliding lid."

"We make boxes."

The family at the other table shifted in their seats. The woman's fragile hands folded into each other. The girl colored her paper placemat with broken crayons. The man, the husband, the father gawked at Hank and Meredith for a moment.

"What else do you do? What's this?" Meredith placed her finger on the chain letter and stared at Hank in a way that made him very uncomfortable. "You don't believe in these things, do you?"

He shrugged again. The corner of his mouth, the corner that didn't usually move, twitched. "Could use some luck."

She pursed her lips. Considered him. Dug into her purse and pulled out a pen. "I'll help." She tore a few sheets from his pad. Hank stared until she said, "Get writing. I'm not doing *all* of them. And then they started in.

"Who's that," the little girl said, but Hank refused to look up from the page. Meredith lit another cigarette. She took a French fry from his plate. His neck was warm and he wished he still smoked. He thought he should smoke. He took one from her pack and lit it with her lighter. It was like breathing the heat from his uncles blacksmithing forge and reminded him of the joy of hammering a seemingly immutable substance into something new. *With LOVE all things are possible*, he wrote.

"Kate, shh," the mother, the stepmother, Hank gathered, hissed in a way that cut through the sounds of the kitchen, the muzak, the clank of silverware, the rumbling of the ice machine, and the pens scratching the surface of paper. Meredith's shoulders raised slightly as she wrote and she tilted her head and sometimes chewed the inside of her lip. Ingrid entered and exited the periphery of his vision as she moved between tables. A few more people came in. Time slowed. He watched Meredith's pen move from one side of the paper to the next. Somewhere in there, for a moment or two, he fell in love.

Then he dropped his cigarette on the red vinyl of the seat. It burned a perfect hole.

"Hey. Don't get my kid in trouble." Meredith slapped his arm. Her eyes widened.

He wiped the ash to the floor. She smiled, so he smiled. She laughed, so he laughed, too.

"I once saw a fat man here." She leaned in, a conspiratorial hush in her voice. "A really fat guy. But he was good-looking. He had a calm. You know the type?"

Hank didn't, but he said he did.

"He took up the whole booth and part of his stomach rested on the table. He ordered a twenty scoop ice cream sundae. Twenty scoops."

"Twenty scoops?"

She lit two cigarettes and handed one to him. "He ate it. All of it. Slowly, too. Spoonful by spoonful. Small spoon. You'd think for the size of the bowl they'd give him a bigger spoon. A soup spoon, but no. He ate until the bowl was empty."

He didn't know why she was telling him this, but he could picture, almost like a memory, the man and his sundae. Clean-shaven. Pressed shirt. Tie tossed over his shoulder so it wouldn't catch a stain. How cold that spoon must've been. Hank imagined him as a sort of hero.

"The whole place was watching him. Couldn't look away. We were rooting for the guy. Though some might wonder what would make anyone order a twenty scooper. Not a drip on his shirt, either. Utterly graceful. He smoked while he ate. A spoon in one hand, a cigarette in the other. He dropped the last butt into the almost-empty bowl." She stubbed her cigarette out. She was really pretty.

Hank wondered if he should ask her out. "Sometimes I imagine what it'd be like to eat a twenty scooper. What flavors did he order?"

"All of them, I guess." Meredith laughed again, but really laughed this time. The family at the other end of the restaurant bore down on their ice cream sundaes, mere double scoops in tall glasses. They only looked at each other. Ingrid leaned against the register and pretended not to care.

He ordered French fries, extra salt, and a vanilla shake to go. In his mother's room, he spooned first sweet, then salt for her as she lay propped up in bed, eyes closed, pressing soft food into the palate of her mouth. He told his mother about the fat man with his twenty scoops of ice cream, his tie tossed over his shoulder, a pack of cigarettes on the table by the ashtray. Hank gave him a silver lighter etched with his initials, and a spoon that had bent beneath the weight of its profession. Maybe, Hank thought, the man knew that people were watching. Maybe he felt beholden to his secret audience. Maybe he needed them.

One of her hands gripped the metal bar of the bed. She lay there dying, slowly dying, a victim of love, unaware of almost everything. The letters in their envelopes were crammed into the creases of the seat cushions in his car. He'd go to the library tomorrow. He'd open a phone book. He'd choose random people. He'd bend the hinge of the mailbox and hammer it back into place. In the afternoon, he'd send the letters off.

LUCKY

On their last trip to Ace Hardware, Kate ran her hand along pendulums of lucky rabbit feet at the register. She slid a pink one off the display and squeezed it into her fist. The fur tickled her palm, made it itch. Itchy palms meant money, her grandma Dempsey told her a while back in her thick European accent. Coated with seventy years of three packs a day, her words twisted around themselves like rusted metal. Kate barely understood what she was saying, but she pretended to and nodded. "She's an agreeable child," her grandmother sometimes muttered. Kate understood that.

The hair on the underbelly of the rabbit paw was feathery, softer than the straight hairs on top. Around the twisted rabbit toenails, the hair was hardest of all and stuck out in angry angles. The wrist of the foot was jammed into a junk-metal cap painted to look like brass.

Down the hardware aisle, her father squinted over a rusted bolt in his hand, comparing it to the large collection of unsullied bolts in hardware store drawers. His glasses, black-rimmed and heavy, slid down his nose.

In the years to come, she'd remember those glasses and his smile when she tried to bring him to mind. The glasses cut his face like black paint or magic marker. She rarely saw him without them; it was jarring when she did. He looked so vulnerable. She'd remember his smile, too, because it looked like hers.

His head was lowered. The skin of his scalp was white at his part, his hair as dark as hers. His face was sallow gold, unlike hers, and lay slack over his sagging cheekbones. She closed her eyes and tried to hear him breathe.

She had a plan. While her father consulted the store worker, a white-haired man whose stomach pushed at the buttons on his red vest like the skin of an overripe tomato, she'd slide the rabbit's foot up her sleeve, then lower her arm and shake it into her jacket pocket. But a cashier appeared. A bent stick of a boy about the same age as her half-sister, Ingrid.

"You buying that?" His lips were too large for his face and their color matched the acne welts that lined his chin. She paid for the rabbit's foot with her allowance while her father was distracted.

On Monday, at school, she'd tell Maddie she'd lifted it. Maddie'd made fun of her the previous weekend when she tried to teach Kate how to shoplift at the Hallmark store and all Kate pocketed was a Fireball, a candy she didn't even like. Still, she'd popped it in her mouth like a triumph and then spit it into her hand when it got too hot while Maddie howled, holding her sides, bending over, laughing on the sidewalk. Maddie made off with a pair of necklaces, two halves of a heart that fit together. She kept one for herself and clasped the other around Kate's neck. The junk metal charm and chain turned Kate's skin black, but she wore it to school, hidden beneath her shirt.

The cashier folded the rabbit foot into a small paper bag. As her father approached, Kate crammed it into the front pocket of her knapsack. The tips of her ears burned and she wandered off towards the entrance so her father wouldn't see. She felt guilty, like she'd been caught, though she hadn't had the chance to do anything wrong.

She *was* an agreeable girl. Strangers said so when they complimented her parents on her heart-shaped face, her frank eyebrows, the waves in her walnut hair. She stepped back and smiled and allowed them to admire her dress and shoes. Kate was a good girl.

When the strangers said, "What an agreeable child,"

Her parents said, "Say thank you, Kate."

And Kate said, "Thank you."

✳

It was a dry, flat January and Kate locked the rabbit foot around the bottom strap of her backpack. She liked the shock of pink, how it tapped against her hipbone when she walked. At school, Maddie jealously fingered the foot. She promised to swipe one, but purple, so they wouldn't match *too* much. Kate liked brushing the paw with her thumb when she thought. She wondered about luck. Certainly, she'd been lucky enough not to get caught stealing it, but then again, she had to buy it instead. She could see no discernible lucky results from the lucky rabbit foot, but also didn't know what luck looked like. Or how luck worked. Or how to tease it out from wherever it was hiding.

Kate's half-sister Ingrid lived with them half the time, less now that she was away at college. When she visited, she kicked her legs over the arm of the sofa and slouched in front of the TV. Her hair went unbrushed and tangled. Her jeans were ripped and she'd taped her shoes and the shoulder of her leather jacket together with silver duct tape. She rolled her eyes. *A lot.* Kate's mother complained that Ingrid had turned into a mean, disrespectful thing. "Talk to her," she instructed their father. "She can't act like this in my house. Send her back to her mother's."

Kate and Ingrid's father would wince, shrug, push up his glasses, and slide next to Ingrid on the couch. "Kiddo, you got to be nicer to your stepmom."

They'd watch TV.

"You been drawing? Anything I can see?"

Like a salve, Ingrid pulled out her sketchbook and he pulled out his and they'd turn the pages and talk.

Some nights, though, they'd fight, and Ingrid stomped out to sleep at her real mother's house, or, they discovered when a police officer escorted her home one time, in her car in the beach parking lot.

That winter, when Ingrid was with them, she watched Kate when her parents went out. Sometimes they'd drive to the Kmart and roam the aisles. They'd pick out the most hideous outfits and dare each other to model them or secretly follow customers through the aisles and sneak items into their carts.

When strangers commented on how pretty Kate was, Ingrid scowled. "What do you know about pretty."

They'd look at her sharply and move on. Ingrid mocked them behind their backs as they walked away. "Smart's better than pretty," she'd say to Kate. "It lasts longer."

Sometimes, rarely, but *sometimes*, Ingrid brushed and braided Kate's hair. "You grow out of pretty," she'd say as she looped a hair band around the end of Kate's braid. "You grow into smart."

Kate remembered the years of braces Ingrid endured. Her overgrown eyebrows, her chewed-up nails, black like rot from drawing with charcoal. Ingrid never cried in front of anyone, but sometimes when she came in from driving alone, or out of her room, or after sneaking cigarettes behind the shed, her cheeks were splotched and puffy, her eyes swollen. Kate thought her sister looked most beautiful when she was either laughing or on the verge of tears.

Mostly, Ingrid ignored Kate, and everyone else. Kate practiced her piano scales as softly as she could when Ingrid was there, lightly sliding her fingers up and down the keys. Or, she lodged herself in the other corner of the sofa and pretended she didn't care that Ingrid wasn't talking to her.

"You know that's from a dead rabbit." Ingrid swatted the rabbit's foot, its pink dingy from travel. "They kill the rabbits and cut off their feet." It was Sunday. "For experiments and stuff." They were alone.

"I know," Kate said. It hadn't occurred to her that there once had been a rabbit attached to the foot. Her neck tingled. Her mouth dried. "It's a lucky charm."

"It's not a lucky charm. Not for the rabbit, anyway."

Kate didn't want to cry in front of her sister. She waited. That night in bed, she curled around the rabbit's foot, pressed it against her chest, and sobbed. "I'm sorry, I'm sorry, I'm sorry . . ." She imagined the rabbit, its button lips screaming, its black button nose split from pain, its delirious button eyes locked on its bloody stumps.

In the kitchen, her father, *their* father, screamed at Ingrid.

Ingrid screamed back.

A fist pounded on the table.

A dish fell and broke.

Her mother slammed a door and stomped down the hallway and yelled at the both of them to give it a rest.

Kate let her sobs be loud since no one was listening. "I'm sorry, I'm sorry, I'm sorry . . ."

The next morning, she latched the rabbit's foot around her knapsack strap and pretended she didn't care. When it tapped her hipbone, she suppressed an impulse to recoil. She yanked it through her hand backwards against the bristling fur. The morning Ingrid left for school again, Kate dug at the frozen earth. She buried the rabbit's foot in a shallow grave between the roots of the weeping willow.

She never forgot that day. It was the day her father died.

While Kate practiced her scales and arpeggios and etudes full volume, her mother read a novel in the master bedroom, and her father drove to the city to visit his mother. He brought her a bouquet of orange roses.

While Kate kicked a soccer ball against the garage door, her mother answered the phone. Her father called to say he wasn't feeling well.

While Kate sprawled on the living room floor, her math homework spread before her, her mother answered the phone again. Kate's grandmother this time. He was too tired to drive and decided to stay the night.

While Kate rifled through her half-sister's half-empty drawers, searching for insights, some small clue, proof of love, the phone rang again.

"Get your shoes on." Her mother's hair was pulled into a tight ponytail. Her shirt was wrinkled. Kate had never seen her leave the house without lipstick. She followed her to the car, hugging her backpack, hastily packed with a stuffed animal she was too old for and a book. The car smelled of plastic and exhaust and seemed louder than usual as they peeled out of the driveway and down the street. Her mother gripped the steering wheel.

An accident on 95 slowed traffic to a crawl. Kate looked into the windows of the cars next to them. On one side, a man sang, his voice trapped in the bubble of his VW. An older woman worked a crossword puzzle on her dashboard, glancing up every few moments to inch forward. A young woman, her blonde hair falling in curtains, chewed her nails.

Her mother exhaled, a taut rope of breath. Kate wondered what people saw when they looked into their window. Perhaps a mother and a daughter on their way to New York for an audition. People sometimes told Kate she was pretty enough to be an actress. Or maybe, a mother and daughter driving in to shop at Bloomingdale's and eat in the cafeteria. Maybe they saw the worry on her mother's face, saw a mother and daughter driving into the unknown, where the best-case scenario wasn't all that good.

As an adult, Kate remembered snapshots of that afternoon: a man in the emergency room pressing a bloody compress to his eye, the weight of time crushing an elderly woman as she turned the pages of a stained *Us* magazine, a nurse rolling on her chair behind the admissions desk; the slimy smoothness of the hard chairs in the waiting room, some sort of hospital blue, the black, rounded cushion of the doctor's stool in the treatment room where they waited; her mother spinning her watch around her cruelly thin wrist, the red splotches that crept up her knuckles, the catching and sinking of her chest. "Things like this don't happen to people like us," she said just under her breath.

Then there was the whisper of the door opening. The doctor's earnest face. His sigh. "He told me to tell you that he loved you very much."

There would be a night, well into the future, when Kate, the mother of a young child, in love with her husband, admired her father for his last words, when she finally understood his last, grave act of generosity: a man on the precipice of the biggest moment of his life, his death, turned back in that moment to comfort his wife. But, at twelve, going on thirteen, she didn't see it that way. Words like *things* and *like* and *this* and *don't* and *happen* and *to* and *people* and *us* fluttered around her head like butterflies. Like moths.

They were quiet on the drive home. Her father's wallet, his keys, his glasses sat in a Ziploc on Kate's lap. The wallet's corners were worn, the stitching loose. It was dark by then and Kate was lulled by the tires drumming against cracks in the road. She thought about the rabbit's foot in its shallow winter grave and prayed that the raccoons hadn't dug it up.

When they pulled into the driveway, Kate bolted inside and bashed the piano keys. Her mother stayed behind, her hands resting on the steering wheel, the car lights on, the motor off. By the time she came in, Kate was practicing Chopin.

"Call your sister." Her mother traced her finger along the hallway wall to her bedroom and quietly shut the door.

Kate cradled the phone receiver between her ear and shoulder and dialed.

"Dad's dead," she whispered.

Ingrid paused at the other end and Kate wondered if she'd say anything at all, but then, she heard a stirring on the other end. "Shit."

"I know." Kate nodded, as if her sister could see her. "I know."

There were other things Kate thought she remembered from those days, but memory is a fine and fading thing: the colored stones of light breaking through the stained-glass windows at the church, despite Ingrid's insistence that it had rained that day. The funeral home parted her father's hair on the wrong side; her mother pushed his hair to the other side of his face, but it wouldn't stay. The centerpiece center stage—a polished silver urn crammed with white flowers, a small group of family and friends looking away. Her father's cheeks, unnaturally rosy, his waxy complexion, his sallow skin forced into a healthy shade of beige; a woman she didn't know leaned into the shoulder of a man in a black suit. She sobbed softly. "What a handsome, handsome man." Kate imagined that Maddie would've step on the woman's foot. Ingrid would stare her down with a bent smile. But Kate was a good girl. She said nothing to this woman stealing a piece of Kate and her mother's own story, coveting it like a party prize.

Her mother's hand, cool and heavy, leaned on her shoulder and Kate stood locked to the carpeting. She wished to escape the claustrophobic weight, to elbow through the crowd, to find Ingrid. To skip laughing and screaming, to pull down that woman's skirt and swing from the men's all-too-serious ties, for alongside the sadness came a giddiness of freedom she didn't understand and would never talk about. She was a good girl. Agreeable. Her shoes were shiny black patent leather with square buckles across the top. Innocent shoes, good-girl shoes. She'd throw them away the following morning, bury them at the bottom of the kitchen garbage. She searched for Ingrid in the growing crowd and found her walking in alone through the entrance to the atrium.

Behind Ingrid, a woman in white sneakers and green tights tiptoed in. Kate's eyes widened, and Ingrid turned as the woman loudly whispered to an usher in a black suit, asking for directions to the aerobics class. When Kate looked back to the casket, her shoulders were shaking from silent laughter followed by a raft of tears.

Late afternoon, dull, dreary, worn away, Kate wandered from room to room at the house. Her mother, beautifully pale, her hair pulled back into a severe bun, her red lipstick, her faded smile, accepted a plate of food from a fellow mourner, which she balanced, untouched, on the arm of the chair. Kate thought about the rabbit foot in its shallow, frozen grave beneath the weeping willow, which made her think of the hardware store, how only a few weeks before. She'd planned to push it up her sleeve and into her pocket, seduced by the danger of its soft, pink fur. She never asked if Ingrid knew the cashier who foiled her plan. She wandered outside.

Ingrid was smoking behind the shed. She waved Kate over.

"Dad smoked a cigarette every night." Ingrid poked the toe of her shoe into a small pile of butts. "Only one. After you went to bed."

"Did you smoke with him?"

"Sometimes. If I was here."

"Oh."

Kate watched her own breath turn white in the cold air. Pretended it was smoke.

"You okay?"

"I guess."

"I'm leaving tonight." Ingrid tossed the spent cigarette and Kate now saw even more decomposing butts, a trail of them littered the ground. "I'm not coming back."

"Okay."

"I'll call sometimes."

"Okay."

"It's not like anyone's gonna miss me around here."

Kate reached for something more to say, something seductive, soulful, something that would keep her sister there. "Who was the lady in the green tights?"

Ingrid lit another cigarette. "I think she's what they call a cosmic joke."

"Okay."

"Listen," Ingrid said, "you can use whatever I leave behind."

When Kate went back to school a couple of weeks later, she imagined the lady in the green tights peeking through the classroom windows, walking in on her in the bathroom stalls, barging through dodgeball in gym class. The first days back were rough, even though Maddie pulled her into the girl's room and pressed her hand to Kate's cheek and cried. She lifted both half-heart necklaces, hers and Kate's, fit them together and held the charms, still attached to their necks, in her mouth. Kate cried, too, because life seemed to evade her slippery grip and she couldn't bear to lose another thing but, when she got home, she rubbed at the black marks the junk-metal necklace left on her skin. She hung her half heart on her bedside lamp and allowed her skin to return to its normal pink.

At night, her mother sat at the kitchen table with the lights off. Kate heated water for tea and they'd wrap their hands around the mugs and stare at each other until the colors dimmed and their outlines blurred and it was too dark to see.

There were things Kate knew. She knew she couldn't be sad for too long. That the weight of new life had to be hidden and carried as if it weighed nothing at all.

In third grade, she'd gone on a class field trip to a cemetery to make gravestone rubbings. The stones were mostly ancient, worn down and cracked. They could barely read the writing until their teacher taped newsprint to the stones and gently ran black crayon over it. There was a boy in her class, a brooding, taciturn kid, whose voice rarely rose above a whisper. At the cemetery, he told the teacher, "I think my brother's buried here." Kate had stared at a cluster of lilies of the valley that day and would not look at the boy, for fear of jinxing her own life. Among the ghosts, no less.

Now she was like him. The school social worker cornered her in the hallway. The guidance counselor arranged meetings for her in his office where with watery eyes, he removed his glasses and cleaned them with a tissue and waited for her to speak. And the music teacher unlocked the practice room. Kate spent her lunches practicing scales and playing pop songs. It was easier than facing frozen, fawning friendships.

After the funeral, after Ingrid left, while the stragglers hovered around her mom, Kate pulled her father's wallet and glasses from her mother's top drawer. She delicately opened the Ziploc, stroked the pitted leather of the wallet, and twirled the coarse thread that dangled from one corner, past the missing stitches. She bent over his driver's license and the school photographs of each of his daughters, the corners fuzzy and bent. In the long sleeve of the wallet, there were three twenties.

Feet hanging off the edge of her bed, her dead father's wallet and glasses on her lap, she outlined the flowers on the quilt with her fingers. She worried she'd never be able to shake the ease with which she'd become an agreeable child. She thought she wanted to, but—well, she didn't know what she wanted.

The not-knowing followed her for the rest of her life, the sense that something irreplaceable had been ripped from her life, something beyond her father, some mysterious something she'd never find again.

Kate wished Ingrid were there.

Out in the living room, her mother curled into the big chair, her lids heavy from Valium. Kate's grandmother grabbed her hand. "He tell me no to call the ambulance. He say is fine. He fix da flower stem. He tell me he's fine."

*

Kate turned thirteen that spring. In the summer, Maddie and her parents invited her to spend a weekend at the Jersey Shore. They rented two motel rooms, side by side, and the girls were given a key which hung from a plastic diamond with scalloped edges. It was too big to fit in the back pocket of Maddie's shorts, but Maddie discovered, anyway, that she could leave it in a cubby by the front desk. That way, she told Kate, they could get into the room if they lost each other on the beach.

While Kate unpacked her overnight bag, her bathing suit, her sundresses, and two twenties she'd stolen from her father's wallet, Maddie lay on her back across the stiff bedspread of one of the twin beds. Her legs swung off the side and the bed creaked and sagged in the center. The swirls of blue and green on the bedspread seemed disingenuous, flat, and fake. Kate's back was to Maddie and she thought she felt her stare, but when she turned, Maddie was facing the popcorn ceiling, her head cradled in her hands.

"Kate?"

"What?" Kate closed the dresser drawer. There were things about Maddie that made her uneasy. Her abrasiveness, her loud willingness to embarrass kids at school, the sharp comments and sense of ownership she had over her friends. If Kate strayed too far too fast, Maddie would reel her back in.

"If we meet boys, tell them you're sixteen."

"What are you talking about?" Kate folded the twenties and zipped them into the inside pocket of her purse.

"Anyway," Maddie said, "it's better to do it early, to get it over with."

"Oh, my God!" Kate covered her face and collapsed on her bed. Maddie threw a pillow at her.

"No! For real. If you lose it early, when you fall in love it's no big deal. Anyway . . ." She turned on the TV, flipped through the channels, turned it off. "Let's go to the beach?"

Kate felt for the twenties inside her purse. She trusted Maddie less and less.

After dinner, the girls split from Maddie's parents and walked the boardwalk. At dusk, the carnival rides lit up and a busker on the sidewalk turned up his cheap amp and sang classic rock to karaoke tracks. The shops along the walk glowed fluorescent.

Maddie swung her purse widely by her knee, stopping every once in a while to see if anyone was looking at them. Kate kept her head down. Her red Keds slapped against the boardwalk. The laces of her shoes popped white; the hem of her dress brushed against her knees. She almost bumped into Maddie when she stepped in front of her.

"You look too young," Maddie said. She pulled the elastics from Kate's pigtail braids. She handed Kate a tube of lip gloss from her purse. "Now smile wide. Now pucker. Now make a kiss." She allowed Maddie to spread the gloss's sticky tip across her lips.

She felt someone watching. Maddie felt it, too. Two older boys suddenly flanked them. The boy by Kate's side slowed. His shirt was open and his shorts loose. His torso was spindly and hard. Kate tried not to stare at his caved-in chest. He chewed on the straw of his Orange Julius. The one by Maddie was shorter, wider, older, it seemed, but not by much. "Hey," he said, "you want a sip?"

Maddie took a long pull and passed the cup to Kate, who sipped, expecting the powdery sweetness and was struck instead by a base bitterness. She made a face. "There's something wrong with it."

Maddie swiped the cup back. "It's vodka, stupid." She popped the top off and drank straight from the cup, turned to the boy and swallowed.

They walked for a while, passing the drink down the line. The boys were rowdy and Maddie made them laugh.

Kate's boy said, "You seem shy."

"I guess I am." She'd never been on a date before and wasn't sure how to act. The boy rested his hand on the small of her back and for a moment, she felt a jab of alarm. But, beyond the fear was the headiness of stepping into a lawless world. The crowds swelled and thinned. Her feet scuffed the fine layer of sand on the wooden walk. Between the night and all the people, she could barely see the beach or the half-moon that hung sloppy and low above the water.

They walked for a while, the four of them. They wandered in and out of tourist shops, the boys bumping shoulders with the girls. Kate thought the boy who liked her, Evan, was pleasant enough. He held the door for her and lightly touched the small of her back. Maddie's boy, Teddy, hooked his thumb through the loop of Maddie's belt. Maddie had somehow arched her back to meet it. Between the perpetual twilight, the twisting lights of the carnival rides, and the breeze that blew bits of Maddie's hair free, she looked older than she really was, as if she'd even willed herself to age for this very moment, a loss of innocence, Kate supposed, though she didn't feel all that innocent, only awkward and uncomfortable. Nothing she'd want Maddie or the boys to notice. She grabbed the drink cup from Evan and in three long pulls of the straw, she tasted melted ice and watered-down syrup and the mysterious desolation of the vodka. Alcohol, she'd heard, made you brave, or at least, dampened the impulse to care. Maddie cast an approving glance her way.

"I want to show you something," Evan said. He pulled Kate to the back of the Sunglass Hut where he took her hand and squeezed it and kissed her at the end of the aisle. She didn't know what she'd expected, or what to do. The mealy softness of his tongue brushed the inside of her mouth and the back of her teeth, searching for hers, which remained limp and lifeless, unsure. His lips pressed hard against hers and his clumsy fingers dug into her ribs. He stepped away. "Did you like that? Was that okay?" She nodded. His chin was splotched with red. She thought of the cashier at the hardware store, his blotched chin, his head bobbing on his long neck, his Adam's apple sliding up and down like a fishing lure.

"Uh-huh." She didn't want to hurt his feelings. They silently made their way to the front of the store where Maddie and Teddy swayed to the music, facing each other with hooked pinkies.

"Meet me at the bench by the soft serve at eight," Maddie said. And then she was gone.

Kate let Evan hold her hand. He was a foot taller and her elbow bent at an awkward angle, his fingers stuffed between hers, causing hers to splay and stiffen. They sat on the steps that led from the boardwalk to the beach and he kissed her again. She tried her best to kiss back and the skin around her face and neck became slimy with his spit. If this was love, she could do without it.

He led her to the beach by the boardwalk and she let him inch his hand into her panties as she leaned against a wooden beam for balance. Then, somehow, they were laying in the sand, the top of her head pressed up against the beam, among the beach pebbles, dried seaweed, and cigarette butts. The boy lay heavy on top of her, breathing against her neck, fiddling with his shorts. In the moment, she wondered if she knew something now that Ingrid didn't. She imagined she was Ingrid and Evan was the hardware store cashier. When she turned her head, she thought she saw the ankles of the woman in green tights, her white tennis shoes slightly scuffed. She started to laugh but felt a blunt punch inside. The boy, Evan, collapsed on top of her, his chin nuzzling her neck, spent. "I'm sorry," he whispered. "That was so fast. You are so beautiful."

They lay on the beach for a moment. Then, Kate pushed the boy off to the side and said, "I got to go."

"Can I see you again? Tomorrow night. At the Sunglass Hut?"

"Yeah," she said. "At six?"

"I'll be there. Promise me you'll come."

She promised, even though she and Maddie were leaving early that afternoon.

Maddie was at the bench when Kate got there, eating ice cream.

She offered Kate a lick. The over-sweet vanilla mixed with the sand and salt stuck behind her lips.

"Well?" Maddie pulled Kate by the wrist down the boardwalk.

Kate shrugged. "What?"

"Did you?"

"Did you?"

"We made out forever, but—" Maddie's lips were swollen, her cheeks rubbed raw. Kate smoothed her own hair behind her ears. She'd long since shaken the sand from beneath her dress and straightened her straps, but what of the rest? What of the sleepiness that had descended? The weariness of realizing that she was alone, raising herself. That no one would know if she made mistakes, not her mother, not Ingrid, not her dead father. No one was watching her grow up.

On the day that Maddie decided to teach her to shoplift, Kate's heart filled her throat while Maddie touched everything in the Hallmark store, picked it up, put it down, smiled at the cashiers, roamed the aisles. Every moment, Kate felt like they were being watched, that security was waiting for them to make a move. She hated Maddie. When they finally made it to the street and Maddie clasped the half a heart around her neck, she felt trapped into their friendship. She felt dirty.

When they walked towards the parking lot and she saw her father leaning against the car, she ran to him and threw herself into a hug. He'd been surprised by the sudden outburst of affection, but he held her close and said, "What's up, Button?"

She'd stepped back and shrugged and said, "I'm just glad you're here."

Now, walking with Maddie back to the hotel room, she realized the weight and worry of disappearing, felt the heft of the loneliness that had been forced upon her.

"Well? What about you?"

"No," Kate said. "I couldn't."

Maddie stomped her feet and giddily pushed Kate away. Kate stumbled, caught her balance and, laughing, pushed Maddie back.

AND SHE DID

Anyone could've predicted that the party'd split in two. The non-smokers stayed inside in Ingrid and Hoshi's floor-thru, lingering in the doorless configuration of rooms—Hoshi's in the back, then Ingrid's, then the living room, the kitchen, the bathroom. The kitchen table, pressed wood and peeling laminate, dragged in from the sidewalk three years ago, was crowded with handles of vodka, rum, cheap wine, and glasses smeared with fingerprints and lipstick. Hoshi's bowls, thrown on the pottery wheel at college, were thick and pooled with glaze. They were filled with clumps of anemic dips and thinning piles of crumbling pretzels. There was music and meaningless chatter. The smokers smoked outside.

Ingrid was with the smokers who'd gathered on the sidewalk. It was one of those silken city nights that lingered between summer and spring. Brooklyn was not yet swampy with its August humidity. The leaking lights of streetlamps and the Key Foods sign across the street dusted the sky. The headlights of cars coasted by like dimming stars. Cigarette embers extinguished themselves. The group lingered by the optometrist office, a storefront beneath Ingrid and Hoshi's apartment. The office was always empty, a shell of a business. The glasses on the display racks, dull with the filth of abandonment, stared bleakly towards the window. The only time Ingrid had ever seen someone in the shop was when she and Hoshi signed the lease on top of the glass display counter in back. Their Armenian landlord's son had pushed the paper across the mottled glass. She and Hoshi, used to their fellow raw and unformed college students, were struck silent by his sculpted beauty, shadowed in the back of the unlit store.

On the first of every month, they slipped the rent check through the brass mail slot by the door and watched it drift to the floor where it languished for weeks until, along with ignored grocery store flyers and other pieces of abject mail spread across the carpeted floor, it disappeared.

Below the curb, a puddle swirled with oil and constellations of tar pebbles. It stretched the lit moon reflections of streetlights along the curve of the street. Ingrid picked up a playing card that had settled at the edge of the puddle. It was the Jack of Spades, creased down the middle, dropped at the end of a shill game. The back of the card was a filigree of blue with tiny bluebirds at each corner. On the flip side, the Jacks' bodies met just below their chests. Their heads peered off in opposite directions.

She stepped into the street and looked up to her apartment's street-side window. Jake was inside. That morning, he'd whispered that he loved her. The words were sandwiched between the whistling kettle and a car horn, but with one finger, he'd moved her hair aside and, tickling her ear with his lips, he said something. Something intimate and strange, and she was sure it was "I love you." Whatever he said trickled down her spine and radiated to the ends of her nerves. The words spun with her blood through her splitting veins and landed like polished stones in the palms of her hands. When he stepped away, he was smiling. His hungry cheekbones blushed; his lips were parted. She liked how his front teeth crossed and how the sinewy muscles along his neck tensed and released.

Before he whispered that thing. Before they'd gotten out of bed. Before they'd even spoken, he made love to her slowly, silently, stretching her arms above her head, his hands clamped around her wrists. Her skin glowed white beneath the weight of his ridged chest. Later, after he'd whispered whatever it was he'd whispered, she wanted to be alone with the feeling of knowing that someone loved her, to memorize the feeling of being loved.

But Jake had stayed with her all day. They cleaned the apartment with Hoshi and Ben, shopped at the Key Foods, walked to the liquor store and back. Set up the bar on the kitchen counter. Took a nap. All the while, those two imagined polished stones that had spilled into Ingrid's palms became mashed and mangled from the carrying of bags and the passing time. They melted back into her skin.

Weekday mornings at five, Ingrid walked west on Grand Street, past Kellogg's Diner, the freeway, the vacant Williamsburg Bank and the burnt-out, boarded up tenements to the pedestrian entrance of the Williamsburg Bridge. Her early-morning walks always began as a landscape in gray, the moon melting into the silhouettes of the buildings and the river's undulant, sleeping breath. By the time she reached the middle of the bridge, the Hassidic women appeared in thick, lined stockings, white sneakers, matching brown wigs, to shatter Ingrid's quietude.

From Delancey, she made her way down Broadway to the Financial District and wove through the streets and avenues to the alleyway entrance of the Bank of America Building. In the fifth-floor employee locker room, she changed from street clothes to the tuxedo hanging in her locker, pulled her hair back into a tight bun, and snapped her bowtie around her neck. Then she helped her fellow waiters prepare coffee urns, lay out breakfast pastries, polish water-stained silverware, and fold cloth napkins into standing fans. At seven, the investment bankers and their assistants filtered in.

In the cafeteria, time moved slowly. Every palatial work shift was a practice in purgatory. The waiters stood at the back of the room, their hands clasped, and waited. They waited for the bankers and their assistants and clients to come. Then, they waited on the bankers through breakfast. They waited for breakfast to end and lunch to begin. They occasionally waited celebratory dinners and cocktail hours. They waited for the bankers and their assistants to leave. They waited for the day to end.

On the day she and Jake met, Ingrid was waiting to go home. She wasn't feeling well.

A tightness in her low back radiated along her spine. She had trouble breathing, and trouble standing still. Her throat was rocky and raw. After the lunch crowd thinned, her manager convinced her to go to the Free Clinic. She did.

There, she waited for the doctor in the examination room, her socked feet dangling off the edge of the paper-lined table. The clammy chill of the table bed bled through her paper gown. She shivered and wondered why hospitals were always cold.

"Are you pregnant?" the doctor asked. He was young. A year or two older than her. One strand of his thick Asian hair poked into the side of his nose.

"No."

"Are you sure?"

"Yes." She'd only been with one man during college, a perfunctory relationship that served one purpose. Her de-flowering came from a place of urgency, a means to end a ticking clock. That had been a few years ago.

"We should check, anyway."

She shuffled to the hallway bathroom in her paper gown, holding the plastic cup.

When the doctor tapped her kidneys, she flinched from a biting pain. He diagnosed a kidney infection and sent her home with a prescription and sample blister pack of antibiotics. The bus bounced on a pothole on Grand Street and pain pulsed up and down her back in radiant spheres. She crawled up the stairs to her apartment and dropped her keys twice trying to unlock the apartment door. By then, the pain raged across her back.

She curled on her side on the kitchen floor, the cool of the peeling linoleum a relief against her burning skin. She shivered. *This is what it feels like to be alone.* Eyes closed, breath metered, she fumbled through her bag, blindly feeling for the antibiotics. Ingrid's nails were cut to the pink, her fingers clumsy with pain. She couldn't rip through the blister pack. She weakly threw the pills further into the kitchen, past the bathroom door. Allowed herself a moment in the luxury of regret. Then squirmed on her side to retrieve them.

Maybe she heard the splash, maybe she didn't, but lying in fetal position, she thought she was delirious, dizzy from pain, when she saw a foot propped up on the edge of the clawfoot bathtub. Then Jake sat up and turned towards her, his hair cropped tight in a wide Mohawk, beads of sweat rolling down his forehead. Ropes of muscle twisted from his shoulders down his arms. He gripped the edge of the tub as she crawled towards him, the blister pack resting in her open palm.

"Open it?"

"Jesus." He splashed out of the tub and dripped water from his naked limbs. Moments later, wrapped in a towel, he cradled her head as she lay on the floor of the bathroom and helped her swallow the pills. She closed her eyes.

"Who are you?" No strength to struggle. "I'm calling the police."

"I'm Jake," he said. "Hoshi's friend. She said I could stay."

"Fucking Hoshi." She surrendered further into his lap.

An hour later, the antibiotics kicked in. He tucked her tightly into bed. She heard him leave and come back. He'd filled her prescription. He brought her soup. He brushed her sweat-soaked hair away from her forehead. Somewhere in there, she heard Hoshi came back. "Jakey!"

"You didn't tell your roommate I was coming?"

"I'm sure I did!" The pitch of her voice rose again, then dropped. "Oh. No. I guess I didn't. You were coming next week!"

By morning, Ingrid was feeling better. Jake introduced himself properly. He was a college friend of Hoshi's—one of the few Ingrid hadn't met. He'd graduated before she got there. He'd spent the last two years working at canneries and traveling Alaska. Hoshi'd agreed to let him to crash on their couch for a week, maybe two.

So far, he'd been there for five weeks and only slept on the sofa once. Ingrid liked waking up next to him in the mornings. She liked the way he smelled of watermelon rind. She liked the way he looked at her and that he walked the city while Ingrid worked and collected stories. She liked his stories. Buddha of Brooklyn, the dwarf prostitute in Hell's Kitchen, the garbage men in the East Village who did pull-ups on the city scaffolding before throwing trash into the back of the truck. For a while, she liked that he walked her to work and waited for her after work to walk her home. But then it felt claustrophobic. She missed the gray loneliness of her early-morning walks and worried that something was wrong with her. That she was incapable of accepting what looked a little like love.

Those days, Williamsburg was a raucous confusion of old Brooklyn and new Brooklyn. The artists and musicians were moving in while Polish grandmothers in housecoats sat on their stoops and eyed the shifting culture. Old Italian men smoked pipes and played dominoes in lawn chairs on the sidewalk. Mormon missionaries, clean-shaven young men with their hair cropped tightly above their ears, strolled in pairs around the city blocks alongside young Hassidic men in their wool coats, side curls, and beards. New York was still a little lawless. Everybody, just a little on the take.

Ingrid turned the Jack of Spades in her hand and straightened it along its bent spine.

She slipped it into her back pocket and thought maybe she'd mail it to her half-sister. She liked to send her small, strange mysteries. Found objects and trinkets without histories. Sometimes she wrote her letters from imaginary people. Postcards and things.

The smokers smoked with conviction. The smoke lifted from their cigarettes like dander caught in a sigh of breath. Music leaked from inside the apartment alongside scales of laughter and chatter. Every few minutes another guest, Kelly Martin or Heather Keene, or Keith Langston or Sam Early, emerged from the building for a smoke or a breath of fresh air, and someone else would go back in.

A cab pulled up to the curb at the same time that Greta Weeks and Dante Coleman lurched through the front door, gripping each other's hand.

Nathalie Madera stepped out of the taxi. Her black Lycra miniskirt rode up her thighs. She balanced on top of her red platform shoes on the cracked sidewalk and tugged the hem of the skirt.

Dante lit two cigarettes and handed one to Greta. Greta bit her lip to keep from laughing, but Ingrid admired Nathalie's hipness, how she cared how she looked, but didn't care how other people saw her. Nathalie was a woman in full bloom whereas Ingrid was stunted, trapped in the nowhere-land between boyish adolescence and womanhood. She nodded as Nathalie passed. Keith opened the door and followed her in.

Greta moaned after the door closed. "She thinks she's so much." She traded her cigarette for a lit joint from Dante. She pulled at it and then passed it to Ingrid. "I mean, really? Does she think she's at Club 54?"

Ingrid tugged smoke from the joint twice, her own cigarette bobbing in the loose grip of her other hand. Her cigarette was only half-lit and choked out an anemic plume of smoke, which curled around Ingrid's fingers.

Dante kicked a crushed soda can into the street. It pinged flatly, like the E string on a strangled violin. "We should do something," he said. "Something really fun. Something we'll read about in the *Daily News*. Page Six. We should do something crazy."

"I just saw a rat." Greta tugged Dante's hand. Feigning a swoon with the back of her hand to her forehead, she crumpled into his arms. "Save me, save me from the wildlife."

He bit down on his cigarette filter and wrapped his arms around her. "Sure, baby. Anything for you."

"I want a kitten. I want you to find me an abandoned kitten on the street. Ruth Gunderson always finds abandoned animals on the subway. Baby birds and things."

"I'd get you a mouse for your house." He snuffed the ember of the joint and dropped it in the front pocket of his shirt.

Ingrid felt for the playing card. She looked up to the sky, to the bright star Jake told her was a planet. The half-moon looked dirty, dusted with midnight blue, ragged, graceless, half-lit, Ingrid thought. The buildings down the block were the same hue as the sky, but darker. So was the street. And the sidewalk. And the parked cars in the absence of vibrant light.

"So . . . what's Ingrid thinking?" Greta asked.

"I'm thinking it'd be nice to walk to the bridge. Look at the water."

"Is it safe? At night?" Greta took Ingrid's dying cigarette and tried to bring it back to life. "I can't believe Nathalie showed up looking like a Russian hooker."

"Hoshi always looks like a six-year-old who dressed herself," Ingrid said. Sometimes Hoshi sneaked into the college's sculpting studio at night using keys she'd stolen and copied as an undergraduate. The security guards assumed, with her pigtails and knee socks and her tiny frame, that she was still a student there.

"That's Hoshi."

Ingrid shrugged.

Jake pushed out onto the sidewalk. "I was looking for you," he said, and took Ingrid's face in his hands. He kissed her. "I missed you."

Ingrid reveled in the swell of owning someone's affection. She wanted those polished stones to rematerialize, so she could place them on display, proof that someone could love her. She hoped he'd say it again. Clearer this time, so there'd be no mistake. Then again, to be loved seemed a grave responsibility. Perhaps too great for her. She was only twenty-four years old and didn't know how to be loved. She didn't know what love was or how to keep it. Maybe she could grab onto it for a minute longer the next time. She'd run away with it, if she could. Bury it. A little bit. A tiny bit. A pinch of it until she needed it. That's what she'd do.

"I want to see if the Buddha's still at the bottom of the swimming pool." He turned to the others. "I met the Buddha of Brooklyn. I left him a gift. Ingrid brought him flowers. We left them by the drain of the empty pool."

"Flower petals."

"Rose petals."

"Carnations, actually."

"Let's go see." He wove his fingers through Ingrid's. Motioned with his head. In the half-moon, his face was a crash of angles. The dark whittled away his eyes. His forehead flashed bright.

"Is it safe?" Greta asked.

Dante said, "Who cares?"

The group of smokers followed them down Lorimer to the abandoned McCarren pool.

The McCarren pool had lain fallow for ten years. A chain-link fence crowned with a coil of barbed wire surrounded the crumbling bathhouse and parched pool. Brick arches tagged with graffiti led past a wrought-iron gate that had, for a time, been held shut with a lock and chain. The gate's iron spindles pointed upwards. Its rungs were dented and curved, pried apart by a crow bar, or maybe a pipe. Long ago, the chain had been cut. It now lay kicked to the side, frozen with rust. At night, dandelions slept with heavy heads. There was trash on both sides of the fence: bent bottle caps, battered cans, plastic bags so tattered that they'd turned to silk and folded around the links like wilting vines. The mattress propped up against the bathhouse promenade was stained and losing form, wasted by the bodies who'd used her: the homeless and drug addicted, the anonymous lovers, prostitutes, and johns. A sweatshirt had molded itself over a set of brick steps. Ingrid didn't believe in ghosts, but she wouldn't be surprised if she ran into one there. Nights in New York were different than days, and forgotten places had heartbeats and secrets of their own. One by one, the group climbed over the fence where a hole had been cut in the barbed wire. This was the first time Ingrid had been there at night. In the dark, the pool looked bottomless. It swallowed the feeble light.

During the day, the McCarren pool was funky and strange, the graffiti weathered with passing time. A giant pink lotus flower on the wide brick wall had browned. A series of colorful tags by 'R.E.N.' hit four walls, the last of the series was tagged with a small and respectful R.I.P. The other tags, some artful, some hasty and slick, popped against the canvas of fading brick.

Two days before the party, two days before Jake whispered, "I love you," if that's what he'd whispered (Ingrid was pretty sure, but not a hundred percent sure that that's what he'd said before he flipped off the burner and poured them both tea), they'd gone to the pool with Hoshi, Ben, and Jake. They'd picnicked on the floor of the empty pool on top of a blanket Ingrid knitted for her final art installation at college. The knots were willfully and wildly uneven. Hoshi brought a bouquet of carnations wrapped in a cellophane cone, and the manufactured red of the petals clashed with the faded-out everything else.

Ben was telling them how his grandparents were at the opening of the pool in the thirties, a triumphant project of the WPA, and how, as children, his grandparents had spent their summers waist-high in the crowded waters, slept outside on roofs and fire escapes, and sneaked into the adult section of the movie theater that was now the dirty Key Foods on Grand Street.

Jake wandered off in the middle of Ben's story to the pool's center. He squatted down and placed something by the drain. Then, he stood and circled the object, like a ritual. At a lull, Ingrid walked towards Jake, imagining she was negotiating the water and historic crowds. The cries of children submerged and splashing.

He squinted towards her and smiled. He stepped back. By the drain was a miniature smiling Buddha statue, the kind they sold on sidewalk tables in Chinatown. "I ran into this guy a few days ago meditating on a park bench. I told him about the pool, this place of peace, the absence of movement, the memory of water. I told him to come here. I told him I'd leave him a sign. I'd met a similar guy praying on a bench in Berkeley. They could be brothers. The Buddha of Berkeley. The Buddha of Brooklyn."

"Wait here," she said. She skipped back to the picnic blanket and stole Hoshi's carnations.

Hoshi frowned. "Please don't break Jake's heart. It's so easily broken."

"He's leaving soon," Ingrid simply stated. She ran back to him.

Someday soon, he *would* leave. In this way, both he and Ingrid were safe.

Greta screamed, her voice throaty, and Ingrid turned to see Dante spinning her above his head, Greta's feet pointed one way, her unsure arms reaching forward, her torso arched and pulled taut.

"Look! *Dirty Dancing*," Dante howled.

Greta kneed him in the forehead. They fell down, laughing.

Kelly sat at the side of the pool, her legs dangling over the side as Sam stood inside the empty pool, his arms crossed and resting on the edge, his cheek leaning against her thigh. All of them chattered and giggled. Ingrid wished they'd stop talking for once.

Here, at McCarren Park's abandoned pool, love was spilling through her fingertips. She felt it slipping away. She touched the palm of her hand to the rough brick, ran it over the crumbling mortar. She wished she could find a corner of silence, the kind of silence that didn't hurt, didn't squeeze like thirst. She closed her eyes and listened for silence between words, between thoughts, between her shallow breath. Her kidneys pinched, a reminder of what they'd been through a few weeks before. She decided she didn't like the gripping sensation love left her with. It made her hungry, lonely, and sad—a cruel craving.

She sensed the shadow of a sigh behind her, but there was no one there. She heard a rustle she couldn't locate in the dark. She felt a presence she couldn't define. Was she counting her own breaths or someone else's? Two glints from the corner of the covered promenade, two eyes, human eyes, empty, sagging circles stared at her. She backed away. A hand landed on her shoulder and she jumped and turned and found herself trapped by Jake's hard chest.

"Oh my god. You scared me."

"It's okay," he said. "It's just me."

"We need to leave," she whispered.

He raked his fingers into her hair. "It's gone. The Buddha took the Buddha. We are blessed." He tried to kiss her, but she pulled away.

"Someone's here. We need to go." She pulled back towards the pool. "Let's go."

They lost track of the group on the walk back to the apartment. Greta and Dante ran ahead. Kelly and Sam fell away. Jake and Ingrid strolled slowly in the cooling night. His hands dug deep into his pockets. He swung his feet, looking for pebbles to kick. She listened to him not talk, tried to understand what he wasn't saying, tuned in to the changes of rhythm, the movement of his hips, the sudden heaviness they carried between them. He looked at her once and blindly landed his hand at the base of her neck. He had a bit of a dangerous look, a coiled anger that made her feel safe. Another moment she wished she could memorize. They stopped at a double payphone, with a scratched window separating the two sides.

He guided her into one. He stepped to the other side and

deposited a quarter into the slot. When her phone rang, she answered it. She heard him breathing on the other end and her heart picked up pace. *Here it is*, she thought. The moment where he'd say it again. The moment she'd know that he loved her, and she'd finally know what love was.

"Hello?" There was silence for a good long while, and she glanced through the scratched Plexiglas between phones.

He was watching her, the receiver to his ear.

"What," she said.

He turned back towards his own phone and ran his fingers along its boxy top.

"I bought a ticket," he said. "Leaving Tuesday."

She waited for more. "When will you be back?"

"Some time, I guess. New York's hard to avoid."

The call was cut off by a recorded operator. The line went dead. Still, Ingrid held the receiver to her ear and waited for an answer.

She needed to hear him say those words again. Out loud this time, without nuance. Without artistry. Flat and simple. Easy love. Love laid on the table for all to see, not like a shill game or a trickster or a stolen thought. But they didn't talk the rest of the way to the Grand Street. He went into the apartment. She lit a cigarette outside the optometrist's office.

He loved her. He'd whispered it. She was sure. He'd breathed it into her ear. She'd felt the words travel through her bloodstream and into her cells. He'd held her when she was sick, before she knew his name. When they made love, he was slow and gentle and touched her in a way that her body remembered throughout the interminable workday of waiting.

He never insisted that she talk. That was another sign. Nothing was forced. Nothing taken. She dragged her cigarette; the smoke coated the roof of her mouth. She didn't like smoking: stale smells, the bitter, earthy, musty taste. Smoking was her father's habit. She'd learned so she could smoke with him. Her poor father, always trying to escape, always hiding. Did he ever tell her he loved her? She was sure he had, but she couldn't remember. She was certain she'd told him the same, when she was a little girl. When love was a given. But he was always hiding, and she was always looking for him. Together, they breathed. Heat in, smoke out. She spit onto the sidewalk and dropped her butt.

It was near two, she guessed, and the party was staggering to its end. The night was flat and falling to earth. Brooklyn was dull. Limp light emanated from the flickering Key Foods sign.

There were still a few hangers-on inside. Nathalie Madera was speaking softly to Hoshi and Ben on the sofa, Kyle Newman's arms were wrapped tightly around Robbie Spade and they danced a slow drunk dance to no music. Jake wasn't there.

Ingrid climbed out of the open window in Hoshi's room and up the fire-escape stairs to the rooftop. He was lying on his back on the blanket she'd knitted for her art installation. He opened his arms and she nestled beside him where she fit in the crook between his ribs and shoulder. She willed him to say the words. Instead, he kissed the crown of her head.

"Where are you going?"

"Phuket."

"Are you coming back?"

"Some time, maybe." he said. "I don't know."

"What's that star again? The one that shines bright?"

"Jupiter."

"That's what I thought," she said. She wondered what it felt like to say those words out loud, to speak them into being. She waited until Jake's breath grew heavy and his eyelids twitched with dreams. They were hard to say, but she said them. Afterwards, it felt good. She decided she'd marry the next man who said those words to her.

And she did.

SOLITAIRE

Winter on City Island is drab. The fog rolling off the water lingers past noon. The island takes on hues of gray: the bloated bark of maple trees, the boarded-up ice cream hut, the lethargic New England Sound beyond the gray stone graveyard where I sometimes drink my coffee.

During summer, things are livelier. The circus of low-rent tourists blows through town: radios and traffic lights and too-tight two-pieces, skin spilling over Lycra. By autumn, we residents, left behind, anticipate the onslaught of moist frigidity. We press our knuckles into the seams of our pockets and hunch our shoulders against the bickering winds.

Winter is lonely here. When Ellen and I first married, I thought City Island would be the perfect place to write. I never got to it, past the handwritten notes in wire-bound notebooks that now lay tangled on a shelf above my desk, stranded.

Saturday, I presided over the last wedding of the season. The ceremony took place in the back garden of Scavelli's, a short walk from my apartment, past the Cumberland Farms and the grave-yard, across the street from the liquor store that charges double in the summer.

That morning, I'd learned that Nate was dead, that he'd been dead for six months. I read his obituary in the alumni journal. No one thought to tell me. Back in divinity school, we were like brothers. Fifteen years later, I suppose no one remembered we'd been friends.

I opened a bottle of Andre for breakfast, twisted the cork, released the weak hiss of gas, and poured into my mug. Always upon first pour, Andre smells vaguely of piss. It reminded me of the sidewalks of Berkeley, and how they smelled of piss. The homeless veterans spare-changing on Telegraph Avenue smelled of piss. The men's room at Blake's smelled of piss. Nate smelled of piss.

That Sunday morning, I might've smelled slightly of the acrid, stale scent of piss. My ceremonial blacks, my uniform, had just made it through the season. With the television on low, a winning game of solitaire in motion, the cat snoring on the arm of the sofa, I read his obituary again, searching for clues. As far as I could tell, there were none.

Nate was born sick. His heart was too big for his rib cage, his legs too short for his body. His oversized head balanced like a melon on his abbreviated neck. His electric wheelchair, loaded with books, was heavier than he was, and at twenty-four, he was already balding. He was smart, though. The smartest in our class. The professors steeled themselves when he began to speak, and we students leaned forward in our chairs. You never could predict where he'd take the debate, whether he'd question the veracity of academic inquiry, the religiosity of science, the love story between God and the universe, how one could not exist without the other. Then, he'd lean back, lips pursed in a scowling grin. He liked winding up the class and then watching it spin. Afterwards, over drinks, he'd mock the simpleton responses his questions evoked. He was bitter in a way that made bitter fun. He liked that my belief in God wavered like a torn and dirty flag crushed between rocks at the ocean's edge, sometimes arching towards the sky, sometimes weeping over battered stone. He liked that the professors didn't like me and that I didn't care.

"My parents declared me an outward expression of their inner turmoil," he told me when we first met. They'd just dropped him off at the dorms. His father was a repentant philanderer, his mother depressed. "After my traumatic entrance into the world, they found solace in religion and tethered themselves to their devotion." I'd never known a cripple to be buoyant, defiant, and strong like he was.

To be honest, I'd never brushed elbows with a man in a wheelchair before. He crushed clichés, preconceived notions. He was a force.

I thought I should write his parents a letter.

For Nate, Berkeley and divinity school were a respite from his limitations and his parents' saccharine fears. He enjoyed the heady discourse of intellectual debate. More than that, he loved our bourbon-fueled conversations and smoking cigarettes at night and the stories of my seductions and conquests and flings.

It'd been six years since we last spoke and twelve since we'd seen each other on the day of my wedding, which had been his only trip east. The gulf between Traverse City and City Island was too great a hurdle for us to overcome. Daily life and small dramas filled the distance between us. Given his moodiness on the day of my wedding, his punctuated breath, his meager enthusiasm, his sideways glances, I know he was not surprised by my divorce some ten years later.

The obituary mentioned none of this.

His memory tracked me as I pulled my raincoat closed past where the buttons used to be and walked crown-first into the spitting rain. The legs of my blacks were shiny and the creases across the tops of my shoes set to crack. Luckily, no one ever looks at the person performing the ceremony, only the bride and groom and the pretty bridesmaids done up like Easter eggs. But for the memory of Nate nipping at me, I was confident in my mercurial invisibility.

The drizzle was subtle, soft, persistent by the time I arrived at Scavelli's. Back in the garden, the ladies' heels wobbled on the pebbled paths and sank into the grass. The wedding programs curled from the mist. The violinist complained that her violin's pegs were swollen and that tuning was a chore. The guests were dressed in muted tones, the threat of winter having faded autumn's palette except for the bridesmaid, a sparrow of a woman swaddled in magenta, who darted towards me. She lifted onto her toes and whispered in my ear that the bride and groom were running late.

"They might not even make it," she said. "Ingrid would be late to her own funeral, but a wedding? All these people? This hideous dress? I swear she made my buy this dress because she hates me."

The bride and groom, Ingrid and Mark, did make it, breathless and panting. The flustered bridesmaid trembled by my side as she stood witness when we convened in the manager's office. I remembered the couple from our meeting six months ago. I thought them handsome in contradicting ways. Then and now, the groom had the arrogance of a man who didn't like a challenge, and the bride, Ingrid, possessed a pristine quietude, polished, weighty, and mysterious, her heart a doorway the groom seemed unworthy of stepping through. Then, I thought she was beautiful. Now, with her flushed cheeks and failing bun, she was exquisite.

Next to her, the groom's hair was bent from the baseball cap now scrunched beneath his armpit. Had I been a shadow of my former self, the self that Nate once knew, I could've enticed her to come away with me and rescued her from the trap of marriage. The groom pulled the marriage license from his tuxedo pocket and slammed it, triumphant, on the desk. It had been torn and torn again and taped back together. The bridesmaid's eyes widened; the bride avoided her stare. The groom smiled stupidly. I signed, as that's what I'd been paid to do.

I hadn't seen it when I first met the couple, but with her eyes cast downward, the bride looked like Anna. Her high forehead, the calm terror that tugged at the corner of her lips, her delicate contemplation, as breakable as a champagne flute. It was because of Nate that I was thinking of Anna. Of Berkeley and divinity school. I smiled kindly when I caught the bride's eye beneath the canopy in the garden. I couldn't look away. Words filled my mouth like boiled wool when I pronounced them, by the power vested in me by the state of New York, husband and wife.

The bridesmaid, drunk from the scent of roses, batted her eyes during the ceremony and later begged me to stay through the cocktail hour. I told her I didn't do that, that I no longer drank, but she persisted.

"Amuse me," she demanded. "Tell me stories of beautiful disasters. Can you tell when something's a lasting thing?" She charmed me.

I surrendered. The temptation of sweet bourbon, the impulse to toast Nate, and her pretty pout seduced me.

She sipped Long Island Iced Teas through a straw. I pretended to listen to her chatter. Across the room, the bride was a vision of poetic melancholy. Nervous elegance. Accidental grace. She took an elderly guest's hand and drew the old woman's knuckles along her brow.

More and more the bride reminded me of Anna. My younger self blushed, remembering spying on Anna from the window of Café Intermezzo as she set up her table of jewelry on Telegraph Avenue early mornings. How I strolled by late afternoons as she packed up, just to catch a glimpse of her moving through space. How I memorized the glide of her hands shaping space as she talked to customers and how her brows lifted and her lips parted when she was thinking of something to say.

I loved her.

The first time I kissed her, I didn't know her name. It was outside Blake's, late night. I hit her up for a cigarette. She lit mine off hers and blew the smoke straight up. Her neck arched around the moon. Two college kids stumbled down the block, screaming with laughter.

She said, "Nothing's that funny."

I said, "I know."

When they turned the corner, I took her chin and turned her face towards mine. I gently kissed her bottom lip. Then I went back inside.

Nate was drunk at the table. Drunker than me. His lids were heavy, and his chin sunk towards his neck. The band played low and the other customers slumped in their seats. The beer was warm and the ice in our drinks had melted. I didn't see her again that night.

"Will you sleep with her," Nate asked. He slurred his words.

"With who?"

"Whoever."

"Not tonight."

As I pushed him home, the weight of his wheelchair kept me standing instead of falling.

The second time I kissed her, I still didn't know her name. It was at Rainbow Food, a warehouse of day-old bread, expired juices, and wilting lettuce. I spotted her by the pasta. Her lips were parted, her breath dangled dangerously. I paused for a while before inching down the aisle. Once by her side, I brushed a lock of her hair from her face.

She half-smiled as if she half-expected me.

I kissed the corner of her mouth. She blushed and started to speak. I wish now I'd stayed to hear what she wanted to say, but Nate was waiting by the register, his wheelchair weighed down with bad wine and stale cigarettes.

"Who will you be with tonight?" He impatiently nudged his wheelchair controller.

"No one, I think."

"I'm lonely, Thomas."

"As are we all."

That spring, Nate watched when I paid her to pierce my ear behind her jewelry stand. He leaned forward on his chair like a spectator at a sporting event. His breath, her breath, my breath folded into one.

The piercing gun punched a black stud through my skin.

My lobe swelled.

She blew on the burning wound.

"Please choose her," he said.

"Not my type."

He laughed scornfully. "You have a type?"

He was with me the next day, too, when I returned and asked her to twist the earring in my ear. And the day after that, when we brought her coffee. By then, he'd stopped asking about her. He grew sullen. I pretended I didn't notice.

The third time I kissed her, I knew her name, but I didn't tell Nate. I fell in love with whispering *Anna, Anna, Anna*. I only whispered *Anna* when I was alone. Or with her.

There were other women. He should've been satisfied with their stories. Bette, with a cursive tattoo *Truth* spun onto her wrist, always wore the top three buttons of her gauzy shirts undone. When the two of us lay naked in the mornings on her mattress on the floor, she read the tarot. I always asked her to pull a card for Nate and then later reported back to him what the card said.

Esther was a movement artist in a political dance troupe. Nate asked me what it was like to fuck a mime. I told him she was a screamer in bed. She once slapped me so hard, I thought she'd broken my nose. Nate insisted there was an imprint of her hand imbedded in my cheek.

Lydia was an activist who always wore black. We had a tryst in the doorway to Berkeley's Admissions Office as the riot police chased protesters through Peoples' Park.

Mary loved baseball.

Jessica loved tea.

Deirdre loved cats.

When I proposed to Ellen, I imagined him witnessing me lowering down to my knee.

In the park when I was with Caroline, he became the black silhouette watching from the trees.

When I straddled Sophia on the campus green, he was the policeman who stumbled upon us.

Since I'd met him, I was never alone. I practiced my monologues, polished my adjectives, rewrote the dialogue, enhanced the character for my audience of one. He knew about them all, every little detail. The timbre of their voices, the notes of their smells, their secret fantasies stolen by me to give to him.

But not Anna.

Anna was mine.

Poor Nate would never know the love of a stranger, the mixing of scent and skin, the excitement fed by orbiting expectations. He had no one but me to live through, to experience the delights of humanity. To light his cigarettes. To push him home when he was drunk. To argue over bourbon and whiskey and beer backs. I suppose when I proposed to Ellen, I somehow let him down.

"The end of an era," I said.

He said, "Indeed."

I decided to write his parents a letter.

Towards the back of Scavelli's dining room, the bridesmaid leaned over the bar, the magenta train of her dress rumpled and spotted with dried rain.

The bride and groom posed in the front of the restaurant for pictures by the windows. His hand clutched hers. I closed my eyes and leaned against the wall, trying to call to mind the freckles on Anna's arm, which I'd once kissed, one by one, as she lay on her side on the carpet in her bedroom and wept, for what, I couldn't remember. I only remember how the inside of her wrist smelled of mango and how her hands were curled into fists, which I pried open and held flat between my hands.

Silverware clanked in the restaurant kitchen. The cooks and the servers fumbled to plate the food. The kitchen doors swung open and whooshed closed. Soft-heeled shoes and the rustling of cheap slacks paused before me. I sensed a leaden gravity. Heard cutting sigh. I knew before I opened my eyes. My ex-wife's best friend.

Cyndi worked for the divorce lawyer in town, Heath Walker. I married almost everyone on City Island. I've counseled them on street corners. I've run into them in the diner. I've watched their families grow. Heath divorced them. Not only did he divorce them, he kept a running tally how many I married that he divorced. "Got another one of yours, Thomas. Makes three this week."

All the years I was with Ellen, Cyndi was never far away. We'd run into her at the diner on Saturday mornings; she'd slip uninvited into our booth. Her lipstick smeared on a coffee cup, on a napkin, on a fork, on scrambled eggs left on her plate. Like a mirror looking backwards, you could see where she'd been. A week before Ellen left me, she gesticulated with her dirty fork while Ellen sipped her coffee, turned away from me. "Two more, Thomas. That makes five divorces this month. Heath says 'thanks for the business.'"

"I marry people who want to get married. Who am I to deny the pleasure of love, even for a single day? You don't deny the dissolution of that love. You revel in it."

She laughed her straw-ridden laugh. Dry as a bone.

Love, I've always thought, is a temporary delight. Aside from Anna.

Now she held a tray of stuffed mushrooms in one hand, a stack of napkins in the other. The mushrooms leaked grease into a paper doily. There was a stain on the lapel of her vest. I skewered a mushroom.

"Things slow at the office? No divorces?"

She stared at me. "Are you drunk?"

"I'm working." I chewed another mushroom and then another, slowly. The bridesmaid stood a few feet off, sipping her drink, holding mine in her other hand. The bride and groom had disappeared from view. The wedding guests started to find their seats. I ate three more. Four more. Five. Six. I'd had one drink, but it felt like three after so many months without. She'd tell Ellen. Ellen would cry and show up at my apartment with boiled chicken and that look. That look. God. That look.

Cyndi scowled and slunk away to circle the room and the bridesmaid returned with a fresh drink. I downed it.

The bridesmaid clamped her teeth around her drink straw and dug into the ice for her cherry.

"My ex-wife's best friend."

"I didn't know you were allowed to marry."

I set my empty glass on the bar. "We're allowed to do all sorts of things."

The wicked bridesmaid brushed the inside of my elbow.

"Really," she said. "Show me."

She led me to the back hallway of Scavelli's, her hands trailing like kite tails. At the ladies' room, she beckoned me inside. I'd forgotten the headiness of flight, the feeling of home that bourbon afforded me. The surprising heat of her. Her body pressed against mine. The cold of the porcelain toilet tapping the backs of my knees. The flimsy stall door rattled against the lock. The hem of her dress tangled around my wrists and bound me to her as I entered her. Her body arched back.

After, she scrawled her number on a scrap of paper towel and shoved it into my front pocket. Beyond the door, a knife clinked against a water glass. The wedding guests' murmurs swelled. A few applauded and the bridesmaid lifted her head.

"Shit. I have to go."

And then, quiet. I was alone. Though I shun the superstitions of religiosity, I felt Nate's spirit hover in the corner, howling with voyeuristic delight. Winded, I looked up and winked. For old time's sake.

In the front of the restaurant, a litany of toasts commenced. There was no leaving by the front door. The serving staff circulated from kitchen to floor. The bartender stood sentry by the swinging kitchen doors. The sky beyond the front windows darkened. The hallway narrowed and the wallpaper turned dingy. From my vantage, the guests had vanished, their party clothes took on a life of their own.

I began to feel generally unwell. The grease from the stuffed mushrooms puddled in my stomach. The ice and bourbon and

Andre champagne I drank for breakfast didn't agree. I craved a cigarette and solitude, an opportunity to spend time alone with memories.

I deeply missed smoking in the courtyard of Nate's apartment building or mine, after the whiskey had settled, the stories had been told, and we'd run out of things to say. There are times that I understand ceremony as the intention to recreate the sensation of being seen, being heard, being understood by an entity larger than oneself. The ritual of smoke Nate and I practiced nearly every night for those three years seemed sacred.

The hallway floor pulsed in time with my breath. Weariness descended, a tiredness that made my limbs fill with sand. I needed to sit. I slipped into the manager's office, a windowless tomb, and sank into the desk chair. Nate's ghost sat with me. He dug in. I was thirsty as dried grass. When we were young men, I'd considered it my duty, to give him life. But now, with his memory hounding me, I wondered what life I had to offer.

Light filtered in from the cracks around the door, tracing the shadows of the desk, the piles of paper, the opened cartons of liquor and wine. There was a tablecloth folded on top of a stack of boxes. I wrapped it around my shoulders and cracked the seal on a bottle of Maker's Mark. The coils of a wire-bound notebook glinted in the meager light. I decided to write Nate's parents that letter. I opened to an empty page.

Dear Mr. and Mrs. Schiffer, I knew your son once.
We were friends.
During divinity school.
I don't know why I went.
I went blank.

The office air was too thick and musty for me to think. My collar closed around my neck. The ghosts, all of them, crowded around me, siphoning my oxygen, coveting my heartbeat, craving my life. All the women I'd been with, even those whose names I never learned, those who would never love me, filled the room. In the middle, I saw Ellen, mad at me for my short-lived career as pastor at St. Mary's, the books I never wrote, the vows I never kept, the child I never gave her.

Outside the office, someone worked the doorknob. At first, I thought it Anna standing there, a benevolent spirit glowing in a halo of soft light. I stepped forward. She stepped back. It was the bride. Her starched dress has softened. Her lips were swollen from drinking wine.

"I didn't realize someone was in here. I'm sorry."

"No," I said. I rested my hand on her shoulder. I fought the urge to kiss her.

"I just needed a minute." She paused and bit her bottom lip. "He loves me more than anyone else ever will." She looked at me expectantly, her eyes welling up, as if I had something wise to say.

I wanted Anna. I wanted to hold Anna as she cried. I wanted to remember why she'd been crying. I swallowed the heaviness of loss.

"He should."

Her hands were clasped above her heart. The sculpted points of her elbows made me swoon.

"I was looking for the door to the garden," she said. "I need a cigarette. I don't want anyone to see."

I brought her to the garden exit. We dodged raindrops to converge beneath the canopy. I motioned for a cigarette. She lit mine off hers and blew the smoke straight up.

"I don't even like smoking," she said. "My half-sister brought these for me. She likes to think she knows me." She ran her thumb over her fingernails. They were short and painted red. "I guess maybe she does." She inhaled, exhaled. "I shouldn't've made her buy that dress."

"We used to smoke Marlboro Reds. Back in the day."

She grinned. "People still smoke them. It's not like they're some antique brand."

"Could you help me drag that bench to that wall?" I dropped the filter into the wet grass. "I'd like to escape without being seen. My ex-wife's best friend is in the house."

She laughed like Anna used to laugh.

We dragged the bench to the garden wall and I balanced on its back and hoisted myself to the top. She watched, her eyes puddles of gray, as I dropped to the other side, the wire-bound notebook tucked into the back of my pants, the tablecloth pooled over my shoulders and dragging along the ground.

At the liquor store that charges double in summer, I bought a pack of Marlboros and a half-liter of Jim Beam. A ritual is not complete without all its pieces.

The clerk was an older man. I'd married his granddaughter. I couldn't remember his name. "You don't look too good, Thomas." He pushed my change across the counter.

He was right. My hair was dripping wet. I'd barely slept the night before. My ceremonial blacks were soaked through. "Thank you."

I fashioned a rain cap out of the plastic bag and held the liquor under my arm. I wrapped myself tighter in the tablecloth. I'd forgotten my buttonless rain coat at the restaurant. The bells on the door jangling behind me as I braved the spitting rain.

We sat on the bench, Nate's spirit and I, in the cemetery overlooking the bloated, brackish Sound. I broke the seal on the whiskey and lit two cigarettes. I balanced Nate's on the worn edge of a gravestone, where it extinguished itself. I splashed whiskey on the ground, then pulled from the bottle. It didn't burn like it used to. I pulled again and gargled until the back of my throat throbbed. It felt good, sitting with the ghost of a man I didn't know as well as I used to. It felt right. The notebook lay flat on my lap.

The dates and names etched on the cemetery headstones had softened with age. To my left, the roots of a maple tree had knocked over a cluster of children's headstones. Ahead, the water looked closer than it was, like I could take a running leap and land in a sand bank by the shallow swells. Nate's ghost had grown in girth and weight. I could almost hear his whistling breath.

Had I summoned Nate, or had he summoned me? He'd been dead for six months, but for me, he'd only been dead since morning. Still, I'd carried his dead weight for decades, pushing his wheelchair wherever I went.

I knelt before him one night and wept in practice confessional. I loved two women. I was marrying the wrong one. He laid his hand on the top of my head.

"You're an emotional cripple, Thomas." He moved over to his bed and told me to sit in his wheelchair. "Do you see how it feels? Do you understand?"

The seat of the chair was warm. The footrests were too high for me and my knee knocked up past my stomach. And yet the chair felt like a throne, like a privileged place. We laughed through tears and snot, him wheezing from his bed, smelling of stale smoke and piss. Me, bound to his chair, also smelling of piss and tears.

"I want to meet her," he said.

He'd never be satisfied.

He wanted what he couldn't have.

He wanted Anna.

But Anna was mine. I scrawled her details on the palm of my hand, lost hours later to soap and water and the shedding of skin. I didn't let myself memorize her, beyond the trail of freckles on her arm. When I kissed Anna the last time, which I didn't know was the last time, I neglected to transcribe the flash of skin, the scent of grace, the delicious gravity of surrender. But he found her. The three of us sat at a table in the basement of Blake's where a bad band played beneath blue lights. A night like every other night. Save for Anna.

When I went to the bar to order another round, he told her

about Ellen. In the time it took a bartender to pour two fingers of scotch, she was gone.

That's how I remember it. But what's memory, anyway, but a handwritten history revisited so many times that the ink has faded, and the paper, creased and torn, is pieced back together with yellowing tape. Memory is a candid photo taken by a cheap camera with an unskilled eye. My memories were squeezed between lips and bodies, strewn onto winter streets, orphaned and abandoned far from their places of origin. Had Nate been as smart as I remembered? Had his bitterness made bitterness fun? Had he worn his anger like a badge? Or had he secretly craved, relished, his parents' saccharine fears? Had he loved me as much as he demanded I love him? Had I loved him, or had I been in love with the sound of my own voice?

Sitting in the cemetery, the brackish Sound just beyond the hill, I knew that if I buried him, I'd bury a part of myself. It didn't seem like a bad idea. His cigarette tumbled from the tombstone. I lit two more and smoked them both.

It felt terribly lonely. No more thinking. Nothing left to narrate. No one to listen. My mind squeezed dry, an unfurnished room, as if someone who'd been living with me all those years had moved out. I drank his share of Jim Beam. All that was left was mine.

The breeze blew between the buttons of my shirt and I knew what I wanted to write to his parents. I'd say that I knew him once. That he wasn't the hopeless, helpless person they cast him as. He was calculating, shrewd, and clever. He knew more than he let on. I'd write how his broken body set him free from the shackles of propriety, just like the edges of my fractured will did for me. I'd tell them that he drank and swore and loved to think. That he lived through me and I'd let him. I'd wreck their memory of him. He might've broken me, but maybe I was broken already.

I couldn't find my pen. I felt for it in my pockets. I looked on the bench and inside the notebook. I crawled along the grass, scrambling my hands along the cracks between headstone and earth. The mud seeped into the knees of my pants. I searched my pockets again. There was the bridesmaid's number. I unfolded it and examined her bulbous scrawl. I ran the paper across my cheek, searched for hints of texture, expecting the scrap to convey the raw silkiness of her skin. Nothing. I'd never learned her name.

FRIDAY HARBOR

Ingrid tracks the poet and his librarian wife through the jagged edges of the swells. They're far ahead, dwarfed by distance. They paddle in perfect rhythm, their oars pushing arched swallows behind their kayak. When they dip, it's the librarian's white bun that distinguishes them from the sharp angles of the waves. And when they bob, the poet's shaggy hair, also white, emerges from the ocean.

Where Ingrid and Kate struggle, the poet and his wife make the paddling look easy. A strip of sunlight shatters a flimsy cloud. A gust of wind blows their boat to the left. They push into the waves.

Gregory glides through the water. He knows the ocean, a tour guide rounding up his tourist flock. The minister and his daughters lack balance and cooperation, but three bodies are better than two and they slog forward. Pete, the other guide, paddles with the minister's wife, a solid woman with a patient smile. Pete has muscle. The minister's wife is sturdy and strong.

Ingrid leans hard on the right-side rudder to keep the kayak from skidding away from the shore, into the center of the ocean. She digs into the barking water and pulls, hard. In the front dugout, Kate slaps at the water, her stick arms barely able to balance the weight of the paddle. She's useless. More than useless. She's weak. Ingrid digs in again. Her stomach's tight, her shoulders pitched forward, her biceps burning. An hour ago, the ocean was a postcard picture, blue on blue. Now it's a moving sculpture, angry white.

She pulls the both of them, and the camp stove, food, dry bags, bottles of wine, sleeping bags, tents, and drinking water, but they are small, and their weighted boat is not heavy enough to outweigh the wind. The poet and his wife, Gregory, Pete, the minister and his family shrink, then disappear into the distance.

"Why are we so far behind?" Kate looks back to Ingrid.

Ingrid grunts through her bared teeth. "Keep rowing." She doubles down.

Kate turns back again and yells, "Do you wish I was someone else?"

"Fuck you," Ingrid yells back, but Kate is already turned forward, squinting into the sun, Ingrid's words swept into a gust of wind. She does wish she was alone, or better yet, with someone stronger than her. She reminds herself to breathe, to not waste energy on these churning thoughts.

In the space between breaths, the small moments of grace when the swells soften and the boat cuts the waves, when everything is easy, Ingrid pretends that she is every bit of the ocean and the ocean is every bit of her. She imagines they are two bodies separated only by the thin membrane of her skin, that the ocean's mysteries are her own, hidden valleys and mountains, volcanoes, and drowned cities. What if they capsized, and she pulled the skirt away from the lip of the cockpit, and dove deep, her body free, her body home, her body floating through blue nothing, her mind—where would her mind go? Someplace else.

But then she imagines buoying to the surface against her will, pulled onto Gregory's kayak, cold and shivering, another story, another cautionary tale for his next group of tourists.

The blister under her right index finger oozes. Her left pinky is not far behind. She checks the horizon for the poet's white hair, the librarian's bun. Gregory's red kayak slows towards land.

Kate turns and smiles. "We're almost there." She slaps her paddle at a frantic pace.

Ingrid keeps it strong and simple, struggling against an impulse to swat her half-sister into the water.

By the time they reach the shore, Gregory's lying in the sun, his shoes off, his battered straw hat blocking the sun from his face. The others are eating their sandwiches.

Ingrid drops her lifejacket into the cockpit, steps out of the skirt, and leaves Kate on the beach, riffling through the hatches. Her legs buckle as she climbs up the hill to the picnic tables. She sits on a warm, flat rock by Gregory and empties her shoes of the pebbles they collected as she pushed the kayak out of the shallows and onto the sand.

Gregory's legs are crossed at the ankles, his arms heavy by his side. He chews a blade of grass. Ingrid watches his chest press the collar of his tired T-shirt with each inhale, each exhale. She wishes she brought her camera, the good one, the one that can almost capture the beauty of movement and the subtleties of space. She wishes she was brave enough to touch him, feel his sun-heated skin. But, she knows these guys with their scraggly beards and honest muscles. They possess a friendly charisma; they've seen a lot. They have easy laughs and interesting stories. They're charming liars with rugged wisdom and when they look at you they make you feel like you're the only person in the room. When they're not teaching scuba in Phuket, they're skiing at Vail, and the few months each year they're weary of the shallow parade of tourists, they shack up with a college girl who's rebelling against her parents, spin her around the world, and then drop her at home and forget her name.

But still, you can't help but fall in love with them.

When he shifts his hat and turns on his side to watch her blow on her blister, she blushes and smiles back.

"Rough ride," he says. "Glad you made it."

"I should've brought gloves, I guess." She turns her hands towards him. He examines the flapping skin.

"Yeah. Probably should've." He lies back down. "Rowing won't be half as hard the rest of the day."

"I think we're too light, Kate and me," she says. "Keep getting pushed by the wind."

"Likely."

"Two lightweights."

He squints. "Nah," he says, "you're a pro."

The poet and his wife wander on the mossy rock onto the other side of the island. The minister and his family lie in the shade, cradled at the roots of a tree. Pete suns himself on the flat top of a picnic table.

Kate crosses towards them, the dry bag's strap dangling from her wrist. She sits on the other side of Gregory and rifles though the sack, pulls out two sandwiches, a bottle of water, a bag of nuts.

"I'm glad we made peanut butter sandwiches," she says. She turns towards Gregory. "I'm a vegetarian. I don't eat meat."

"Probably better that way," Gregory says. "Less to keep track of."

Leaning against the rock, Ingrid watches Kate delicately pull apart her sandwich, delicately hover by Gregory, delicately turn her face to the sun. Kate's beautiful, at times, painfully so. Her fingers and wrists are so fine, her stature so slight, that if she didn't wear shoes, the wind, the air, the ethers might float her off the ground. In certain light, with her black hair and her alabaster skin, she glows. Sometimes when Ingrid looks at her, she sees the child she once was, standing at her mother's side, twelve years old, crying and confused in the crowd of mourning strangers at their father's funeral. Her cheeks a perfect blush, her eyes watered-down blue. At these moments, the tangle of their lives loosens. *Relationships between half-sisters should be half as complicated*, she thinks. *But they're not.*

Ingrid's small but solid, a plodding pedestrian trapped in a gymnast's body. Her friends call her "handsome," which she takes to mean mannish. It doesn't much matter to her. Her looks keep the rabble away. Where Kate inherited their father's fine features, his Roman nose, his denim eyes, Ingrid inherited his mind.

She draws, like he did, but in broad strokes. Charcoal on palettes of thick paper. When she is not working, her hands are silty and black. She paints her short nails red to hide the ash beneath her fingernails. She's like him in other ways, too. She's read through his entire collection of books, from Philip Roth to Bulgakov. She shares his lips and the shape of his eyes. Sometimes she makes bread, like he did, finding therapy in kneading the dough, drenching the crust in egg yolk or butter. The only thing she hopes she didn't inherit from him is his heart, which quit when he turned forty-six.

She works near Wall Street, selling expensive watches and bands to men with ties and collars too tight for their thick necks. Sometimes she doodles at work in ballpoint pen on the ends of spent receipt rolls. She watches the workers swing their briefcases through the crowds of people just like them and draws their sunken eyes and stooped shoulders and imagines her father among them, a bogged-down dreamer, his artistry hidden in the pockets of his three-piece suit.

Sometimes she reads at work, leaning against the display case, a bottle of Windex on the floor by the register so she can wipe evidence of her elbows off the glass. When she's bored, she synchronizes the watches so that they tick in time, one loud second after the other. She listens to the time tick away. She dusts, she polishes, and runs an electric broom over the gray carpeting every morning. She waits for the front door to jingle. She thanks the postman, and flirts with the beat cops who sometimes bring her coffee or watch the store so that she can slip out for lunch. She lets Jerry, who washes windows up and down the street, try on Rolexes and TAG Heuers and Movados worth more than his yearly salary. He holds his arm back and whistles and says, "I see the future. And the future are great."

It was Jerry who told her about the whales. The look on his face when he told her how he once saw one breaching when he was a kid is what made her want to go. "They're big," he said. "Bigger'n you can imagine. There's majesty in all that bigness."

"What're you thinking?" Gregory asks.

Kate's wandered to the rocks. She stands against the breeze, her

Lilliputian fists digging into her waist, one foot on a rock like a hunter stepping on fallen game.

Ingrid shrugs. "Thinking about . . . whales, of course," she says. "And the homeless guy, the window washer, who told me to come here. And why he was thinking of whales. I'm thinking of my husband, who was supposed to come. Last week, he said he loved me. This week, he's probably moving out. But that's how things go. I'm thinking that all people really want is to sleep with each other. Uncomplicated affection. The sooner we all admit it, the better off humanity will be."

Gregory laughs at that, pulls on his shoes and pulls the rim of his hat over his eyes. "I guess it's time to go. Should be a nice easy ride the rest of the way."

The water *is* calm the rest of the day. The group glides into the campground at dusk. Ingrid softens with the smells of brine, wildflowers, and rotting leaves. She walks with Kate up the wooded path to the tents.

The wine they brought is peppery and hard and they sit with the others. The minister quotes Saint Augustine. His daughters roll their eyes. The poet and his librarian wife talk in low tones, giggling. Kate's cheeks are flushed by her second mug of wine. Gregory tells stories to the group about his last trip with a family of five who hated one another.

The family, similarly charged magnets, slept in four corners of the field, their tents as far as they could get from one another, the father in the middle of the field. He drank beer for breakfast and scowled at his scowling wife. His wife wore mascara and foundation every day. She looked flawless, even at six in the morning, even on a kayak in the middle of the ocean. Most of the time, she wore lipstick, too. The pouty children knew how to twist and turn for their bright selfies. Drunk, the father slipped Gregory a hundred dollars and took him by the shoulders and swore that they were the happiest family on Earth, on the best vacation money could buy. And then, he started weeping.

Pete nods, his doleful eyes fixed on the group. "It's true," he says. "It's all of it true."

There are other stories, too. Encounters with angry gulls, a transsexual madam in Thailand who fell deeply, madly in love with Gregory and followed him back to the States only to be deported before she left the airport, a one-legged skier in Colorado, a young woman with Downs who insisted on learning how to dive.

Kate leans into Gregory's stories and pours wine into his mug. She passes the bottle to Pete at the grill. Pete is younger than Gregory, with a long face and crooked teeth. His boots are taped together with duct tape, his flannel too long in the body, too short in the arms.

Ingrid watches Kate. Kate watches Gregory. Gregory, catlike, watches Ingrid until she pours the last of the bottle in her mug and wanders to the dock. The water's still. The librarian leans against a post, her bun frayed, wisps of white framing her face. She points to a bird. "Marbled murrelet," she says. White bird, black wings, coasts across the sky. Ingrid squints towards the sunset, focuses on the pinks and blues her father would've painted versus the black-gray smudges, the clean white, and the sepia Ingrid works with.

She feels for the thick space between her and Gregory. Gregory is up on the grass, drinking wine with Kate, clearing out the kitchen with Pete. The space is invisible, but it's a living, breathing thing. And then Kate rips the distance apart and runs to Ingrid's side.

"I wasn't sure where you went! You know what I was thinking? I was thinking about Dad. How he would love this. Don't you think? He'd be really happy."

She asks about their father almost every time they're together. *What was he like when he was younger? Did he love Ingrid's mother once, as much as he loved hers? What do you think he was thinking before he died? Do you think he knew he was going to die?*

No one noticed that his heart was failing, but the alarm had been set from his birth, a ticking clock that grew as loud as the synchronized watches at Ingrid's watch store. His death left Kate, twelve, with a mystery she'd never solve, and Ingrid, at twenty, with a reason to never go home again. Depending on Ingrid's mood, she answers in different ways.

She wants to ask Kate questions, too. *Did he sing to you? Did he rub your back until you fell asleep? Did he yell at you for no good reason? Did you ever catch him crying behind the shed?*

Ingrid sleeps outside, a few feet from their tent. Her pillow is a balled-up sweater. The earth fills the contours of her spine. She sleeps lightly, dreams she's in a rowboat in the pond at Central Park. She rows. Her father's at the stern. She's concerned because he's been dead for twelve years, but he keeps coming back; the pages of his story are dog-eared, the margins marked up with notes. He's drawing pictures on the water with his finger, now running his pinky over his brow, now pushing his black-framed glasses up the bridge of his nose. They propel the boat under the footbridge with colorful graffiti, intricate patterns.

Ingrid starts awake. It's only when Kate's around that she has these dreams.

There's a light drizzle, and sprinklings of rain collect in the corners of her eyes. Gregory kneels by her shoulder.

"I want to show you something," he whispers.

She slips on her sneakers and follows him down the path. The air is dotted with moisture. A cricket song hangs in the air. When they are far enough away from the tents, he flicks on his flashlight and leads her to the kayaks.

Their paddles jangle the water, soft mallets on a wooden bell. The island is a silhouette, black against midnight blue, the moon covered by clouds.

Gregory lifts his paddle. Ingrid does the same. They coast,

carried by the current. In turns there's the smell of brine, followed by the sweetness of flower, of musk, Gregory's and then her own scent, a mixture of salt and honey.

"Look," he says. He stretches the tip of his oar towards the water by her side. He draws a round arch and scribbles back. Veins of gold and green light up just under the surface of the water.

She takes her oar and does the same. The same green and gold veins follow the path of movement. He uses his hand. She uses her hand. The veins weave around their fingers and then disappear.

"What is it?" she says.

He shrugs.

The gold makes way for the hull of the kayak, marking where they're going, where they've been.

Back on shore, he takes her hand. He kisses her forehead as her father might've done. And then, she kisses him.

"I'm too human," he says. He kisses the corners of her eyes, the corners of her lips.

"I'm too married," she says. But she follows him gently up the path.

Later that night, the early before morning, she leaves him where the trees end and the mowed grass begins.

She slides into her sleeping bag; Kate stirs from inside the tent.

"Where were you?"

"I just got up to pee."

"Were you dreaming?"

"Go back to sleep."

Ingrid lies awake until dawn.

At six a.m., the dew hangs in the air and the sun promises to rise. Ingrid, cupping the warm coffee, watches the fog roll off the water. When she was young, when their father was her father only, she'd find him at the kitchen table on mornings like this, looking out the picture window to their backyard, a family of deer grazing on his garden. Some mornings she'd find him with his drafting pen hovered over a paper napkin or watching the ink bleed into the hollow of a man's face, a city melting into perspective, blurred trees and birds.

In high school, when her father was no longer hers alone, when she lived between two houses and the picture window gave way to her mother's condo and her father's new family, he would leaf through her charcoal drawings with his drafting pen. He drew on top of them, correcting proportions, angles, lines of actions. He knew where contours could be extended and where lines should end. Young Kate would sink into the corner of the couch and pretend to listen. She fidgeted and posed, languid and feline, vying for his attention.

After breakfast, the group sets out to Friday Harbor. From the back of the kayak, Ingrid watches Kate, her child-sized life vest pushing up against the hairs on her neck, the stiff body of the vest making an immobile tunnel for her body, her arms the only part in motion as she strokes the water with the tip of her blade.

Gregory's kayak glides between tourists. One moment he's nestled alongside Ingrid and Kate, the next, circling the poet and his wife. Today, the kayakers travel as a tribe and Ingrid can hear the others speak.

Gregory expounds upon the virtues of the gull.

The minister blathers to the group about Sedna, goddess of the whales and narwhals. When his youngest asks what a narwhal is, he tells her, "The unicorn of the sea." She doesn't believe him.

The poet and his wife make plans for dinner.

The trip ends at two. The group loads their kayaks onto the trailer of the pickup van and drives back to Friday Harbor from the launch. They pull in at the far end of Main Street. The corner's choked with cars rolling onto the ferry dock, tourists, and summer residents. The poet and his librarian wife hop off the van and disappear into a puff of words. The minister and his flock bottleneck the van door with their gear as Pete unloads the back of the van. Kate and Ingrid wait for the others to exit in the last row.

"Dad would've loved this, don't you think," Kate says.

"He was afraid of water. Couldn't swim. City kid."

"He would've liked it except for the water. He would've liked the whales."

"We didn't see any whales."

"He would've like the idea of whales. I think. Right?"

"Maybe. I guess. I don't know."

Kate sighs, "I'm going to miss Gregory so much."

Outside the van, Kate wraps her arms around Gregory's waist as they say goodbye. He returns the gesture, lifts her feet off the ground in a bear hug. When he sets her down, she plants herself at Gregory's side.

When Ingrid looks at Gregory, his eyes trap hers. She knows these guys. She knows how they operate. And still.

She shoves two twenties in his hand. "For you and Pete," she says. He pulls her in. "Thank you," he whispers, as if he's sharing a secret.

All the while, Kate stands smiling, squinting into the sun.

A crow picks at the pebble by their feet as they walk towards the hotel.

"The crow," Kate says, "the smartest of all birds."

"According to who?"

"According to they."

"Compared to what?"

"To humans."

"That's stupid," Ingrid says. "You can't compare birds to people."

"Why do you always do this?"

Because you always want what I have, Ingrid thinks. *Because you are always there, trotting beside me to remind me of what I'm not. Because I'm the only one to know that he loved me more than he loved you. Because you keep finding me, keep coming back, keep trying to make me love you. Because you'll never understand.*

The Rocky Bay Bar is lit by cruel fluorescents reflected on laminate floors as the band unpacks their instruments. Five guys, middle-aged, polo shirts, two of them balding, one of them bald, tune their guitars and rattle their drums with one hand, and carry a bottleneck beer with the other. Townies, tour guides, and tourists in dusty Keens and cargo pants. Five sailors in their Navy whites sit at the bar. Everyone else is dressed in faded blacks, browns, and blues. Ponytails, blue jeans, crumpled shirts.

The minister and his family sit in a booth, their table littered with greasy plates and scraps. The minister sips two fingers of whiskey, his daughters slurp melted ice and Coke, his wife drinks herbal tea. Ingrid and Kate pass by their table with a quick smile and nod.

They take a high two-top in back, and Pete swaggers in and waves to them from across the dance floor. His hair is wet, his dirty flannel traded for a clean one, too long in the torso, too short in the arms. He drags stools from another table and squeezes them between the women. "Gregory's coming," he says. "Ahh, the real world. The real world has craft beer. And showers."

"Real world for you," Ingrid says. "We're still on vacation."

"Ingrid's on permanent vacation," Kate says. "Sort of. That's what my mom says. But, I mean, she works."

Pete lifts Ingrid's beer. "Cheers to that." Sweet, affable Pete.

Both Ingrid and Kate feel the heavy warmth of Gregory's arms on their shoulders before they see him. He smells of whiskey, beer, pot, tobacco, soap. He buries his face into the curve of Ingrid's neck and then does the same to Kate, who stretches to offer him more. "Are you really leaving?"

Ingrid and Kate nod.

"Really? Tomorrow? Really?"

"We have to. Really," Ingrid says.

Kate sighs.

He pouts like a forlorn child. "Really? You have to?" He looks at her, and her body remembers him inside her and she feels the ghost of a swoon. "Well, let me buy you a beer."

The band plays standards with a swing beat, jazzy and cool. Ingrid's heart presses against her chest bone. She's dizzy. Maybe it's the beer after three days of pushing water, three days of granola bars and canned spaghetti. Three days watching Gregory watch her. Three days of Kate.

When Gregory returns from the bar, he looks deflated. In the water, he's graceful, but on land, he's just another guy. He hugs a waitress and waves the small packet of rolling papers at Kate, Ingrid, and Pete.

"Come smoke with us?" Kate slides off her stool. Pete follows.

"Go ahead," she says. She runs her thumb over the condensation on her beer. "I'm good here."

Her beer tastes medicinal and she pushes it aside. She watches the dance floor spotted with children and their mothers pushing against the beat. One of the Navy sailors, clean-shaven, clean-cut, circumnavigates the dancers and stops at her table. "Do you want to dance?"

She hesitates. She doesn't know what she wants, but she holds out her hand. The sailor pulls her into the thin crowd and then suddenly pushes her out and they are skipping through a triple step, as if they'd been dancing together for their whole lives. The air isn't heavy like the water was, and the centrifugal force, the spinning, the twirling, the turning makes her laugh.

There's Kate climbing back up onto her stool. Next there's Gregory, his eyes red and glazed, his hand resting on Kate's back. The sailor turns her out and pulls her back in. Pete lifts his beer, Kate leans against Gregory's arm. And who cares?

Ingrid smiles. The sailor smiles. The band smiles. Gregory,

drunk, smiles, too. *Kate can have him*, she thinks, even though neither of them ever will. *I had the best of him. I had him longer. She can have him last.*

ALMOST ALWAYS

Ingrid's directions read:

"There's a basketball court on the corner of Third and Sixth. There'll be boys and men playing on one side of the chain-link fence. There'll be people on the other side watching the game. Hoshi's apartment is a half a block east. It's a fourth floor walk-up. It's above a bar. The bar's name is always changing, so I don't know what it is, but there's an old oak doorway next to another old oak doorway. The first doorway is Hoshi's. There's no buzzer. Yell up towards the fourth floor when you get there. She'll be listening for you."

Nine hours earlier, Kate'd been in Los Angeles. *Lost Angeles*, she secretly, silently called it. Now she was in New York, lugging her suitcase up the subway stairs. She'd met Hoshi once—at Ingrid's wedding. She vaguely remembered ponytails and platform shoes. A giggle that made other people giggle. She'd been effusive in her affection. Kate wasn't used to that.

She found the bar. She counted up to Hoshi's windows. She wasn't a yeller, but she yelled.

"Hoshi! Hoshi—it's Kate. I'm here." In the moments between Kate yelling and Hoshi poking her head out of the window, Kate's pulse quickened. *What if Hoshi wasn't home? What if she was on the wrong street, at the wrong bar, outside the wrong apartment building?* But Hoshi appeared, waved, and disappeared again. A minute later, she burst from the front door and pulled Kate into an aggressive hug.

"Oh my God . . . you look just like your sister . . . same hair . . . same eyes! Oh wow. Super. You made it!"

Together, they yanked Kate's suitcase up the crooked stairs.

"Mailbox key sticks, so press the hinge when you turn the key." Thump. "Thick key is the deadlock." Thump. "Green key—the next lock down, twist it twice." Thump. "The key with the red nail polish works the back basement door. Into the secret garden. Ever read that book?"

Tired from travel, Kate wheezed as they climbed. Still, she was relieved that her day was four floors away from ending. Hoshi would leave in a couple of hours for an eight-week visit to her family in Japan. Ingrid had arranged Kate's stay. She'd collect the mail. Water the plants. Dog-sit Hoshi's teacup Yorkie, Max.

Kate's return back east was not a triumph. Everyone knew that. It hadn't been as hard as Kate thought it'd be to admit defeat, though. It'd been almost sensual, melting into failure. Bones softening. Skin luxuriously unmasked. The chill that accompanied vulnerability was painfully satisfying. In L.A., people looked away, wishing that they, too, could give up. No one called it what it was. But Kate knew. She whispered it in private. *Failure.* She'd started wearing sweats to the grocery. Stopped coming on to the boys who worked in the mailroom at William Morris. As a hostess at P.D. Chang's, she refused to seat the *important people* by the window. She left drunk messages on people's phones. To her mother: *I never liked playing the piano.* To her friends: *I'm too fat to be successful here.* To Ingrid: *I wish just once you'd say you loved me.*

That Ingrid was the one who brought Kate back, well, they didn't talk about that.

Hoshi's apartment was small. The shower was in the kitchen and the living room was a slip of a space, steps beyond the front door— more of a hallway with a sofa than a room. Even the oven was slim, crammed in, half the width of a regular oven. A cookie tray could slide in lengthwise. The apartment was dark. Shaded on the windowed wall by a brick building so close that a person could touch it. Hoshi kept a bowl of sidewalk chalk on the window sill and sometimes drew on the other building.

"Like lists?"

"Like a canvas." Hoshi demonstrated. "Like the O. Henry story." She drew a leaf.

Normally Kate would nod, tight-lipped, but she was too tired to lie. "I don't know that one."

"The leaf one. Where she doesn't die because the painted leaf doesn't fall?"

"No."

"It's famous."

"No one reads in L.A."

Max lifted a sympathetic eyebrow and sighed from his bed in the corner of the kitchen.

That night, when she was finally alone and sitting on Hoshi's bed, Max butted up against Kate's leg. She wished Ingrid would call, but knew she wouldn't. Ingrid. A wolf who displayed affection in stealth. She'd do it when it was needed most or least expected. Kate had learned over time not to pursue Ingrid. That seizing those moments always led to a hasty retreat.

She liked being new in town, the freedom that accompanied solitude. She liked that no one was looking at her. She dove into the thrum of the city and let it carry her. She liked living in someone else's space, too. She flipped through Hoshi's Japanese books and ran her fingers along the characters from the top to the bottom of the page. She imagined living in a world where language was white noise.

She walked. One among millions traveling from one building to another. Here, for now, Kate didn't have to be anyone at all. Bowing to pressure from her mother, she signed up for the LSATs. Her first two weeks in New York, she dutifully carried the LSAT work book from café to coffee house to park benches and the library. Her third week, she interviewed for an assistant position at a corporate law firm in Times Square, another surreptitiously-delivered gift of aid from Ingrid who worked at different law firm designing graphics for their in-house newsletter.

For the interview, Kate dressed up. She wore eyeliner and pantyhose and bought a pair of pumps which she carried in her bag as she walked forty blocks up to the firm. The *Operations Team* was comprised of actors and writers who waited, two to each small office cubicle, until a frantic legal secretary barked orders at them: *Make copies. Order dinner. Pick up take-out.*

All her life, Kate dreamt of growing up to be like Ingrid, but now, with both of them living in the city, both working at law firms, the crisscrossing of experience felt like a paper cut.

Kate's co-workers were good New York transplants who'd escaped the trap of living their parents' dreams. Kate was the only one on the team planning on law school and they found that novel and amusing. By the end of the week, she started telling them she, too, was an actress in order to fit in, straight from playing an alien in L.A., neglecting to mention that it was to hand out energy drink samples at the West Hollywood Hallowe'en parade and that her handler had dragged her into the crowd in order to conduct a drug deal. *What are you working on now,* they asked. She answered: *This.*

By the middle of her first week, she'd mastered the copy machine. By her second week, she'd memorized the phone numbers of the Chinese take-out and the deli. By her third week, she'd settled into the fog of waiting. Along with co-workers, she practiced the methodical slowness required to stretch a simple task across an eight-hour shift. She arranged the plasticware in the breakroom. She refilled staplers. Sharpened pencils. Anything to stave off the voracious boredom of office life.

On the Tuesday of her second week at the law firm, Kate woke with an overwhelming feeling of joy. The island had thrown open its arms and invited her into a warm embrace. People said New York was a small town. Kate believed it. It was a beautiful day, stunningly so. Three steps into autumn. The sky was as blue as it'd ever been.

She walked Max to the river. They zig-zagged through Greenwich Village past carriage houses and brownstones. There was breeze off the river that morning and a calm only cities know. She and Max sat on a park bench and Kate closed her eyes and wished that she'd always feel like this. Like someone somewhere secretly loved her and that person was worthy of her love in return.

She wore Hoshi's hoodie over her pajama top and a skirt over her pajama bottoms. The toes of her pink Uggs had turned gray with soot. Her hair was unbrushed. No one cast a second glance. She'd escaped the shackles of beauty. She was set free.

She and Max watched a barge amble up the river. She tripped over Max's leash. Max yelped as she twisted away from him and landed on her knee and the heel of her hand. It burned before she even looked at it. The swelling red of the skin beneath her skin was flecked with sand and dark pebbles of tar. Even that, even the sting felt right. Staring at the scrape, she stepped forward, into someone else. His hands clapped on to her shoulders, then pulled back away.

"You okay?"

"Oh, sorry." He looked nice. Suit. Tie. Good shoes. Her mother always told her to look at a man's shoes. She showed him the scrape. "Not paying attention."

"My mother used to have Yorkies. She put little bows in their hair." There was something in the way that he said mother. *Mother.* Trepidation. *Mother* was always such a loaded term. Unlike *father* which always sounded so simple.

"You sure you're okay?"

She nodded and dug her hands into the pockets of Hoshi's sweat jacket. There was something unfamiliar in the pockets' emptiness. Something missing. A wave, shame. A flood, deep and ugly, swelled and she pushed her hands deeper into the pockets. "Empty."

"Huh?"

"I lost my keys." She rushed back the few steps to where she fell. Nothing. They looked around the park bench she and Max had sat on. They looked in the grass. No keys. The world seemed suddenly very large and the keys so small.

"Maybe walk back the way you came?"

On that beautiful day at that beautiful hour, the path Kate traveled to arrive at that moment yawned open. The streets crumbled. She saw rivers of road. Wilshire Boulevard. The La Brea Tar Pits. The Grove. The lost keys a throbbing augury. *Lost Angeles* laughing. She thought she'd never leave that spot by the Hudson. She'd turn to salt.

"Here's my number in case—I don't know." He handed her a business card.

"I have to go." She drifted away with Max by her side.

Keys—lost. Money—locked in the apartment. Phone—locked in the apartment. Friends—none. Dog—needs shelter. Work—can't call. Bar below Hoshi's– doesn't open until five. Fire escape—too high to reach. Windows—locked anyway.

She stepped into a bodega.

"You can't bring a dog in here," the cashier said, leaning forward. The shop cat stared from an empty shelf by the door. Kate burst. Sobbing.

"Can I use your phone?"

The cashier then nodded and took the phone from its cradle behind the counter. He handed it to her. "What's the number, darling?"

Ingrid would know what to do. She had to have a key. Anyway, Ingrid's was the only phone number she knew by heart. She contained her tears by staring at the candy bars. Bright lines of yellow wrappers. Butterscotch Life Savers. Chocolate. Mints. Gum.

"Hi. It's me."

"Where are you calling from?"

Kate couldn't stop the sobbing from coming on. The bodega owner handed her a napkin. "I'm in my pajamas."

There was a pause on Ingrid's end. "Are you okay?"

"Locked out." She tried to stop crying. Scrunched her face. Bit her thumb. "I'm sorry," she said to the phone. "I'm sorry," she said to the bodega owner. "I'm sorry," she said to the floor, to Max, to her mother. To *Lost Angeles*. To the energy drink people who hired her to play an alien.

"Take a cab. Whatever. Just get here."

" . . . "

"Okay? Okay. I got to get ready. I'll meet you outside." Ingrid hung up the phone.

Kate handed the receiver to the shop owner. "Sorry. Thank you."

"No problem," he said, his voice soft. "You'll laugh at this tomorrow." He wiped the phone with a napkin. "I promise. You have friends. It's okay."

"Okay." She doubted him. "Tomorrow."

Kate half-ran to Ingrid's apartment, a breakneck speedwalk up Sixth Avenue, the dog panting in her folded arm. It was coming on nine. *Stupid. Stupid.* Kate was making both of them late. She ran the last two blocks.

Ingrid was waiting on the stoop, dressed for work.

"Okay. Hurry!" Ingrid held the front door open. "Let's go." Both clambered up the stairs. "I set out clothes. Will be big for you, but—" They burst through the apartment door and swept past Ingrid's husband. Kate barely saw him as Ingrid rushed her to the bedroom. But she heard him.

"She brought Hoshi's dog? Really?"

"It's for a couple of hours, Mark." Ingrid shut the door.

"I hate this yappy thing."

"Mark! Don't make things worse." Ingrid shook her head. "He's impossible."

Kate kicked off her shoes. "Will Max be okay?"

"He's just whining. Max'll be fine."

"Fucking Hoshi," they heard him say.

Ingrid pointed to the clothes laid out on the bed. "Change." She slipped out of the room. Just outside the door, Ingrid and Mark's voices went low. Kate stepped into the skirt. A fine checkered pattern, black and white, a flat bow at the waist. The skirt spun on her and rested on her hips. The shirt, a black blouse, was loose and long in the arms. Ingrid's shoes didn't fit at all. Kate slipped on her pink Uggs again. Maybe at lunch she'd buy a pair of shoes. Cheap flats.

Ingrid was sitting on Mark's lap on the sagging sofa, his arms locked around her waist when Kate emerged from the bedroom. Ingrid stifled a laugh. "Tuck in the shirt. Roll up the sleeves."

"I look bad."

"You'll live."

Mark leaned forward and rested his chin on Ingrid's hip. "You wearing those shoes?"

"I have to." Kate's hands slapped against her thighs. Her lip quivered and *dammit* she didn't want to cry in front of her sister and definitely not in front of Mark, but—

"It's okay. Don't cry. In ten years, this'll be story for your kids. Jesus. I can't stand it when women cry."

Ingrid hit her husband's shoulder. "Shut up."

"Thanks," Kate said. "Thanks for helping."

Ingrid shrugged. "What else was I going to do?"

And then they were off, trotting down Tenth Avenue and across 50th Street. It *was* a beautiful day and Kate already felt the urge to laugh, even as she wanted to cry. She was commuting with her older sister, going to work. *Commuting.* A casual moment. Despite the shame of losing the keys, the pink Uggs and spinning skirt . . . Kate wondered if this was what happy was. *Everything,* she thought, *everything, will be okay.*

On Ninth and 50th, a crowd had gathered around an electronics store. Kate wanted to press on, but Ingrid slowed. They were watching the T.V.s in the shop window.

"What happened?" Ingrid stepped into the group.

Kate followed in her shadow.

A man turned, his mouth hanging open, his eyes wide. Kate lifted onto her toes. It didn't make sense. Televisions played silently behind the glass. She pushed her way to the front.

"Another plane just flew into the building." Then the group, the entire group, Kate among them gasped one collective breath, as a tower of the World Trade Center crumbled in real time to the ground.

They stayed and watched it fall again.

And again.

And again.

And again.

Until the second tower fell.

Mark was in bed when they got back. The apartment smelled of weed. Ingrid paused at the kitchen sink. Ran water until it was clear and filled two glasses. She handed one to Kate, who tip-toed back to the open apartment door and shut it.

"You want coffee?" Ingrid had already turned on the stove. The burner flashed fire into flame.

"Sure."

They moved like that, around each other. Kate reached into the refrigerator for milk. Ingrid filled the kettle with water. Ingrid tapped coffee into the French press. Kate rinsed mugs and placed them on the counter. Max watched from the living room sofa.

Every movement made a sound. Every sound hung in the air. Crisp. Cutting. Kate couldn't imagine how Mark was still sleeping. How he'd slept through it all. She and Ingrid sat at the crowded kitchen table. Ingrid leaned her head against the wall. Eventually Mark stumbled in.

"Thought I heard something. What're you doing back?"

"Turn on the news."

He shuffled into the living room and pushed Max to the floor. "Holy shit." They heard the click of a lighter.

"Could you not? For one day?"

"Baby," he said from the door jamb, a smoking bowl in his hand. "Today, of all days, is a day to smoke."

The three of them sat on the sofa and watched the towers collapse again. This time in slow motion.

Wherever Ingrid lived, she found a way onto the rooftops. This rooftop was nothing special. Warped tar. Dirty brick. A bent wrought-iron railing, ten inches high. A flat, forsaken place. Kate picked at the tar. Ingrid leaned against the crumbling brick. Both held their coffee mugs, the warmth leaching into their hands. This was the sort of day that lived forever. And *yes,* Kate thought, if she had kids, she'd tell them the story.

To the north, the sky was beautiful; the downtown air was stained with the bitterness of fire, the melting of steel and plastic. A helplessness impossible to articulate. A quietude as well.

Ingrid pushed her cellphone towards Kate. "Try your mother again."

Busy signal.

"They're okay, right?"

"The mothers? They're fine. Worried about us."

It was true. Kate's mother was always fine. Unflappable. Cool. Never harried. Never rushed. Kate'd only met Ingrid's mother a couple of times. Only in passing, though once as a teenager she'd seen her at K-Mart and followed her through the store. It was around Christmas and Ingrid's mother had picked up an ornament of mirrors, a tiny disco ball, and stared at her broken reflection in the tiny squares for the longest time. After she'd left the store, Kate returned to the ornaments and did the same.

Is this what people did when bad things happened? Did they remember strange moments? String them together? Tell themselves stories?

"Dad used to work down there, right?"

"Yeah. Wall Street. I used to try to imagine him walking down the streets when I worked at the watch store."

Kate felt the last of the warmth in her cup of coffee bleed into her hands.

"My mom never recovered from it," Ingrid said. "She never let him go. Never understood why he left, I guess. When he died, she was wrecked. Funny how one person can hurt so many. He wasn't that special, you know? Dad. He was just a guy. And probably not that good a guy."

All morning they'd watched footage of people hanging out of the building windows, waving white paper for flags. A couple holding hands leapt out of one of the floors, caught on camera and trapped in midflight. People diving. People falling. People plunging. For years, their families would scour the photographs and film footage. Search for clues. Wonder at the moment where grace met fear and pain and surrender crossed paths. Ripped from a fading fabric.

"He left because of me." The end of her father's life had begun with her. The end of a marriage. *Talk about failure.* "I'm the asshole."

Ingrid took the mug from Kate's loosening grip. Gently placed it to the side. And for the first and only time in Kate's adult life, rested her arm around Kate's shoulder and pulled her onto her lap and let her cry.

"Are you gonna have kids? Kate asked. They were still on the roof. The sun was slipping. Mark had been up and gone back in. Downtown, smoke mingled with the clouds.

"I don't think so."

"You don't want them?"

"It's not that." Ingrid turned her back to the smoke. "I'm in my thirties. It just doesn't seem like it's gonna happen."

"Are you afraid Mark will leave you?"

"God no. He can't even get it together to change his underwear most days." She sighed. "No one'll ever love me like he does."

"I don't want children," Kate said.

"Give it time."

"I don't want to be a lawyer."

"You don't have to be."

A plume of black smoke shot straight into the air. "Strange days." A howl, grief, rose from the windows below. Ingrid leaned over the ledge. On the sidewalk, outside the apartment building, a collection of flowers and candles had gathered and swelled. Ingrid's face lost its color. "Shit," she whispered. "My neighbor's wife's a flight attendant."

After that, words ceased working.

On Saturday, Ingrid called Kate.

"I want to see," she said. "Mark won't come."

They walked from the West Village down past Canal Street on the east side. Ingrid brought her camera and stopped to take pictures every few moments. The streets were quiet. And then, they were silent. Ingrid and Kate crossed an invisible line. The color blanched from the trees and the sidewalks were haunted and hollow. Flat emptiness. Dead pigeons in the ash. Live pigeons stumbling on the sidewalks. The air tasted bitter. They walked.

There was a hollow stillness in the streets, the kind ghosts carry, the kind that turns bones to chalk. They stopped at the watch store Ingrid used to work at. Ash had pushed its way under the door and into piles and dunes that reached the edges of the display cases, poetic in that way that sand takes on sound and sheer curtains hang.

The watches were still in the display cases. Ingrid cupped her hands to the window. "They're still ticking."

Kate looked ahead. There were no footprints in the ash.

"I want to be a nurse," Kate said when they'd made it out of the dust and back into sunshine. Another beautiful day. They stood on the corner by the basketball court. A slow gentlemen's game in progress. A sparse mob watched behind the chain-link fence. The city would become a gentler place for a while.

"A nurse." Ingrid nodded. "Good. The world needs nurses like you."

"Don't tell my mom."

"I don't talk to your mom if I can help it."

"I'm not going back to the law firm." She had Hoshi's place for another few weeks. She had a little bit of savings. She'd figure it out. "Should I give notice?"

"I don't think it matters."

Kate knew what would happen, but she threw her arms around Ingrid anyway. Ingrid stiffened, then softened, then stiffened again. Like a wolf, she placed her hand on Kate's cheek, then took it back. A moment so brief that Kate wasn't sure it happened. She smiled. Nodded. Disappeared underground to catch the subway without a word.

On Monday morning, Kate took the train to Pace to visit the nursing school. The subway car was quiet. No one spoke. People sobbed silently instead. Hands folded. Eyes drifting. Hearts open. Sorrow mingling with grace.

Kate thought she recognized the man she'd met at the park when she'd lost Hoshi's keys. He was wearing the same suit. He wiped his mottled cheek with the base of his hand, then ran it back across his nose. Their eyes met and parted.

They got off at the same stop. "You found your keys?"

She shook her head. "Spares."

He was tall, but not imposing. His arms hung easy by his side. The strap of his messenger bag cut across his tie.

"Well," he said, "I'm glad you're safe. I was wondering about the girl who lost her keys."

She wanted to say something kind. Something that would touch him. Words failed. "What's your name?"

"Brad."

"Kate. Nice to meet you."

They walked together up to the street. A bike messenger sped past them. A taxi swerved and honked. The sky was incredibly blue if you looked in the right direction. City pigeons. City of litter. City of abandoned dreams. They stopped at the door to a café. He offered to buy her coffee.

"You won't be late for work?"

He shrugged. "Doesn't much matter, does it?"

City of cracked sidewalks. City of tired buildings. City of strangers. City of brownstones. City of brick. City of a single star.

It was a planet, really. Kate knew that. But it glittered like a star.

THE DARLING DEMPSINI SISTERS

Val rings the doorbell. She rings it again. She presses the bell button a third time, so hard that the tip of her finger bends back. A chill runs up Kate's spine. She shudders at the muted *ding dong*, an innocent sound. The Open House sign swings from a mud-flecked post at the end of the drive, dolorous in the late spring spatter of rain.

There are three of them outside. Four, actually, if you count the baby, who's not yet born, but is big enough *to* be born. Kate-with-baby stands a few steps behind Val, gaze trapped on Val's bending finger, on the emergent white roots of her dyed black hair, on the stretched and tired fabric of her fitted dress. The knit of the begonias across her thighs is wilted. Flecks of exhausted elastic dot the landscape like snow. Dandruff. Flower lice. Is there a such a thing as flower lice? If not flower lice, lice lice, little beasts Kate will likely come to know in the years ahead when her child starts school.

Since she's been pregnant, she notices small things. Small details. Small smells. Small sounds. Small feelings. Small memories, too.

Brad stands next to Kate, his hand absentmindedly resting on her shoulder. Kate didn't use to mind the casualness of his touch, his comforting weight, but since the beginning of her third trimester, she's become leaden under the force of gravity. She feels squat. Corpulent's too jolly a word. She feels like she's sinking into muddy ground.

Today is Saturday. On Saturdays, Val looks at houses for sale and imagines her life within the fading walls of other people's abandoned dreams. She fantasizes about chucking her caked-up kitchen appliances and replacing them with Brand New Things. She'll buy a Kitchen-Aid mixer. Carnation Pink or Crayola Orange. She'll buy a chrome coffee-maker—a fancy one, one that steams milk. She'll buy a hanging fruit basket and fill it with ripe oranges that match her orange Kitchen-Aid mixer. Life will be clean. Lines carefully drawn. Dust will never settle. The roof will never leak. Mushrooms won't sprout in the corner of the basement and the curtains won't stain. She'll plant tulips in the front and mums along the walk and Clark will come crawling back in the early days of summer in time to mow the lawn.

"Did I tell you he left his shoehorn?" Val shakes her head in a pitying way. "He loves that shoehorn. He uses it every day. Clearly, subconsciously, he left it for a reason. I *feel* it."

She rings the bell a fourth time.

The baby kicks at the closing-in walls of Kate's uterus. Kate tugs Brad's hand. "Let's go," she mouths.

Val's fingers are narrow, her fingernails as bendable as the plastic take-out containers, used and re-used, stacked in her refrigerator. A psychic once told her she has psychic fingers. Because of this, she sometimes rolls her eyes back towards the top of her skull and shivers with *knowing*. For instance, she *knows* that Kate and Brad are having a girl, even though they are having a boy and told her so. She *knows* that Clark, her third husband, will beg for reconciliation—sooner rather than later. She also *knew* that her elderly neighbor Mr. Handkopf would succumb to a cancer so fierce that it'd turn his bones to chalk. He passed away from a stroke before that could happen.

She is very nearly always wrong.

She slams the base of her palm into the doorbell now, color rising in her cheeks. To Kate, her mother-in-law looks more and more like a sack of over-ripe fruit. She glances at Brad, then quickly away, for fear of him reading her mean thoughts. His face is frozen in a placid smile.

The baby fidgets in a fussy, underwater way. Kate, on the second week of her maternity leave, is floating between states of being as well. The other maternity nurses and doctors and orderlies on the floor threw her a lukewarm shower a week before she left. They are no longer enthralled by the miracle of birth, which they witness on a daily basis. For them, birth is not a mystery. It's an industry. Giving birth is a lonely business. Kate is lonely.

She runs her finger down her t-shirt, along the raised brown line that appeared one morning a few weeks ago and slopes over the roundness of her belly. Change is terminal. She closes her eyes.

"You okay?" Brad tugs her ponytail.

"Maybe we should go?"

"Just give it one more minute."

Val cups her hands over the door window. "I see someone. Movement. I see sandwiches." When she straightens up, she leaves two greasy parentheses behind.

The baby hiccups. *Please*, Kate silently prays, *please don't let my baby be born in Ohio.*

"I'm going to need to eat soon."

"Just one more minute. Please."

Kate reaches back and feels for the arms of the Adirondack chair, poised artfully on the porch. She eases herself into the slanted seat. Once down, she realizes that she won't be able to get back up without help. She's wedged in.

"They're coming!" Val blots her lips and smooths her broken hair. "I look like I could buy this house. Like I could afford it. Like I fit in?"

"Sure, Mom," Brad says. "Of course."

The door cracks open and a turtle-faced woman peers out. Val barrels past her. "What beautiful sandwiches!"

Brad hesitates. He always thinks twice. Kate usually loves that about him. He cares that others feel cared for.

"You coming?"

"I'm good."

"It doesn't mean we're moving here."

"I know."

"And we would never move here." He drags his arm dramatically across the barren landscape. Hills of dirt, two half-built houses. A rusted bulldozer and a yellow crane. The skeleton of a tree swoons against the famine of beauty. The house is a counterfeit colonial. Drab blue. Plastic shutters. "It's fun for her."

When Val visits them in New York, she learns the entire flight crew's names. She applauds the plane upon landing. She spills onto the baby grand at Don't Tell Mama's and belts three torch songs in a row.

"She's done this my whole life." Brad says.

"I know."

She insists on going to Lord and Taylor before they open so she can drink free coffee and stand patriotically when the pianist plays the National Anthem, her hand clawing at her heart, buried deep beneath her bosom.

When she leaves, Kate and Brad joke that she suffers from Attention Addiction Disorder. But when she's there, Brad defers to her. Every single time.

Kate means to smile, but the baby punches her bladder. She winces instead. Brad follows his mother inside.

Past the porch railing and the undeveloped wasteland, the sky is starch white. The sun sears through the stinging haze. She hasn't been able to take a full breath for a couple of days now, the baby's grown that big. She thinks of the infinity of DNA combinations. Memory, cell meeting cell, egg choosing sperm, the coupling and uncoupling of it all. How the baby seemed to will itself alive. She considers the millions of micro-mistakes she makes every moment of every day. Mistakes that don't seem like mistakes at the time. Mistakes that seem like good ideas. Every decision, a turn of a key.

Muted laughter pings the window. Kate's outside of it all. Her life has been hijacked. Her body belongs to the baby. Her neck is thick, her ankles, thick, her hair, thick. Her pointy chin is rounded and soft. She barely recognizes herself anymore.

Brad pokes his head out of the front door and offers her a sandwich.

"Turkey. We'll leave in a minute. They have a gas fireplace in there. You turn it on with a dimmer switch. She's telling the real estate agent about her fantasy flower garden. You know my mom."

"Okay."

"I promise." He goes back inside.

He promised that Monday's job interview in Columbus was a lark. An excuse to visit his mother before the baby was born. An exercise in upward mobility. At best a job offer could be leverage against his position at Edelman. A raise. A promotion. A new title. She believed him until he bought new razors and a new suit. And pointed out every swing set in every lawn on their drive to Mayberry.

She imagines the baby outside of her, sleeping on her chest, his skin softer than the soft skin on the inside of Brad's arm. The baby's heartbeat is different than her own. She can almost feel his sleeping breath. Can almost smell his sweet, newborn scent.

What if her life is never hers again? What if the baby steals it? What if Brad falls in love with someone new like her father fell in love with her mother, leaving Ingrid's mother behind? Ingrid used to hold Kate when she was a baby. The first time they met, Ingrid was eight and Kate three months old. Infant Kate reached for her as if she recognized her half-sister. Ingrid would never admit it, but she reached for Kate, too.

What would Ingrid do?

She'd run.

Ingrid would run.

Harnessing gravity, she'd slouch in the incline of the chair until chin met belly. She'd crab walk *out* of the chair and slide to the floor, skootch herself to the stairs, and pull herself up by the railing. Then she'd waddle to the street, pregnant as she was, and flag an idling car and drive to Florida or someplace. Someplace far away, only to be heard from in a series of enigmatic letters and packages like the ones she used to send Kate when Kate was still a kid and Ingrid an adult. A checker piece, grooves packed with city dirt. A rusted hinge missing its door. An antique crystal from a chandelier. Strange letters from a fictional pair of enchanting circus sisters, the Darling Dempsini Sisters, who rode horses bareback, flew on the trapeze, and balanced precariously on a tower of mismatched chairs. Kate admired the imaginary sisters. She envied their kinship. When one of them took up the escape arts, Kate decided to as well. She read about Houdini, how he'd worn a key-sized pocket on the inside of his cheek, the graceful way he fooled others into helping his act. She learned, in theory, how to escape a straightjacket. But now, all this is useless. There's no graceful way to escape a visit with one's mother-in-law, the birth of a birthable baby, the strange and mysterious prison of a happy life.

Impatient, enigmatic, never-waits-for-anyone Ingrid doesn't want the things other people want. But Kate wants to be like her.

The raw wood snags at the collar of Kate's cotton shirt. She yanks herself away from the splinter and skootches forward on the seat. She wants to see if the crabwalk will work. Feet on the ground, chin to her belly, she inches forward until her back is arched over the seat, her head cramps in the hard corner where the edges of the chair meet. One more push and she's on the floor, free. It turns out she doesn't need the stair railings to stand.

The rain picks up, melting veins of mud down the dirt piles. *When did those letters end? Where did they go?* As sudden as a craving, she needs to talk to Ingrid, to ask her about the Dempsini Sisters. But Kate's phone is in her purse and her purse is in the car and it's raining.

"Fuck it," she says to whoever's listening. She steps into the mud and the rain.

But then the front door opens and she's no longer alone.

✳

It's Sunday. On Sundays, Val treats herself to dinner at the Bonanza Steakhouse. She arrives at five, as the keyboardist pulls his electronic keyboard from the back seat of his car. As she takes a tray from a stack by the register, slides it towards the cashier, and orders the House Special, the keyboardist fills a cup at the soda fountain and plugs his keyboard into the outlet in the corner by the salad bar. By the time Val is seated at her favorite table, a booth at the far wall beneath a blow-up photograph and a cow with a tag in its ear, the keyboardist plays his first notes.

But, today, there are three of them. Four, if you count the baby. They line up their trays on the metal tray slide, Val in the lead, Brad in the rear, Kate trapped between. A man in a paper chef's hat takes their order. His teeth are rimmed with yellow. His name tag drags down the wide collar of his uniform shirt. The nametag is also rimmed with yellow. The color of aging. The color of neglect. The color of bad lighting and cheap toothpaste and a life where Too Many Hard Things happen at once and all the time.

They move down the line. Val pauses, so they all pause, at the cups of chocolate and rice puddings and shivering Jell-O cubes. They pick up tiny tubs of steak sauce and sour cream flecked with dry chives. Val lingers by the steam table. The keyboardist plays. The steam from the steam table blows wisps of Val's hair as she hums the words of the unsung song.

The baby kicks. Kate winces. *Please,* she quietly breathes, *please don't let my baby be born in Bonanza Steakhouse.*

At the potato bar, a server stands stoic, her chef's hat wilting in the fever of steam heat. Her nametag boldly states DEBRA! Below her name, a button screams: ASK ME ABOUT OUR HOME-MADE APPLE PIE! A mole hooks the corner of her mouth and pulls her lower lip into a lopsided frown. She's still. It's like she sprouted from that very spot. Everything in the steakhouse is bolted down, the tables, the chairs, the all-you-can-eat toppings bar. Perhaps Debra is bolted down, too. Kate shifts her own leaden feet, lifts one and then the other, to make sure she still can.

"Mashed, baked, or fired?" The serving spoon dangles from Debra's loose grip.

"A taste of all three."

"Can only do one, hon."

"My daughter-in-law's pregnant," Val whines.

"'Less you pay, can only do one."

"Rob gives me three."

"Rob ain't here."

Val's eyes flutter behind her lids. Kate grabs onto her tray.

Brad leans in. "It's okay, Mom. I'll pay for extras." The baby rakes an elbow across Kate's abdomen and Brad bounds back to the register.

"You are a very unhappy woman."

Debra purses her lips and crosses her arms, the serving spoon cradled in her elbow. The keyboardist has reached a refrain. Kate eyes the distance between the potato bar and the front entrance, estimates the time it'd take to reach the double doors. She'll hitch a ride to Manhattan. She'll knock on Ingrid's door. It wouldn't be the first time.

Brad returns with a new receipt which he respectfully shows Debra. "Thanks," he says with an apologetic shrug.

Val blinks and mascara flakes onto her cheeks. "Boys do love their mothers." Triumphant, she thrusts her tray towards Debra. "Extra butter, please."

Beneath the cow photo, Val lines up three single serving bottles of wine and pours her first into a plastic cup. The three of them saw at their steaks with plastic forks.

"You know how I know Clark misses me? I *feel* it. And then there are the things he left behind. His toothbrush. His toolkit. Wool socks I bought him for Christmas. He loved those socks. I don't know if you know what it feels like to *feel* something . . ."

"I feel things." Kate's plastic knife bends from the pressure. Brad hands her a new one.

"You lose your senses in the big city. Too much noise. Too much electricity. Too many rays."

"I like living in the city."

"I *feel* it like a cold stone in the middle of my chest."

Kate smooths her napkin, runs her finger down the raised skin on her abdomen. She looks up towards the cow photo. The cow's black bedroom eyes stare back at her. A hunk of chewed flesh sticks to the back of her throat. "I like the parks. I like the people. I like the museums. There are lots of things to do."

"So many people. So many *types* of people."

"Mom." Brad stops sawing his beef. "Please."

"Lots of interesting people," Kate says.

"You'll change your mind once you have the baby."

"I need to use the ladies' room." Kate slips out of the booth and rambles past the salad bar. The keyboardist nods in her direction. A man with a bolo tie yells from the bar. "Twins!"

"No, there's just one in there."

"Well don't squeeze that puppy out in here."

"Can you imagine," the woman sitting next to him gasps, clearly imagining it.

Kate picks up speed. "That's the idea."

Beyond the beaded curtain is an overstuffed settee shaped like a pair of kissing lips. In her less-pregnant days, Kate might've thrown herself onto the cushions in a pose of feigned ennui, and begged for a photo, but today, after splashing her face with water, she eases into it, leaning back where the upper lip dips. She wants to call Ingrid, but her phone is in her purse and her purse is at the table.

Conversations pick up in the bar. Aggressive laughter. The shaking of ice. There's an open window at the far side of the bathroom, above the hand dryer, beside the sinks. The Darling Dempsini Sisters, masters of adventure and escape would have no concerns, slipping through the window. Violet would cartwheel one-handed onto Lily's shoulders. Lily would somersault down the exterior alley wall. Ingrid once told Kate about a time she ditched a bad date with her ex-husband, slipped through the restaurant kitchen, stole into her own apartment while he was waiting for her to return, packed a bag. She left a note.

There are a million ways to escape. Kate's afraid of them all.

She's also afraid of having these thoughts for the rest of her life.

She runs the faucet and splashes her face again and wonders if she could pull herself up onto the sink, lift onto the sill, and crawl through the open window. She suspects she can't, but decides to try. Her joints are supple and free in anticipation of the baby. Pulling onto the soap pump, her front foot planted in the sink, her back foot leaves the floor. The window edge is almost within reach. She reaches.

The beaded curtains part. Debra stares at her, her hat wilted, her fish-hook mouth gaping open, her shoes, white Keds, stained with gravy. She silently holds out her hand and gently, kindly, helps Kate back down.

Brad's childhood bedroom is in another house, long since sold, the remnants of his broken family painted over by another and then another and then another. Val keeps track of the old house's new families, though she's only walked through an open house once, which made her cry. The kitchen had been renovated, the fireplace revitalized. The floors were new. "The Forniers have been erased," she announced in the living room just before she was escorted out. "Squeezed dry, Polished. Torn up. Throw away."

Kate and Brad sleep in the guest room of Val's condo. The bed sheets are patterned with lilacs, the quilt with daisies, the curtains with black-eyed Susans. The chaos of blooms glows in the bleeding moonlight. The carpet smells of Febreze. Brad smells of ivory soap. Kate lies awake, arms and legs curled around her sleeping stomach. Brad snores lightly.

"Will you rub my back?" She gently elbows him. She wonders if the baby will grow up to look like Brad or like her father who's been dead so long that despite the family photos, she barely remembers what he looked like. She doesn't remember his voice, but she does remember the perfect half-moons in the beds of his fingernails. She remembers the essence of his smile, but not the smile itself. Brad's groggy hand finds her back and rests there.

"You promise?"

"I mean, if the offer's too good to turn down . . . we'll discuss. I promise."

"Too good to turn down?"

"We could raise our son in a house. With a yard. And swing set. And a sand box."

"We can do that in the city, too. He can have friends who don't look like him."

His eyes are still closed. Hers are open. "We'll figure it out."

"I'd miss my sister."

When they were growing up, the days Ingrid was away at her mother's or at college were interminable for Kate. In Ingrid's absence, Kate saved up words and stories about the Dempsini Sisters. For the longest time, perhaps longer than appropriate, Kate insisted that they were real.

"She needs me."

"Ingrid doesn't need anyone."

The baby pushes, hands and feet, against Kate's abdomen. "She needs me. Even if she doesn't know it."

"I know you love her, baby, but your sister barely talks to you."

"Doesn't mean she doesn't need me. And I know she loves me, too."

"*I* love you," he says. "And the baby. I love all of you."

It takes some effort, but she pulls away.

*

"You promise," Kate mutters when Brad wakes up. "You promise?" she asks as she follows him to the kitchen. "You promise," she reminds him as he buttons his shirt.

"I promise," he says as he kisses her goodbye, but when the screen door latches shut, a waxy emptiness drips over her. She doesn't believe him. She goes back to bed.

By existing and not existing at the same time, the baby is trapped between worlds. Kate is trapped between worlds. She's childless, but she's a mother. She's not herself, but she's no one else. She can't remember life before pregnancy and can't imagine life after the baby is born. She's never alone, but she's lonely.

What if, after birth, the baby doesn't reach for her?

What if he doesn't recognize her?

What if she doesn't recognize him?

He will feel so alone.

She tells herself it's Ohio, but she's afraid these feelings will never go away.

Where are those letters, those things Ingrid sent? A music box dancer. A key. A red glass bead. The Darling Dempsini sisters, trapped in a stack of letters. She wants to call Ingrid, but her phone is in her purse and her purse in in the kitchen and it's eight and she's probably sleeping, and Kate can hear Val puttering around. Maybe she'll try Ingrid at nine.

It's Monday.

On Mondays, Val speeds-walks the mile loop inside the Macy's Mall.

"A walk will be good for you. Fresh air."

"Inside the mall?"

"There's fresh air in the parking lot *to* the mall. It's a big lot." Val looks at her own reflection in the dark window of the microwave. "Clark'll be the only man to remember that I was pretty once."

To escape from a straightjacket, you first need to know how to get *into* the straightjacket. Make yourself as big as possible. Make yourself as small as possible. The rest falls into place.

To escape talking to an ex-boyfriend or a boss who made a pass at you in New York City, duck into a bodega and hope that they are not going into the same bodega.

To escape the womb, leave the same way you came in. Make yourself as small as possible. Surrender every muscle, every bone, every plate in your skull to contract and squeeze the fluids from your brain. Will yourself into a brighter, colder world.

There is no way to escape a Monday mile through Macy's Mall with Val.

Beyond the sparkling Macy's entrance and the perfume girls who spray floral scents, beyond the make-up artists, and the scarves, and the urns of plastic blooms—hyacinths and oleander, cosmos, petunias, daffodils, and pussy willows—Val will imagine her life in the gleaming aisles of no one else's stuff. She'll chuck her caked-up kitchen utensils and burnt pots and pans and replaced them with Brand New Things. She'll cook cellophane bags of imported pastas and dried beans. She'll buy an electric griddle and a deluxe George Foreman Grill. She'll buy a Lime Green Kitchen-Aid mixer or maybe Florida Blue. Life will be cheerful, saturated with hues of joy. Book clubs will gather in her kitchen, the postman will stop in for tea, and Clark will come crawling back in the early days of autumn in time to rake the leaves.

"And I want to buy the baby a dress."

"It's a boy," Kate says. "He's a he. A nameless he. But a he."

"Don't be so sure. Those sonograms are often wrong."

"No, they're not."

"Well, you just don't know until you have it."

Kate doesn't notice when Val turns left on Brint Street. She's still thinking about the dress. Not that the baby will mind.

They wait a red light. When the light turns green, Val turns down a side street. Under her breath she mutters, "I *know* it's a girl.

I *feel* it." Her face darkens. She drives slowly, hands gripping the steering wheel, bendable nails pressing into her palms. She turns down a cul de sac.

"Where are you going?"

"Just one errand."

The houses on the street are low to the ground and close together. A different sort of suburban neighborhood, the kind that exists in a liminal space between cities and towns. Morbid thoughts float through Kate's mind. *Brad's bought a fixer-upper. My mother-in-law's a mass murderer. I'll never leave Ohio alive.* Kate reaches for her phone as they pull up outside a house with a rusted swing set, the poles flecked with blue enamel. Ingrid's number's on speed dial. "Clark left his razors." Val leaves the car running and slips out.

Kate eyes the keys in the ignition. She's sure she'll fit behind the steering wheel. Wedged in, perhaps, but it's a small price to pay for escape. But then Val's mumbled words untangle and Kate hears what she said moments ago. She watches Val cross the lawn slowly, a used razer in her hand.

"Val, wait," Kate bursts out of the car. She lands squarely on her feet. The breeze brushes by. "Val. Stop."

Then Kate is on the porch, blocking Val from the doorbell.

"What about Macy's? What about the dress?"

Val persists. Kate grabs the razor and chucks it into the lawn. "Don't do it."

"He left it for a reason."

"Because it's dull."

Val heaves one painful breath, then another. Along the porch railing, a half-used bar of soap. A single, clean folded sock. A screwdriver and a stained t-shirt. "His *favorite* shirt. Why would he leave it outside?" A toothbrush. A coffee mug. A ballpoint pen. Val straightens. She reaches for the doorbell. Her finger hovers. Kate holds her breath. Then Val turns away. The baby burps.

"He must not be home." She walks to the car.

Kate follows. They idle for a bit as Val bites her lip.

"He's the last one," she says. In the rear view mirror, she examines her face, wipes the smudge of her eyeliner, blots her lipstick on the back of her wrist. Kate suspects that is a new part of Val's Monday routine.

Val parks as close as she can to the front entrance of Macy's. "There's enough fresh air between here and there," she says.

They pass a child's purple purse, an owl smashed by the tires of a car. A used pair of blue latex gloves. An old man posing as parking lot security even though the lot is empty.

The baby kicks. *Please,* Kate mouths, *please don't let my baby be born in Macy's parking lot.*

The inside of Macy's is even brighter than Kate remembers. They pass the perfume girls, the urns of plastic flowers. Val pauses when a makeup artist calls out, "Want a free makeover? I'll make you beautiful. *More* beautiful."

"Love one," she says, flirting with make-up artist, a young man in a pristine lab coat. She turns to Kate. "Would you like a makeover, too?"

"Sure," Kate says.

"Boy or girl?" He points to her belly.

"Who knows?" Kate nestles into a chair at the counter and waits her turn.

The makeup artist wipes Val's makeup off with a sponge and warm water. Beneath the base and the mascara and cream blush is a plain and easy beauty Kate wishes her mother-in-law could see.

SWEET JESUS

We painted the apartment together the first time, every wall white. "Landlord White," he called it. That's how we saw ourselves back then, like we were tenants in our own lives. We drank beer and had sex in the paint spatter, on plastic tarps. "Blue-collar sex." And then we buckled up and painted some more.

We settled into a Landlord White sort of groove. I left for work in the mornings, he played gigs at night. We fought in whispers. He'd say I didn't need him enough. I'd say "I don't need you at all." He'd say I wanted too much. I'd say he didn't have much to give—I was paying the rent. He'd call me cold. I'd agree. The nights we fought, we fell asleep tangled together, as if insults were as intimate as secrets. I never thought he'd stay for as long as he did. But, he did.

A year in, I painted over the Landlord White. I started with the kitchen. Spring Green. I bought the paint months before I had the guts to pry the can open. Even then, I was too nervous to commit to smears of color. I was a photographer, and it seemed to me that the world and fate did a better job mixing color than I ever could.

So, I waited until Zach was on tour and hired the old guy who hung around the hardware store. He was always smiling, always sweating. He had a gap between his front teeth. He was like an old coat, nothing to look at, but it kept you warm all winter, so you loved it for that. I paid him one fifty, cash, bought rollers and trays, and let him into the apartment one morning before I left for work.

When I got home, the kitchen was sour apple green and the old man lay passed out on the foyer floor, a dried roller stuck to his shirt. He was splattered with green and cheap bourbon. I whispered his murmuring body awake and shook his shoulders until he was able to stand. After he left, I scrubbed his Spring Green outline off the floor.

Zach said two words about it when he came home. "Bright," he said. "Green."

"I like it," I said. I didn't.

That night, he slid his fingers to the roots of my hair and held tight. "When you said on the phone that something had changed, I thought you'd gone and cut your hair."

I decided the green would stay.

The place was a wreck when I moved in. There was a hole in the bathroom floor where tile should've been. The grout was rotted away. The plywood beneath it had turned black. Seventy years of paint plastered over wallpaper bubbled and peeled off the foyer and bedroom walls. The living room window was cracked, its spiderwebs held together with a Grateful Dead decal. I mopped the grime from the floors three times and then scrubbed on my hands and knees with dishsoap to wear away layers of city sludge and still, I couldn't get it all up.

I found a cross of palms in the corner of the bedroom closet, and a flattened shoebox lid on the living room floor. "Save Jesus," was scrawled in black marker on the lid. The pen was faded in places. It'd been close to dry when the writer wrote. I imagined the nib pressed flat and feathered as it bled the last of its ink.

I dragged a ratty futon from my friend's apartment in Williamsburg to the subway, up the subway stairs, and then down the hill. I slept in the previous tenant's filth until my bare feet wore it away. I told my sister I'd never marry again. I meant it, too. I was happy to be alone. I'm not the sort of woman who needs a man, or anyone, really. Four weeks later, I met Zach while I was filling in at the bar I used to work at. One of his bands was playing in the backroom and he kept coming up to the bar between sets to flirt.

I took him home and let him stay. Kate didn't say anything except maybe, "Are you sure?"

I wasn't sure, but he traveled light. I liked that. He was easy. His voice was thick like clay after a rain. He didn't have much. A duffel bag of T-shirts. Two pairs of jeans, a trumpet, a toothbrush, a razor. There was a callus in the center of his lips from his horn's mouthpiece. He swaggered when he thought no one was watching. Sometimes he'd sway to music no one else could hear.

I hoped, after the Spring Green, that the apartment would fall into color, but it took a while. Six months later, I bought a gallon of Seattle Grey and pushed the furniture into the middle of the living room, stacked the books in corners and doorways and rolled paint on the walls. Then came Italian Ice in the foyer, then Oleander in the bathroom. Zach didn't help this time. I did it all myself.

Then came the Buttermilk in the bedroom. When I moved half the bedroom into the living room, with the desk and shelves still pulled away from the walls, Zach promised to paint with me. By that time, we knew the end was near.

The morning before he left, I told him he could keep his stuff at the apartment while he was on tour, as if he had anything there.

We were painting perpendicular walls, our backs turned towards each other.

"Why would I, Ingrid?"

"When you get back, we can talk."

"What's there to say?"

"Please don't be like this," I said.

"We've lived the life out of this thing."

I might've slapped the wall with my paintbrush or banged the paint can closed. I turned my head away from him so he wouldn't hear me cry.

The night we met, when I was bartending and he played with the band, he stayed past closing and I topped off his drink, and mine, until we were both drunk. He emphatically insisted that everything was alive and that everything had a soul. "This bar, this barstool, the spirits." He clinked the ice against his glass. Rocks, water, mountains. Even thoughts. Even relationships. Even love had a beginning, a middle, and an end.

I said, "Amen. I guess."

We painted for a while. There was the sticky sound of bubbles popping as the rollers rolled thick Buttermilk. Someone in another building was playing salsa. The sound bounced up the alley brick and lingered on the fire escape.

"It's not worth fighting over." He dropped his roller in the tray.

"We're not fighting."

His feet bristled the tarp as he walked out.

I heard the clatter of keys on the kitchen counter. Heard him zip his hoodie. Heard the apartment door open, then close. I finished painting my wall, then his, two coats. There was one more wall to paint—the long wall—but I didn't feel like painting anymore.

I stayed longer than I meant to at my sister's house that night. I didn't tell her about Zach. I didn't want to get into it and she didn't need to know. Kate was born under a bright star, as beautiful as she is smart. She married well and moved through life with grace that inspired both awe and envy. Even giving birth was easy for her. Five minutes of pushing produced a sweet infant who grew into a sweet, toddling little boy, Pierre. It's hard to take advice from her.

We drank sangria on the back patio of her house in Brooklyn, a city lot on the bleeding edge of Park Slope. Neither of us was self-conscious about digging past the ice and brandy with our fingers to retrieve slices of peach. Orange and red paper lanterns hung lifeless from roof to fence. The sky in their part of Brooklyn perpetually cycled through shades of gray. There were flecks of Buttermilk yellow on my knuckles.

That morning they'd found a baby bird, Sweet Jesus. She pronounced the *j* as an *h*, the Spanish way. Her husband caught two stray cats stalking something across the street. The starlings screamed, dove in and out, tried to spook the cats with chaos, but they persisted. Brad shooed the cats away and saw Sweet Jesus, fallen from his nest. The starlings calmed. They'd given their baby up for dead. "But he rose again," Kate giggled. "Nature is kind and nature is loving but it sure as hell isn't sentimental. It's a little cruel, too."

The fledgling mistook the back of Brad's right shoe for its mother and followed it across the street, tripping along the way, and into the house, then through the house and into the backyard, where it hung close for most of the day. Every hop, it got stronger, started running, and even tried spreading its wings.

In the evening, it nestled against the empty shoe.

"We're worried he won't make it through the night," Brad said. "The alley cats are stalking the fence."

"He'll live if he learns to fly." Kate filled my glass, then hers. "I should've had you bring your camera. You could've done portraits. Jesus and mother." She pointed to Brad's beat-up tennis shoe. The bird tugged gently on the shoelace.

Jesus's beak was wide for his tiny face, bright yellow and orange. His eyes swallowed his head. Beneath his dappled feathers, his skin was raw pink and scaly and splotched with gray. His neck stretched long and vulnerable. Brad fed him chopped egg from his palm as Pierre squatted next to him, his chubby fingers sneaking towards the little bird's back. He'd been warned not to touch Jesus, not to crush him, not to get too close, but he couldn't look away. It was the golden hour, and rose light broke through the gray and landed between Pierre's pointed finger and the pebbles by Sweet Jesus's orange feet. I wished I'd brought my camera, too.

Kate laid her hand on Brad's bent shoulder. "The cats are screaming from the bathroom. We can't keep them in there much longer."

"He'll learn to fly."

"Fly," Pierre whispered. "Fly. Fly."

"Do you ever think about how different we are?" I watched Pierre turn towards his mother. Brad reached for Pierre. Kate brushed the back of Brad's neck. The bird hopped over a crack and stretched his wings for balance, and pecked on the concrete.

"Half-sisters, half alike."

I shook my head. "I'm taller," I said. My features were thick where hers were fine. I had a shitty day job designing internal newsletters for a law firm; she didn't need to work, but she did as a nurse in obstetrics, a job she chose because she wanted to work in a place where there was more good news than bad.

"We share the half you don't see."

We sat for a while, all eyes on the bird. It grew dark. I drank too much. I stayed too long. I didn't want to go home.

I rode sideways on the subway back uptown. The rocking of the train caused a comforting queasiness. The city was quiet. It often was in the summer. It was late. The thick syrup of sangria coated my tongue.

The apartment door was unlocked. At first, I though Zach had come back, that I'd find him sleeping in bed. I was giddy and angry and sad. I called his name. He wasn't there.

What I remember most was the eerie calm and how the usual chaos of furniture seemed different. I'd become accustomed to the desk pulled diagonally from the wall, the books listing in piles, the bookcases, twin towers, emerging in the middle of the living room. My framed photographs were stacked in the corners. Black garbage bags stuffed with linens were shoved beneath and between chairs. All of it was shadowed and backlit by the city's perpetual dusk.

Then I saw the gaps between things. The computer was gone. The television, too. My camera. I tripped on a tarp. In my bedroom, the dresser drawers were pulled out, my clothes lay strewn on the floor. The window was wide open; the paint cans that had been lined up on the radiator stared into the room from the fire escape.

I slammed the window shut, shoved my underwear back in the drawer and retched over the toilet until the day was purged. I called the police.

I waited for them on the kitchen floor, the only room that had escaped molestation. I called Zach. I could've left a message. I could've said *something happened*, or *I'm sorry*, or *I need you, I do*, but, instead, I hung up after the first ring.

The beat cops came at two: one young, one older, one tall, one short, one bald, one with hair so short and thick it looked like doll's hair. Both square, the corners of their bullet-proof vests pressing up the fabric of their blue shirts. The elder drew his gun and tapped on the closet doors. Then, he yanked the doors open. No one could fit in the closets, let alone hide. The younger took notes.

"Did you touch anything?"

"Yes."

"Why?"

"Because the window was open. My underwear was on the floor."

He clicked his pen and asked what was missing. I recited what I knew. He asked why I'd been out so late. He asked if I had a boyfriend. I didn't know the right answer. Was that what Zach was? We never called ourselves anything.

I curled into the yellow chair, the only piece of furniture in its right place, while they spoke in low tones about where they'd rather be.

I wanted to be somewhere else, too. With someone else.

There was a night when I was half-asleep and Zach wrote secrets on my back with his finger. I pretended to be dreaming. He whispered in my ear, "This is real." I'd pressed my body into his. I wanted to be there again.

Forensics came at three and rolled my fingers in ink. The officer's hands were twice the size of mine, the dryness of his skin made his palms feel like silk.

"You're painting," he said. "Big job. Nice color."

"I don't like it," I said. "Reminds me of my childhood. Unhappy childhood."

"It's hard to tell on those little chips."

"Your windows don't lock," the other officer said. He'd been dusting for fingerprints.

"I know. They never did."

Before they left, the officer took a paint roller handle from the floor and jammed it between the upper and lower windowpanes and told me to call a locksmith, to put up a window gate.

There'd been a gate when I first moved in. It was rusty and dented and opened with a rattling whine. It cast lines of crisscrossed shadow across the room in the mornings that traveled up the wall by afternoon. I took it down first thing. I never wanted to live like that, behind bars.

The officer shrugged. "That's the world we live in."

They left at four. I pulled a blanket from the bed and dragged it to the kitchen. I slept on the kitchen floor.

I woke up with an aching rage, the hard wood of the floor chewing on my hip. Outside the kitchen window, the branches and leaves of the malformed ginkgo in the courtyard bobbed as a pigeon landed, then launched itself back into the air. The ceiling was spattered with Spring Green, smeared evidence of the drunk painter. My eyes stung. My mouth was dry. My stomach filled with cotton. My fingers were inky from the fingerprinting. The cops, the sangria, the baby bird, Sweet Jesus, crashed in. I reached for my phone. 6:42 a.m. No messages.

I hope you never know what it is to have someone come through your home, uninvited. To walk in through the fire escape and out through the front door and rifle through your life, deciding what of yours is of value, what's worth leaving behind. I hope you never experience waking up where everything has changed, even though most everything looks the same, and the only thing you can do is wrap a blanket around your shoulders, open the freezer, pull out the coffee, grind the beans. Turn on the stove. Light the hissing gas, watch the flame catch blue.

I called him again. I let the phone ring. I hung on, but didn't talk. I let the message ran out.

Did I care about the television? I hardly watched. Losing the computer was rougher. My photography portfolio, gone, but I never sent it out, anyway. Credit card numbers, bank accounts, emails. I could change my passwords. The camera and my hard-won lenses were now in someone else's hands, someone who wouldn't understand them.

I thought of the bird and Pierre's fascination, the back of Brad's sneaker, the lanterns, water-stained from a drizzle no one remembered. If Kate had asked, if I'd brought it, a piece of me would've been saved. A small piece. One small thing. But it was only bits of plastic and glass, conduits that worked in ways mysterious to me; magical, even, but it didn't have a soul, or even stories. If we ever spoke again, I'd tell Zach so.

I willed him to call. I knew he wouldn't. He never liked doing anything that he didn't think of himself.

The bedroom, especially, seemed different, as if paper cutouts had replaced my real life. The bed, the dresser, the radiator cover, the unpainted wall were caricatures of themselves. My life in a box. The paint cans lined up on the fire escape, the paint-roller handle jammed between frames like a jagged question mark.

They had taken my wedding rings, too, which I'd buried under a spill of costume jewelry. There were two thin, white-gold bands, one flecked with diamonds. My ex-husband Mark and I bought them in the backroom of a Chinatown jewelry shop. The diamonds were chips, leftovers, swept off the jeweler's floor, their size commensurate with the length of our marriage, but they caught the light and were the only proof I had that someone had loved me once.

I imagined the thief dropping onto the fire escape and sliding the window open. I saw him quietly step through, place his sneak-ered feet on the floor. He must've been tall, with long legs that straddled the window and reached over the radiator. I watched him rifle through my drawers, find nothing he wanted. I followed him down the short hallway, past the bathroom. A stack of books in the far corner of the foyer had been knocked over, or maybe they toppled on their own. He bent down to unplug the computer, the TV, picked up my camera bag as if it were a lady's purse. Did he let someone in through the front door to help? Was his heart racing like mine at that moment? Did he wonder what he was doing or to whom? What did he think of the unpainted wall, the furniture pulled away, the unmade bed, everything where it wasn't supposed to be?

I examined the paint roller jammed in the window and the smear of Buttermilk yellow it made on the glass. The fingerprinting dust collected in the rim of the sill. I scooped my clothes from the drawers and dumped them on the bed. I meant to wash everything that he'd touched, but I didn't have quarters. He'd taken those, too.

In the kitchen, the water boiled to a hiss and forced itself through the coffee grinds. My heart turned to crude oil, my tongue bitter earth. I sat in the yellow chair, my feet folded under my hips. When I brought the mug to my lips, it rattled against my teeth. My hands were shaking that hard.

Off the A train at Columbus Circle, a man, painted silver, dressed like the Statue of Liberty, stared me down. A canvasser approached me with a clipboard. I turned my back. A homeless man, the same one who was always there, reclined on one arm on a flattened box, his feet black and cracked, his toenails curled around themselves, his ankles swollen. Now I was the cardboard cut-out, a visitor pasted onto the world, barely able to reach the ground.

Halfway up the block I realized that I didn't remember getting dressed, and I stopped and looked down towards my feet. I was dressed, flats and blue jeans. My hands snagged in my hair. I pulled at the knots with my fingers. Kate called when I was just outside the bank. I'd left her a message earlier.

"Come to dinner," she said. "Take a cab. We'll pay."

The bank was almost empty. There was a teller hidden behind the plexiglass screen and a banker, a woman, my age, maybe older, sitting in the cheap labyrinth of carpeted cubicle walls. She had mousy brown hair cut into a pageboy. The static from the walls caused certain strands to float off her head. "Can I help you?"

"I hope," I said. My smile came out crooked. I felt heat on my cheeks, heat on my neck, heat at the tip of my nose. "I need to change my account numbers."

"Come with me," she said, and led me to another desk. She disappeared and reappeared with a box of tissues and a plastic cup of water. She held them out to me. Mascara was flaked like stars along her cheek.

My lips twitched, then broke into a full tremble. My throat clenched, my lungs tightened. Then my stomach punched in, my shoulders stooped . . . and then came the wracking, primal gulps of air. I couldn't stop myself. The banker stood beside me, her hand flat and heavy on my shoulder. I sobbed. For the longest while, I couldn't stop.

"I'm sorry," I said when it seemed like I was finished. "Everything's shit."

She eased into her chair on the other side of the desk, opened her drawer and pulled out some forms.

I blew my nose. "I didn't mean to cry," I said, "but there's so much to cry about."

"I know," she said.

I believed that she did.

When I got home, I sat in front of the unpainted wall, the last bits of Buttermilk to my right, a paint tray layered with Buttermilk over

Oleander over Italian Ice and Seattle Gray to my left. I thought about writing something on the wall—a date, a secret, a thought that I could lock in with paint.

The roller handle in the window cast a snake's shadow. I felt that I never wanted to open that window again. I drew a dot. A period. That was all.

I didn't take a car to my sister's house. I took the subway. She asked where Zach was and I told her that he didn't know what happened. I told her that he'd gone. That he hadn't answered his phone when I'd called and that he likely never would.

"You should tell him," she said. "Maybe he can help, financially."

"I don't need help," I said.

"Why don't you ever let anyone help you?"

"I don't know."

We sat in the back and drank Bloody Marys. "I thought it fitting for the occasion," she said darkly. "Brad makes the best mix, don't you think?"

Brad joined us and Pierre climbed on his mother's lap and laid his head on her shoulder. "Sorry about the break-in," Brad said.

"I'm almost finished painting," I said. "One wall left. And the trim."

Kate laughed. "Finally, right?"

We sat still for a moment, the four of us. Pierre chewed on his thumb, Brad looked at his shoe, Kate smelled her son's hair. I couldn't meet their eyes for fear of crying.

The thing was, the thing I was thinking, but couldn't say: it didn't feel good, any of it, but it felt right, like the hand of God had reached through the window and taken everything that distracted me from something else. Some unknown something. A something I'd find out about later, after the swelling subsided. Zach and I were buying time, putting another quarter in the slot because there was nothing better to do, but we weren't making anything. The photos, the few hard copies that hung in coffee shops and galleries, looked limp. They had no meaning, no life. Not even to me.

The cats pawed at the picture window.

"The bird," I said. "Jesus. Where's Sweet Jesus?"

"Oh," Kate said. She looked gravely at her husband.

"Tell me. No. Don't tell me. Tell me."

"Do you want to tell her, or should I?"

"Don't tell me," I said.

"Pierre, you tell her."

"I don't want to know."

Pierre slid off his mother's lap and arms wide, he toddled across the patio. I bent over to catch him and he hugged my neck.

"He flew," Pierre whispered. "Jesus flew."

TRIPTYCH

1. THE DOOR

For the first half of her life, Ingrid was an artist in search of a medium. As a child, she drew, first with crayons, then pencil, ink, and, finally, with charcoal. In college, she sculpted amorphous beings with howling eyes that looked like they'd ooze away while you were sleeping. She made stick puppets for a while, Indonesian design, American imagery. For a short time, she tried graphic design, including working on an in-house newsletter for a law firm, but got fired for rebelling against the insipid ideas of her supervisors.

Desperate for a medium, she bought a camera and studied photography for several years. She sold a few pieces, hung in a couple of galleries. Her ex-husband encouraged her to shoot portraits of high school girls and dogs and families. She lacked a passion for it, though, and when her camera was stolen, she felt strangely at peace, as if an ailing limb had been amputated. The relief was quick, and paralyzing. For weeks after the burglary, she sat in a patch of sunshine on the roof of her building and waited. She decided to do two things: she decided to get a tattoo and she decided to fall in love.

Ingrid was never interested in mundane characters. So, though her heart wasn't in it, she agreed to a date with a salty, motorcycle-riding, recovering alcoholic of a Soto Buddhist monk. Set up by a mutual friend, they agreed to meet in the East Village for coffee.

Ingrid was in a funk. She yearned for the stinging of a tattoo, the act of being drawn upon in a real and permanent way. Hours early for her date, she wandered the village. A decrepit and shaking old man sat in a lawn chair by a barber pole in front of a tattoo parlor on First Avenue. The withered parchment of his arms and neck was covered in ink that had lost its color. The blacks turned green, the reds, pink. Only the blues had stayed true. Though the owner of the salon, he no longer worked on account of his Parkinson's disease. His passionless son carried on the family business. She wished there was more to the story, that she agonized over finding the perfect tattoo. But she didn't. What she wanted and what she chose was a sailor's tattoo—a sparrow in the traditional style. Dark lines, simple colors. No deeper meaning, no sense of artistry, no longing for a dreamscape in which she understood everything and nothing. The only answer she had to the inevitable *why?* was *I don't know.*

She longed to go beyond words, through a doorway with a doorknob she couldn't find. The tattoo and the doorway were not mutually exclusive. On the roof of her building she promised herself to follow her impulses, to see where they led. In this instance, they led to the tattoo artist, a tired young man who'd grown up in the shadow of his father, unable to find a worthwhile rebellion.

The needles bit against the soft skin of her forearm. The swallow's wing spread diagonally from the corner of her elbow to the curve of her arm. She watched as the tattoo artist scratched the red of the swallow's breast and back. The ink mixed with Ingrid's blood, which bubbled to the surface. For someone who'd been numb for the past five months, it was a relief to feel something.

The swallow tattoo was the first of three occurrences to take place while she was waiting for her unknowable something.

2. THE DOORKNOB

The date was the second occurrence, which was pleasant enough. Not exactly earth-shattering.

Jacques Vargas was classically handsome, though a little short and broad from shoulder to hip. His lips were buttery, his features so simple that he resembled a children's drawing come to life. His gold-rimmed glasses left red ovals on the bridge of his nose. He spoke in a low voice, which caused her to lean into his words. He swore his three months at Rikers led him to the doorstep of his salvation. He wasn't her usual type.

"It hasn't worked out with your type yet," her sister pointed out.

He was already at the café when she arrived. She slipped into her seat. She started to apologize for being late, but he lifted his hand to stop her. They sat silent for three minutes. The fresh tattoo itched. The waitress broke their quiet.

They skipped the small talk.

Looking into his eyes was like falling down three flights of stairs.

She agreed to a second date.

After her date, on the subway ride uptown, something like a worm of pain punctured the breast of the bird tattoo. It swam through the maze of her veins, shot into her heart, and tangled itself into a sloppy knot. Though she had nothing substantial to cry about, she cried anyway. She pulled her sunglasses over her eyes, hung her head, and let her tears blanket her cheeks and slip between her lips. By the time she reached her apartment door, her head pounded. She slid down the doorjamb between the kitchen and foyer, pulled her knees up to her chest, and sniveled like a child who's skinned her knee and cried, not for the pain of it, but for the shame of falling.

A memory emerged.

She was six and lying in the bed of her parents' darkened bedroom. She colored a princess in a coloring book, mauve and purple, the same colors as her mother's varicose veins, which Ingrid found mysterious and beautiful, the mystical tails of fairies swimming below the surface of her mother's skin. Her father lay on the other side of the bed, laboring for breath. He'd taken the day off work on account of it. He wore his red bathrobe. His glasses leaned against the lamp on the bedside table. She wasn't used to seeing him without them. She asked if he needed water and he winced and said, "No," and then, "I love you, peanut," and then, "Can you get your mother?"

Leaning against the doorframe, she could feel where he used to kiss her on her forehead.

They drove to the hospital soon after Ingrid's mother shooed her away. He stayed for two weeks and came back home a changed man. Pensive, impatient. Easy to anger. His first heart attack took his soul. The second heart attack took his life. When it came up in conversation, Ingrid told people that her father died twice.

The crying lasted a week. The first two days of the storm, she suffered through work. The second two days, she called out sick and curled up on the apartment floor, pressing her cheek against the cool wood. On the fifth day, she dragged herself from her apartment to the roof of her building, where she lay on a bench in her oversized sweater and sobbed. It was May, a cloudless spring. With the constant breeze, she remembered stories of her grandparents and great aunts and uncles pushing their mattresses out to their fire escapes in Yonkers and the Lower East Side to sleep outside on nights like this.

By her second date with the monk, the following weekend, she seemed a little better. The tattoo had crusted and healed, the scab over the sparrow's heart flaked. Tiny points of her pale skin broke through the ink. The imperfection fascinated her.

They met at a café on Christopher Street and planned to walk to the water. They sat outside, the only two; the afternoon was turning brisk and threatened rain.

She showed the monk her tattoo.

"Why?" He cradled her elbow in his hand. "Why now?"

"I guess I wanted to feel something."

"Can you feel this?" He ran his thumb gently along her forearm. She considered whether she liked the touch of his skin against hers.

"Yes, of course."

"Can you feel this?" He pinched the skin on her wrist; she pulled her arm away.

"Yes."

"Could you feel those things before the tattoo?"

"Of course."

"So that's not why you got it."

"Maybe the bird chose me."

"Well, that's a different story."

Jacques flagged the waitress, who'd been neglecting their table. He ordered a coffee. Ingrid ordered wine. The waitress walked back inside.

"In training I had to light fire for a *homa*, a really important fire. But, the wood was moist and wouldn't catch, except for a young, weak flame along its edge. Before it snuffed itself out, I scrambled through the brush and found dry twigs and tended the fire with my bare hands. I wasn't thinking. I wanted to prove myself. In the end, the fire lit, but never grew. But my hand, suffered the consequence of my ego. A ritual cleansing. A lesson in no-body-ness. The fire, not me, caused the burn. The fire simply did what fire does. It fired."

"Once, someone stopped me on the street and asked me if I was someone," Ingrid said. "I said, 'No, I'm nobody,' but they didn't believe me. They asked me for my autograph. I gave it. It made them happy for a moment."

He leaned back in his chair, his lips pressed into an enigmatic grin, his arms crossed. He blinked. She wondered what it would be like to date a recovering-alcoholic Soto Buddhist monk.

"What are you thinking? he asked.

"I don't know. You?"

He paused, lowered his gaze, then lifted it. Looking into his eyes was like slipping down a rocky hill.

"That's the beauty of it," said the monk said. "I'm not thinking anything at all."

There was something seductive in the teasing hope of connection, a fine filament of silk tying one person to another. The subtle pull between Ingrid and the monk grew muscle. As they walked to the subway, they hardly spoke, but they understood each other, nonetheless. Barely acquainted, neither friend nor lover, they were part of one another. The unknowable something between them comforted Ingrid for most of the week, until he failed to meet her at the coffee shop by her work. She already suspected there might come a day when he evaporated, dissolved into the non-material existence he sought, though she didn't think it would happen so soon after they met. She waited on the bench outside the café and worried the sadness that lingered behind her stormy clouds would reappear. She feared for the worst. For herself and for him.

It came for him.

It was a motorcycle accident. He was thrown from his bike. He suffered a stroke on account of his injuries. She found out a week after he'd stood her up when their mutual friend called her.

"Should I visit him?" she asked her half-sister Kate.

"Do you want to?"

"I do."

"He might not recognize you," Kate said.

"He'll still know I was there."

She visited him.

Over the course of the week, he'd shrunk and aged. His glasses were gone. The stubble on his shaved head was growing in, dark brown flecked with gray. The respirator whistled as it injected air into his lungs. His lips chapped, his mouth slack, his head sunk into the pillow. Looking into his eyes was like looking into a dull and scratched mirror. He didn't recognize her, or anyone, but she sat with him as he lolled and spasmed, strapped into a wheelchair by his hospital bed. Was he aware of his unraveling? Was he relieved? Was he in pain? Or did he feel nothing? And, did he dream? She stayed for an hour and vaguely promised to return another day.

Her grandmother once told her that the soul was made of thousands of tiny birds who lived in a tree rooted in a person's heart. When a bad thing happened, the birds scattered. Sometimes, they lost their way and never returned home. The monk's birds were adrift. No compass to lead the way home.

She never did see him again.

3. THE KEY

In the weeks that followed Ingrid's swallow tattoo, her prematurely shortened association with Jacques Vargas, recovering alcoholic and Soto Buddhist monk, and the unlocking of the memory of her father in bed, masking his fear during his first heart attack, one more thing happened. Ingrid didn't think much of it at the time.

On the fifth day after meeting Jacques for the first time, she pulled herself from her apartment floor, to the roof of her building. She found a spot of sunshine, wrapped herself in her sweater, and started her convalescence by looking out to the Hudson River. Rarely did it occur to her that she lived on an island, and a relatively small one, but, overlooking the water, she was comforted by the feeling of floating and the notion that everything in her life, from her apartment to her problems, was small as well.

Window boxes and potted flowers placed in bunches lined the roof. Each cluster belonged to a building resident, their own attempts at capturing a corner of beauty for themselves. One planter was overtaken with weeds. Ingrid wondered how it had happened. Had the seeds from the crabgrass pushing up from the cracks in the sidewalk floated up six stories? Or had they piggy-backed in the dirt of a transported plant? She wondered about the plants, so far from the ground. Did they experience the particular sensation of floating, too?

The door scraped open and an older woman, one of the two who lived in the building's sole basement apartment, stepped through. She hugged a battered wooden painter's box, the kind Ingrid's father used to have. It doubled as an easel when the top lifted and the box turned around. The woman's name was Alice, and she always wore a cotton house dress over rolled-up jeans. She and her companion, her wife, drank their coffee on the building stoop in the mornings, and Ingrid often walked past them as she trudged out up the hill on her morning commute. She admired them for their inability to be anything other than who they already were: two old lesbians in love. It seemed so easy. Ingrid rarely spoke to them, and then, only in cryptic small talk or building gossip, two languages New Yorkers are fluent in.

Alice set her easel on the picnic table and pulled a crumpled, extra-large, paint-spattered man's shirt from beneath her arm, shook it out, turned it backwards, and stepped her arms through its sleeves. Ingrid watched her from the bench. Alice unpacked the box and locked a cheap canvas into the flimsy easel. She dotted paint on a plastic palette. Then, she smeared sky blue across the top, never aware of Ingrid sitting a few feet away, the fringe of Ingrid's sweater brushing her chin as she drew her arm across her running nose.

For the next three nights and on the weekend and after work, Ingrid made it her avocation to sit on the bench on the roof and secretly wait for Alice. She painted the same views, altering between the bridge, the barges, the Palisades on the other side of the river, the sun, the water, the skyscrapers on the southern tip of the Manhattan, where the twin towers, in miniature, once crowned the island.

A week after Ingrid's second date with the monk, Alice turned towards the bench, pointing her paintbrush, gunked up with green. "Why are you always here?"

"I'm sorry," Ingrid said, "I didn't want to bother you." She gathered her sweater tighter and got up to leave. "Sorry."

"I can't get the green right. See the green in the trees where the clouds break?" Alice frowned towards the dimming sky.

"Try a smudge of red and tiny dot of white."

Alice shook her head. "I'm no good at mixing. I'm afraid."

"You can always paint over. Nothing to be scared of."

Alice thrust the palette towards Ingrid. "You do it." She watched as Ingrid mixed the color.

"I used to mix my father's paint."

"Don't get it on your sweater," Alice said.

"It wouldn't matter if I did." She handed the brush back to Alice, who dragged the fresh green across the canvas.

The evening after Ingrid visited the monk in the hospital, a pink and orange sunset tore past the backlit bridge. The access door was propped open and Alice's easel was out, though she was nowhere to be found. Ingrid assumed, correctly, that she forgotten something in her apartment.

Ingrid sat at the picnic table, in front of the blank canvas, a white stamp interrupting the setting sky. She picked up a pencil. She knew she'd apologize for it later, but it seemed like a good idea to fill in the small rupture. First, she sketched the clouds, riotously nuanced with shades of gray. A lurking pink insinuated itself into the outer edges of everything, and a sharp orange ripped the calm away. She took a paintbrush, squeezed color on the palette. She stroked the cables of the bridge that connected sky and water and the headlights of the cars.

The painting was ponderous, mired with simplicity. Ingrid forgot about Alice, forgot to listen for her footsteps. With a fine brush, she painted a small bird, two frowns meeting a dot in the middle, like she drew in grade school. She painted a few more. When she got to painting the last bird, she noticed that the hard end of the paintbrush pointed to her swallow tattoo and the swallow pointed to her heart. She'd drawn the little birds a map to find their ways back home.

COOKIE AND ALICE

The bedroom was dark. It was always dark. It was in the back of the building, ground floor. The building across the alleyway stood on the upside of the hill, its first floor a floor higher than Cookie and Alice's apartment. It blocked even the peripheral moonlight, scraps of silver that might've otherwise wound their way through the city buildings and alleyways and in through the bedroom windows.

Cookie slept alone on the queen-sized bed in the dark bedroom, curled into herself as closely as her ample breasts would allow. She slept on the right side of the mattress, which sagged under her weight. The left side of the bed was empty: untangled, buoyant, unburdened, unused.

It was raining. Curtains of water pooled into little rivers in the alleyway. The downpour, a staccato plinking of water against glass, against concrete, against itself, and the sharp moans of wind infected her dreams.

While Cookie dreamed, the sand beneath the building that blocked the moon twisted under the relentless weight of water. It belched, then bellowed as the crush of stone stuffed between the building's steel beams rolled. The cracked cement weakened. In her sleep, Cookie heard the soprano tinkling of breaking glass. The retaining wall gave. A rush of wet sand poured through the shattered windows. Sand rolled over her like a blanket of cool silk. It filled the pockets of her eyes and nostrils and ears. Half-dreaming, half-awake, she clawed it away.

Sand. Earthy, damp, clammy sand. Fractals of sea glass and starfish, weighed heavy on her legs. A matching pile lay over the covers where Alice used to sleep. It plugged the windows. The room was darker than its usual dark. It was midnight dark.

She stretched against the sand blanketing her legs and reached for the bedside lamp, feeling her way past its spiked ceramic flowers. The bulb glowed gold. The sand formed dunes from the window to the cracked plaster walls. In the brief passing between sleep and waking, she'd invented a celestial hourglass that shattered overhead. Now, struggling through the haze of unfinished dreams, she knocked the sand off her legs and slid down a pile at the edge of the bed.

On summer nights, she slept in a pink cotton nightgown with a wide, white frill along its edge. The hem landed at her thick, freckled calf. Her plump toes gripped the brown-sugar sand as she skidded to the closet. She wrestled the door open enough to slip an arm inside and grab at whatever she could reach. Alice's purple down parka.

The parka's zipper strained over Cookie's stomach. The pink nightie twisted around her hips. She jammed her feet into her sneakers at the front door. With her purse swinging from her elbow (*like the queen*, Alice used to say), she stepped into the hallway. Her sneakers squeaked on the marble floor.

Dawn's humidity hung heavy. Beads of sweat lined the underbelly of her chin. Her arms were stuffed sausages in the parka sleeves. Alice had been smaller than Cookie, or perhaps Cookie had grown since she'd retired. Her feet felt larger than her shoes. Her brain felt larger than her skull. Her grief felt larger than the body that contained it. She pushed the creaking side alley door open and walked to the front of the building.

The super's window was cracked open. "Arturo," she whispered loudly, operatically. *Sotto*. Loud, but not too loud. Loud enough to wake Arturo, she hoped, but not loud enough to wake the neighbors—the buildings were planted so tightly together. "Arturo . . . wake up . . . something's happened."

Arturo grunted.

"Something's happened." She tapped on the glass.

Lights switched on in adjacent buildings. Windows slid open. A woman hung over the ledge of her window frame, half-in, half-out, watching. People were always watching.

"Wake up." Cookie was frantic now, though encouraged by Arturo's second grunt. She pulled at the zipped-up collar of the parka. Summer air rushed in. The white frill of her nightie clung to the back of her knees.

"Who's that?"

"It's me. It's Cookie. Something's happened."

"Why you wake me? What for?" He coughed his smoker's cough, leaned on the windowsill, his face drawn long in the dark, his eyes pockets of black shadow. "Go home, Cookie. Go to bed."

Cookie wished for Alice who could explain anything. Alice who liked everyone. Alice who knew a little bit of everything. "Please." *Where was Alice?*

He sighed and cleared his throat. "Gimme a minute."

Sand.

Tons of sand.

Dunes of sand piled into soft mountains, grain upon grain gripping the brick of the building where Cookie and Alice's windows used to be. Mist settled onto the piles, on Cookie's wiry strands of gray, on Arturo's glasses, on the paper of his cigarette. The flashlight dropped beside his knee. The beam shrank into a moth-sized moon on the ground. His mouth fell slack. Cookie gasped.

"Oh. Shit," Arturo mumbled. He flicked his cigarette into the sand.

Cookie tugged at the sleeves of the parka, scratched sand from her scalp Her ankles glowed white; the hem of her nightgown hung translucent. They stared, the two them, at the blue dawn shadow that lined the dunes.

Where was Alice in all of this? Where was competent, even-tempered, ever grounded Alice? In the ground, of course. Cookie sighed. Alice was in the ground. She lay beneath clumps of fine, brown dirt, nothing like the clumsy sand. The coffin hung, suspended by nylon straps so astringent, so orange, that it hurt to look at them. There'd been a small group at the burial. Cookie couldn't remember who. That day, the dirt had been contained to a single pile next to the square hole. The walls of the hole were almost smooth, aside from the fine weave of roots, hairs and webs of grass stretching along the dirt walls. Alice: sleeping, her face thick with makeup, round puddles of rouge on her fallen cheeks. Her body flattened by gravity. Her dress spread like a table cloth, bunched in corners between her dead arms and the silken cushions of the coffin. Bunched between her legs. Bunched behind her back. Held tight with hidden safety pins and tape. Cookie knew all the tricks.

The doctor said, "stroke," but Cookie suspected it was something else that had stolen Alice away. Ticks. Spiders, maybe. A pinprick that let the air out of her lungs—a slow, invisible leak. It didn't matter much. She was dead, having beaten death in that she hadn't expected to die that night, or anytime soon. She'd closed her eyes in the dark bedroom of their dark apartment and said goodnight and kissed Cookie's temple. She woke once to use the bathroom. Cookie felt the mattress rise when she got up, but had fallen asleep before Alice climbed back into bed. Her labored breath invaded Cookie's dreams, but Cookie's dreams were always being invaded. In the morning, Alice was cold.

Cookie discovered dead Alice after coffee and her walk beneath the bridge and along the river. She'd once seen a man jump off the bridge and then heard what sounded like a crash of breaking glass, but she never saw his body hit the water. She imagined he'd arched towards the sky and, in the moment she blinked, a fine nylon string yanked him to heaven.

It was on her birthday that she saw the man jump. Alice baked her a cake and frosted it with pink icing. Cookie seemed to remember, as she and Arturo stood in the alleyway and the dark lifted around the dunes of sand, that she'd baked herself a birthday cake last night—before the sand poured in. She'd frosted it pink, like Alice had done. She could *almost* see it on the kitchen counter, plastic wrap tented over toothpicks to keep the cockroaches out.

"What do we do?" Arturo squinted at the sand. He chewed the filter of a fresh cigarette. His hands cupped the flame of his lighter.

The alley door scraped against itself again. Gail Fowler, in her white sneakers and ankle-length khakis, her fists balled, beelined towards them. The sun grew muscle. She stopped short at the dune. She punched her fists into her side and pursed her skinny lips. "Well, don't just stand there. Clean it up."

Arturo let loose a rattling cough that shook itself into laugher. "Clean it up, she says."

"It's my birthday," Cookie said. She knew in the confusion that she'd forgotten something.

Arturo dropped his cigarette butt. "Happy birthday, Cookie." He stubbed out the embers and rubbed his eyes with the heels of his hands. "Happy fucking birthday."

"I think I made a cake."

Having untangled her legs from her neighbor's, and tugged her hand from under his sleep-weighted head, Ingrid wrapped herself in the top sheet, which had wadded up at the foot the bed. She'd pushed her hair from her face and padded over to the window to listen to the quiet commotion unravel in the alleyway.

She left the lights off. She didn't want anyone to see her naked but for a sheet after midnight in her neighbor's apartment. She was a quiet woman: private, stoic, even, and sometimes she wondered if this was the reason love evaded her. Her neighbor was a sound sleeper. He kept his bedroom blinds drawn and the artificial night inside outlived the real night. On days she didn't work, they stayed in bed past noon. She wasn't fooled into thinking it was love that kept her knocking at his door, though sometimes when she watched him sleep, she ran the tips of her fingers gently over the ends of his blond eyelashes and secretly, silently wished she'd hear him say the words. Just once. She would say them back just once and that would be that. Other times, when he bragged about his success in graduate school or played his guitar a little too long, it was clear to her that their relationship had an expiration date.

Until then, however, it was convenient that he lived down the hall.

She'd woken to a crash that sounded like a thousand tall dominoes falling into each other, in that artful, controlled, entropic way. There was movement. Building windows opened. Lights switched on. There was a rustle in the alley as the heavy rains subsided into morning drizzle. Her neighbor hadn't stirred. He could sleep through anything.

From the open window, she'd heard the scraping of metal against metal. Standing at an angle, she caught the edge of the alley access door pushing open. The beam of a flashlight lit the floating drizzle. Ingrid stuck her head farther out the window and rain landed on her face like melting snow. The beam bent around the black garbage bags, piled by the gate, the flowerpots that lined the side of the building, and Arturo's lawn chair where he smoked away most of his mornings and evenings. Its nylon weave had stretched into a relief of his angular behind.

Arturo then appeared, holding the flashlight. Behind him was another neighbor. Half of a lesbian couple who lived in the basement apartment. Ingrid had known the other half for a few months, before her sudden death, though they'd all lived in the same building, the same *existence* for years. The couple used to sit on the front stoop in the mornings, drinking coffee in amiable, enviable silence as the world walked by on its way to work.

Alice had been the friendlier of the two, cocksure in her old age, her round apple cheeks pushing her eyes shut when she laughed. Ingrid sometimes watched her paint the downtown skyline or the Palisades or the bridge from the roof of the building, her cheap canvas balanced on her cheap table top easel on the picnic table on the roof. It'd been Alice who tricked Ingrid into painting, who helped her fill an emptiness that ached like a broken rib.

Cookie was the quiet one. She passed weight from one side to the other, foot to foot, like an impatient child when Alice stopped to talk. She seldom made eye contact, though she'd flutter her eyes up and sometimes whisper a sudden smile, a gap-toothed laugh before staring back at her hands. She'd been a costumer and still, sometimes, the ends of threads stuck themselves to her sweaters and hung from the deep pockets of her jumpers. She was shy to the point of pride. To talk with her, Ingrid intuited, was to cause discomfort. She'd left a card and flowers outside their door after Alice passed. She'd watched the funeral from the back of the small group of onlookers and slipped out before the preacher's closing prayer. Since then, whenever they passed each other, Cookie looked away.

In the alleyway, the flashlight beam stopped and fanned at the base of something Ingrid could barely make out, and only when she pressed herself against the wall and squinted diagonally through the window. It was something foreign, something big. Something that hadn't been in the alleyway hours ago, when her neighbor gingerly moved the straps of her bra down her shoulders and kissed her neck as if he loved that part of her.

She watched the scene unfold from her neighbor's living room until the sirens of the first fire trucks rammed through the alleyways and windows. Then, she shed the sheet at the foot of the bed and crawled over the length of her neighbor's body until she'd nestled into his arms. She pressed her back into the warmth of his chest. He was a dead weight, dead to the world and she both admired and disapproved of his ability to sleep the day away. She considered him undisciplined. Questioned his commitment to his art. He didn't work like she did, in the minutes and hours between the painful numbness of their respective bread-and-butter jobs. She sketched every morning at six and painted when she got home from work. On weekends she sometimes refused to leave the apartment building and threw herself into the manufactured memories she painted on a collapsible easel by her barred bedroom window.

She turned. Shook his shoulder. She pushed on his chest, but he barely moved. "We need to wake up." He slept the sleep of the dead. "The fire department's here." More trucks more sirens. "Something's happened." Should she slap his face, pinch his nipples? Lick the inside of his ear? How did you wake up someone held captive by sleep? Kiss him—like in the fairy tale. She smoothed his hair away from his forehead.

He had a baby face, round and full, made even rounder by his receding hairline. His lashes were tipped with white and oozed a sexy blandness, a seductive apathy, an interest not in the person he was talking to, but in the negative space between them. The curved inside of an empty vase. There was a single freckle where his eyelash met his eyelid.

She tickled him under his arm. He stirred. "James, we got to get up." She heard voices in the hallways below. Boots clomping up stairs. Fists pounding. Men laughing. She kissed the corner of his eye. "Wake up, wake up." He stirred. "We're being evacuated. You might want to get dressed." He smiled, eyes closed, stretched his arms wide, then hugged her strong and close. Sometimes she thought she might love him. "Better get dressed." He didn't move. She squirmed her way out of his sleeping embrace, stepped into her underwear and pulled her dress over her head. She slipped out the door before the firemen knocked.

*

Cookie was thinking about the cake while she sat on the sidewalk curb. She called to mind the silkiness of the flour, the satisfying way it snowed from sifter to bowl. How it drifted into a soft hill.

Two buildings had been evacuated. The inhabitants milled on the corner and down the block. Some lingered at the doors to the café, which was set to open at nine. Alice's purple parka tipped past the points of Cookie's knees. Sweat rolled down her back. It was summer in the humid city and packets of down crinkled when she lifted her arms to twist her hair into a bun. The sun had turned itself all the way up.

For a moment, Gail Fowler's voice rose above all the others with a call to sue the building owners. The retaining wall, she declared, had been compromised for years. She'd called the city zoning commission at the first appearance of the crack, witnessed from her fourth-floor window, and then weekly over the past five years as she watched it grow. Her voice trilled and wavered, *staccato, pizzicato,* plunking, driven, and strange as she wrestled her anger with fisted hands. The displaced nodded and grumbled in sleepy bemusement. Gail Fowler was always leaning on some complaint or another. Complaining was her avocation. She had a reputation.

Other words floated to the top of the din and bobbed down the side street. *Coffee. Sleep. Work. When will they let us in?* Alice was a word that formed from all the other words. Cookie mouthed her name as sweat and sun stung her eyes. *Alice, Alice, Alice. Where was Alice?*

There were days when it felt like Alice was sitting next to her on the building stoop or sleeping on the bed, or heading home from her book club or down from the building rooftop with her paints. Cookie still heard Alice's robust singing echo through the first-floor hallways. She could still see the rivers of veins stitched across Alice's thick calves, which were not as thick as Cookie's calves, lumbering up the hill, her paint box and easel crushed between her elbow and her ribs. Cookie buried her nose into the collar of the parka and tried to smell whatever bit of Alice still lingered, but there was nothing of Alice left. Instead, she smelled her own sweat and diesel from the trucks toiling up 181st Street.

Cookie wasn't sure she believed in death, having seen a man jump from the bridge but never reach the water. It would be like Alice to do the same. Perform a sleight of hand. To leave for a moment to prove that the fabric of a relationship endured beyond its ending. A lover can stop growing old, stop talking, stop brewing coffee, stop sleeping late, stop breathing, stop living, and still stick around. Her clothes hung in the closet. Her toothbrush was crammed in the cup by the bathroom sink. Her paint box waited for her on the bookshelf in the living room. Love lingered.

What if Cookie died? What would happen to the love? Would it *still* linger? Would it keep itself alive? Cookie wanted to die, sitting on the curb in Alice's purple parka, sleeping alone on a half-sagged mattress, baking a cake for two that only one would eat, but Death (or was it Love) wouldn't set her free.

The corner was blocked off with twisted caution tape. Four fire engines lined the side streets. Arturo chain-smoked beneath a hardened city tree. The bridge shimmered over the sliver of river she could see from the middle of the hill.

After she'd seen the man jump and heard the sound of breaking glass, she sat on the rocks by the river and waited for his body to float by. It didn't. Was it possible for a person to disappear, for their molecules to disperse into the ether like glass in a kaleidoscope? To become part of the sky?

"Drug hit," said the cop who smoked a cigar every morning by the Irish pub. "Happens all the time. People thrown from the bridge. They don't think two thoughts about it." She told him how the man had arched, his back bowed, his feet pointing towards the sky. She described the sound of breaking glass.

"Belly flop," the cop said, mimicking the dead man's landing with one flat palm hitting the other. "Body hits water. Makes a terrible sound."

But it'd been a perfect dive. She'd caught her breath. The beauty of it.

That morning, when she got home, there was a pink frosted cake on the kitchen counter that Alice had baked. When she saw Cookie's tear-stained cheeks, she took her face in rounded palms, kissed her across the hairline, and rubbed her ears. Later, they sat at the picnic table on the roof of the building and ate the cake without bothering to cut it into slices. The bridge loomed. The car headlights inched along, coming and going. The water was a deep, pearlescent blue. Cookie made a birthday wish on a candle stuck into a pile of crumbs. They kissed, pink icing between their teeth. She didn't remember what she wished for. Sitting on the curb, she wished that she'd wished for that moment to last forever, or at least a while longer.

Cookie thought about the pink frosted cake currently on the kitchen counter, the one that Alice hadn't made because she wasn't there, wasn't sleeping beneath the sand in their dark apartment after the heavy rain washed the retaining wall away. Her brain felt like a melting crayon. She closed her eyes and searched her memory for the feel of Alice's hand in hers. She strained to hear Alice's belly laugh. What had she wished for on that last birthday night with Alice? Tonight, she decided, when she blew out her birthday candle, she'd wish to remember.

"Did you remember to lock the door?" A swell of misplaced panic pulsed the spindled vein on Ingrid's temple. The commotion, she thought, was an opportunity for an uninvited someone to slip into the building. It'd happened to her before. She'd left her apartment with a certain amount of possessions and returned to find a good number of those items missing. Open doors were an invitation. A psychic once told her that her father had given her what he'd thought of as a gift, but was truly a curse—a wall of protection around her heart. As above, so below. When you open a door, walls come crumbling down. It wasn't that she was afraid to love, or that she didn't know how to love. It was only that—with all of it—no one ever wanted to be the first one to say it. Even in her family, no one ever said "I love you." And so, love was left unsaid. She *preferred* the doors closed, the structure intact.

"No one's getting in." The neighbor had found her outside, given her an approving smile. She'd kept their secret secret.

At each entrance, two firemen and one cop stood, arms crossed, chatting. Her neighbor knocked her shoulder with his. "It'll be okay." He never flirted with her in public. She wasn't sure she liked being a secret anymore and had planned to tell him, but then they fell asleep and the retaining wall collapsed and now they were in a squall of personalities making the best of being locked out on the sidewalk when they should be sleeping.

There were times when she thought they had something good between them, when he sat so closely to her on the subway that she felt the heat off his skin, or when he slipped notes under her apartment door. When he snuck into her unlocked apartment late at night and curled around her when she slept. When he brushed against her in the elevator.

She blocked the sun with her hand. Down the sidewalk, Cookie sat on the curb in her puffed purple parka. She looking like a wilting grape. Ingrid watched as she pulled the spine of a down feather from the seam of the coat and released it into the air. The feather floated onto a spray of grass growing from a crack in the sidewalk. Cookie squinted into the hazy sunlight, the glare that reflected off the bridge. Her lips moved. She was talking to herself.

"She must be so hot." Ingrid stood.

"Where are you going?"

"To give her water. Poor lady. To see that she's okay."

"Who's she talking to?" The neighbor stood, too, dusted off the back of his jeans. Love was something that crossed Ingrid's mind more than she wanted it to when she was near him.

"Don't know. Herself, I guess."

To love and be loved seemed like something mysteriously simple. Sublime, fragile, as destructive as a hurricane. Once love blew through, there was no end to the damage it wrought. She'd seen it in her mother when her father left, and in her stepmother when her father died. She'd seen it in her half-sister Kate, her endless thirst for the approval of others, her knack for fitting the world into a picture she wanted to look at. Only her little nephew gave love, like it was boundless and free. But he'd take it back as easily as he'd given it away. It was safer to be alone with paints and canvas, or under the heavy blankets by the bedroom window, pretending she was lying on soft grass or on the sand by the ocean. She liked being alone. Or, maybe, honestly, her aversion to love had something to do with fear.

She lightly touched Cookie's shoulder. "Are you okay?"

Cookie looked up. "There was a lot of sand."

Ingrid knelt and offered her water from her water bottle. "It's a little warm, but…."

Cookie drank. "Oh! It poured in. Oh, wow. While I was sleeping. Look." She shook sand from her sleeve. "Like an hourglass that broke from above."

For a time, Cookie saw the woman in the mornings when she and Alice drank coffee on the stoop. Those mornings, life was drained from her face, her bag dragged down her shoulder. She was a fish, swimming uphill against the tide and then down, underground into the depths of the train station. Her eyes were gray and watery, far apart. Her hair was usually pulled back, always coming loose. She looked different now. Clear. Bright. Her hair had fallen into dark ringlets.

Later in the mornings, Cookie sometimes watched the man garden on the roof. His hairline receded dramatically from his temples, leaving a spray of baby hairs abandoned on his forehead. Cookie knew them, but didn't *know* them. She couldn't remember their names. She couldn't remember if she'd ever known their names. She couldn't remember if she was supposed to remember.

The heat was getting to her. The down parka. The pebbles on the backs of her legs. The bottoms of her bare feet sticking to the inserts in her sneakers. If she wasn't such a prudish woman, she'd unzip the coat for a moment and fan herself with the flaps, but the nightie was wet with sweat. She couldn't bear revealing her drooping breasts, her tired belly, to the world. And she knew people were watching. Since Alice left, people were *always* watching. From corners and doorways. Behind counters. On the sidewalk. Through the cafe window. They never spoke, but they always watched.

"Are you okay? Is there someone we can call?"

Cookie scratched sand from behind her ear, flicked it from beneath her fingernails, shook her head. "I made a cake. I'd like to eat it before the cockroaches do."

Heat swirled up from inside the parka and swelled to the tip of her head. She baked slowly inside. Internal combustion. Rising heat. The absence of heat from Alice after her night of fitful sleep. Cookie left the light off, tiptoed out of the room to let Alice sleep a little later, then a little later, and then a little later, until it was too late.

"What a day, huh?" The man, the neighbor (*What was his name? Alice would know. Where was Alice?*) leaned in and took her hand and helped her to stand. Her nightie rode up and twisted around her waist. Her thighs chafed. Little black pebbles of tar, fractals of tires, tumbled from her calves.

A murmur rose from the transient crowd. The café waitress opened the doors. The vagrants piled in, clamoring for coffee and early morning Bloody Marys. It was two minutes past nine, but they'd been up for hours. Cookie'd been up for hours upon their hours. She swooned. The woman and the man *what were their names?* each took an elbow and led her inside.

Ingrid pushed sideways through the throng, five deep at the café counter, and pulled Cookie to the back of the restaurant, where tables were filling up. Cookie's thinning skin, loose over her knuckles, slid on her bones. Her fingernails were ridged and brittle—cheap plastic toys. Ingrid stepped around a couple and grabbed a two-top by the window. Wasn't this what she was supposed to do? Make sure this drifting woman had the slightest semblance of attention, of care? To let her know that she had not been forgotten? In that purple parka, she looked like Macy's Thanksgiving day balloon coming to life the evening before the parade. It was enough to make Ingrid laugh and then regret laughing. She was a horrible person for thinking things like that. Hadn't Cookie lost her anchor? An anchor so sturdy, the waters so sharp, that she'd been sent unmoored in a river that flowed in two directions at once.

Ingrid floated in life, too. Floated from boyfriend to boyfriend. *Serial monogamy*, her sister called it, Ingrid's attempts to tether herself to the ground while inching through life. She never had the patience to drag someone else along. But then the gentleness with which her neighbor, her lover, helped Cookie into a chair, brought her water, made sure she drank, the ease with which his tall body moved through space, the grace of his presence made her crave some sort of something more. Perhaps the reason Ingrid found it impossible to love was that she, herself was impossible. In all ways. But especially, to love.

The three of them squeezed around the table. Her neighbor leaned his chair back on two legs. Cookie dropped her head in her hands, then blotted her face with a napkin. She puffed her cheeks and blew a single hair from her forehead. She shrugged. Ingrid took Cookie's hand and held it. Cookie dug her flimsy fingernails into the flesh of Ingrid's palm.

*

The air conditioning turned Cookie's sweat clammy, the feeling some people sometimes described as death. But death, real death, felt heavy and smooth. Polished. Cool to the touch. Sweat pooled beneath the collar of the coat. It dripped down her neck behind her ears. And evaporated from her eyelashes and tumbled in drops to the table. She wiped a grain of sand from the corner of her eye. She hadn't noticed before, but now she felt sand at the bottom of her shoe and between the folds of her skin. Her lungs were bags of sand. She opened her purse and pulled out a battered pack of tissues. She blotted her face, her neck, her hands. She stowed a clean tissue up the sleeve of the parka.

The woman and the man smiled expectantly, both leaning towards her, their shoulders nearly knocking. They made a nice couple, Cookie thought.

Her tongue went dry. They watched. She drank water. They watched. The coolness of the condensation on the glass teased Cookie, trapped in Alice's purple parka stuffed with the feathers of dead birds and Cookie's shriveling skin. They watched. Cookie scratched her palm. *What were their names?* Alice would've known, would've whispered it in Cookie's ears. Cookie closed her eyes to try to hear Alice's voice. She didn't. When she opened her eyes, the couple was watching. They stared at her until she couldn't take it anymore.

"Bathroom," she whispered, *sotto,* loud but not loud. The sand drained from her fingertips, from the bottoms of her shoes. She made her way to the back of the restaurant.

The bathroom was windowless, yet it was not nearly as dark as her apartment. The lights were dim, the red walls, dingy. There was a sloppy cobweb in the corner of the ceiling. Spun in a hurry, no doubt, by a hungry spider. She ran water and splashed her face. She swished it around her mouth. She smoothed her hair and pulled the parka zipper down to the center of her chest and peeled it away from her soaked skin. Her nightgown was sopping wet and see-through. The white cotton frill around the neckline was pasted upside down across her sternum. Color rose in her cheeks. She sat on the edge of the toilet. She craved the breeze off the water, the river in the shadow of the bridge. To sit on a rock and wait for the jumping man to swim by. To join him. Her eyes drifted closed.

In that darkness, she saw Alice stretching her limbs at dawn in their dark bedroom. She reached for the luxury of Alice's hand in hers, then resting on the side of her hip. Alice kissing her forehead. Alice whispering *Happy Birthday, baby girl* even though she knew Cookie hated birthdays. Alice balancing the cake, carrying it to the elevator, pressing the button with her elbow. Sitting in the roof by the dwarf apple tree and the black-eyed Susans. "The man desired privacy," she told Cookie. "It was an accident that you witnessed his flight. For this, I am certain, he is sorry." They danced, slow. They swayed. Cookie made a wish on the cake's crumbs. What was that wish? She wished she knew.

On the other side of the bathroom, there was the rising din of conversation. The scream of a coffee grinder. The clatter of silverware. A tray of glasses dropped and broke. Someone knocked on the door.

"Be right out." Cookie shut off the running water and pulled open the door. It was too much for her. Much too much. She pushed past the waiting people.

"Wait," the wide-eyed woman called from the table. "Cookie, come sit."

"Let her go," the man said.

Cookie pushed past the bottleneck crowd at the front of the café and onto the street.

"Where the hell are you going?" Gail Fowler grabbed her by the arm, tight grip, white-sneaker tapping. "Cookie, sit."

Why, Cookie thought. *Why Gail why now why?*

"You're not well," Gail said. "Not that you ever were. But you walk around like a ghost. Like ghost who's seeing a ghost. You talk to yourself. You're unhinged. Think I'm the only one who notices?"

People were always watching.

"They'll take you away."

Why was everyone always watching?

"It'll make them feel good about themselves."

"I don't like you," Cookie said.

"I don't like you either. Never have. Stay here. I'm getting you water."

"I already drank." Cookie's voice rang shrill and dry. She crossed her arms, her purse swinging from her wrist. The parka crinkled. A feather poked out from a seam.

"So help me. Drink more."

Gail took two steps, three steps, four towards the café. Cookie stood, still as a rock until Gail walked inside. Then she hustled down the hill, the parka rustling, rising around her knees, her feet sliding in her shoes. She looked back once, camouflaged by a struggling city tree. Gail hadn't returned.

The river was at high tide and the water spooned the glacial rocks. She looked towards the bridge and waited for the man to jump. She held her hands out. They still felt like her hands. She kicked off her shoes. Her feet still looked like her feet. The hem of her nightie twisted around her knees. She unzipped the parka and dragged it away from her skin and stepped into the river. She felt full. Heavy. She lay back on the water, arms stretched towards the bridge, towards the sky, ready to catch whoever fell.

She felt like sand.

At dusk, the fire trucks pulled away from the curb. The engineers declared the buildings safe. The politicians went back home. Cookie's neighbors, Ingrid and James, curled together in secret in his apartment. Ingrid worried the corner of the pillowcase in her sleep.

As Cookie huffed up the hill, her ankles swollen, her shoes filled with sand, her hem listing sideways, and her purse jammed onto the puffy sleeves of Alice's purple parka, Ingrid woke with a start from a dream she didn't remember. She slid from under the weight of her neighbor's arm, slipped her dress over her head. Barefoot, she walked up the two flights of stairs to the roof.

"What a strange day," Cookie whispered to no one in particular.

Cookie's apartment door was crisscrossed with yellow caution tape. There was a business card, The Red Cross, jammed in the crack between door and frame. She stretched the tape away. The door was unlocked. The apartment was dark. It was always dark. Her footsteps were muted by a sprinkling of sand, spread by the heels of the firemen's boots. The shadow of the dune loomed beyond the bedroom door. In the stillness she knew she'd finally been forgotten.

The cake was on the counter. She took it and a fork and a bottle of Jameson, which she'd also forgotten about, and shoved a candle and a book of matches into her purse. Her sneakers squeaked on the marble of the hallway floor. She pressed the elevator button with her elbow.

The night had cooled and air rushed at Cookie as she stepped onto the roof. She didn't see Ingrid sitting there on the bench. She stripped the husk of the parka away. A feather stuck to her skin and she released it over the side of the building. The breeze carried it. The wrinkled clumps of her nightgown fell free.

The bridge was lit in silver. The leaves of the apple trees stirred. The black-eyed Susans were gray. The pink of the cake and the pink of her nightgown were gray, too. As was the candle, the matches, her purse which she set on the building ledge. The candle rolled over the ledge and Cookie watched her last wish plummet towards the street. She was too tired to cry.

She pressed the fork into the cake, took a bite. She'd forgotten something, salt or vanilla, one of those intangibles Alice always remembered, the sort of ingredient that made a cake taste good.

Ingrid stood. Her skin glowed like a ghost. She was straight and young, like Alice used to be. Her bare feet gripped the brick. Her hands in the light of the bridge and the moon trembled with hope. Cookie knew it wasn't Alice walking towards her, but she let herself believe. Icing coated her teeth. She sipped a little whiskey to wash it down.

THE BUTTERFLY COLLECTOR

Raymond booked the trip because he wasn't afraid of death. At seventy, he thought he should be. He lied to Mayung about it. Said it was a tourist expedition for amateur entomologists to help a university professor collect butterfly samples from the floor of the Amazon.

As a boy, he'd treasured a hunk of amber with a fly frozen inside. He kept a perfect, dead bee that he found on his mother's windowsill in one of her empty jewelry boxes, laid like a semiprecious stone on the cotton padding. For his eighth-grade science project, he collected fireflies in a jar and set them free in the classroom, where they lit up like sickly constellations when he turned off the lights.

His sentimentality was hard-earned, he insisted when Mayung jutted her lips. At seventy, the road ahead was straight, short, and flat. He'd earned a winding view backwards. Reliving one's boyhood fantasies was one of the luxuries afforded to old men.

He mentioned the expedition to Mayung the month before he was set to leave, even though he'd bought his tickets three months earlier. He made a show of seeking her approval and she made a show of giving it. In a circuitous way, it was her fault he discovered the trip in the first place. He found the ad while flipping through an issue of *Shaman's Drum* at the store where Mayung wholesaled imports from her sisters in Malaysia—hand-sewn eye pillows and beaded scarves. While she haggled with the store owner, a doughy, double-chinned woman whose voice sounded like chimes being dragged along cracking concrete, their boy played with the shop cat and Raymond, half-watching, half-listening, leafed through the magazine. The shop cat draped itself across a stack of books, tail twitching as it offered its neck to the boy's tiny hands.

Raymond wondered if he loved Mayung. If she loved him. Their engagement had been transactional; their marriage, the same. The boy's birth and life bookended his own.

The advertisement was printed on a quarter page of the magazine's flimsy stock. Its illustrations were intricately green, vines turning into snakes, a shaman morphing into a jaguar. The twelve-day retreat promised a traditional *dieta* with plant medicines, healings, spiritual teachings, and *yage*.

Raymond tried *yage* once on a business trip in Ecuador, twenty years prior. His travel partner, more adventurous than he, brought him to a town on the outskirts of Quito. The *curandero* refused to serve gringos, but sent his greasy-haired son, a teenager in a Metallica T-shirt and a grass skirt, to preside over the ceremony. They drank the washed-out, bitter brew and sat on the ground for two hours, waiting for something to happen. Nothing did, and they tripped out of the compound and into a town fair, drank beer, and hailed a motor-taxi back to their hotel. That night, Raymond dreamt of his father, memories he'd long forgotten. Since then, those same memories wound their way into his dreams and, sometimes, his waking life. He couldn't shake them.

The group met at the Hotel River Fox in Calle 7 in Pucallpa. Raymond stumbled over the crumbling, uneven sidewalks after a sleepless night in a cheap hotel room, where he'd had to spin the fan blades by hand to get the motor working. Six feet and bald, he towered over the Peruvian pedestrians. They pointed at him and gawked. Past the bodega's yawning garage doors, past the vendors selling Inca Soda and bottled water, *sin gas y con gas, uno soles,* past the arcade and the bakeries with sickly sweet desserts in their outdoor display cases, a young boy pulled against his mother's grip to ask Raymond in polite Spanish if he could touch Raymond's hairless head. Though Raymond wanted to shake them off, disappear into the homogenized anonymity of his enclave in the States, he bent down and allowed the child to scratch at his sparse stubble. After running his hands along the horseshoe of Raymond's stubble, giggling, he stepped his foot next to Raymond's and heel-toed three times before he reached the end of Raymond's hiking boot. The child's mother noticed Raymond's uncomfortable shifting from foot to foot and called her son back.

There were eleven in the group plus Don Julio, their Peruvian guide, thick as a tree trunk with a baby face. The travelers included a threesome of backpacking twenty-somethings with embroidered bags and sandals and a bookish graduate student with gold-rimmed glasses. There was a soft-spoken doctor from Croatia who sat stoic in the corner, and a striking couple; the woman looked older than the man, though it was hard to gauge her age. She moved with the calm of the dragonflies that Raymond chased as a child. Her boyfriend? Husband? Partner? was affable, easygoing, handsome. Easy to talk to, it seemed. She perched on the edge of the lobby sofa seat, posture perfect, humble elegance. He curved into the cushions, his arm laid nonchalantly across her thigh. Raymond was the last to arrive, and the oldest. He barely huffed his hello before the group walked out to the sidewalk, where Julio hailed three taxis.

They drove two hours out of the city on desolate dirt roads. The passengers gripped the door handles as they bounced towards the Ucayali River. At a port town, they transferred to two dugout boats that labored for another two hours into the Amazon. One by one, the travelers pulled themselves from the bank of the river into the jungle and walked on foot for thirty minutes into camp.

Raymond's *tombo* was set off from the others, which lined the river. His was secluded, sheltered by brush, shades of green broken by a shock of pink hibiscus and the blues and yellows of the hummingbirds that fed off them. Entangled in the canopy, the sun weakly dappled the forest floor with pebbles of light. Birdsong colored the guarded landscape, though the birds themselves lived in the sky and only visited earth at dusk. As he lay on his hammock, two Blue Morphos glided by, alternating between the royal blue of their opened wings and the humility of dirt-gray undersides.

A week before he left for Peru, he and Mayung took the boy to a butterfly exhibit in the city. When one landed on Raymond's head, the boy laughed.

Raymond thought of the time he laughed at his own father, who'd dribbled catsup down his chin. The mistake left young Raymond with a cut lip and a bruised cheek. He had learned by then not to cry.

When Mayung lifted the boy for a better look, Raymond bent down. The boy gently ran his fingers across Raymond's scalp and gasped as the butterfly, incandescent green and oily black, fluttered away.

Raymond set his pack on the slat bed and untucked the mosquito net that hung from the ceiling. It smelled of mildew and soap. The Blue Morphos flew through again, one chasing the other.

The moisture curled the pages of his blank journal. His money and passport were folded in a Ziploc bag so they wouldn't turn moldy. Everything—shirts, shoes, underwear, his butterfly net— was in plastic baggies. Mayung had packed for him. She made him buy a pith hat with a black mosquito net sewn onto the rim. He put it on and lowered the net over his face.

Did he love Mayung? He cared for her a great deal. She cared for him. There were days when he wanted to do something to make her happy. Buy her a gift. Flowers, maybe. But doing so seemed to him a great act of bravery. He never knew what she might like. When he announced their nuptials five years ago, his friends clapped him on the back and congratulated him. Their cap-toothed smiles spread with admiration as if marrying a much younger woman was an accomplishment worthy of admiration. There was nothing admirable about it.

Truth was, he didn't know why he'd married her, only that he'd come into his office more than once to find her crying, her cart of cleaning supplies as depleted as she was. He allowed her to gather herself. She brought him *kiuh*, which reminded him of the sweets he'd tasted as a young soldier in Vietnam. Then, somehow, they were married and she was pregnant and the boy was born. It hadn't felt right, but it hadn't felt wrong, either.

In his journal, he traced the outline of a new butterfly that landed on the knot of the hammock rope. Its wings were orange and black, the colors of the Monarch, but the tips were laced with white. His drawing was clumsy; he hadn't sketched in years, and then only straight lines and perfect circles, boxes, gears, plans.

In the brush outside his hut, two bits of fluff, the downy ends of white bird feathers, vaulted from a leaf, floated at the top of the arc, and landed. The feathers launched again. Raymond started to sketch the mysterious Fairy Bug. He wandered to the edge of the path to look at it, but the bug was gone.

At dusk that first day, Julio called the group to the *maloka* for the ceremony of *yawa panga,* a fierce cleansing. Cross-legged, they leaned against the round walls of the prayer hut as he sang *icaros* and blew *mapacho* smoke, rich, dark jungle tobacco, over the medicine. His Peruvian lilt looped around his words. "The *yawa panga* is good medicine. Strong. Hard medicine. But good. Tomorrow you'll see it in the eyes of the others. Clear eyes are clear souls."

They drank river water, gallons of it, cup by cup, until it thickened into silken sludge. Then, they purged for hours, water in, water out, into their buckets. Later, they dumped their purge onto the roots of the surrounding trees. Still later, after the ceremony had ended and they'd been escorted back to their huts, sounds of retching penetrated the damp darkness of the jungle. Raymond's stomach turned to acid; yellow bile burned his throat.

Throughout the night, he was shaken by the crunching of brush. He huddled beneath the mosquito net, curled around himself on the sheets Mayung had ironed, folded, and packed. A haunting, quivering prayer drifted into his hut. He marveled that a simple song could frighten him when death did not. He felt a presence. Blurred by the mosquito net, Julio, dressed in white, hovered by his bed. Raymond squeezed his eyes shut and pretended to sleep.

He did fall asleep at some point. He dreamed the memory of breaking his arm in a bad landing from a swing at the park when he was eight. As he lay on the ground between the roots of a maple, his injured arm was fused to the sand beneath the swing set. In the dream, and in life, he lay locked to the earth for hours, watching wind ripple its way through the tree's branches until a neighbor stumbled upon him. In the hospital, he cried from fear and pain until he heard his parents hurrying down the hallway, which was a featureless gleam of light in the dream. He wiped his nose on the cuff of his shirt and erased his tears. "Boys don't cry," his father stated often over the course of his childhood, until Raymond came home from high school one afternoon and his mother greeted him in her bathrobe, her eyes rimmed with thumb strokes of red. "Don't go into the basement," she said. First the ambulance came, then the coroner. Raymond and his mother stood at the top of the stairs as they carried his father's stiffened body out.

At sunrise, Julio and his helper brought a plastic pitcher of tea, a tart, pink brew, *bobinsana*, "To bring in dreams."

"I don't want any more dreams," Raymond said.

"Then why come all this way?"

"To stop the dreams. You were singing prayers last night. You came to my hut."

"No," Julio said. "No. I slept. I slept like a log. Like the toad in the shade of a log."

*

When they left, Raymond dug a granola bar from the bottom of his bag. Mayung had packed them, too. He chewed slowly, felt for it swishing in his waterlogged stomach. He folded the wrapper and buried it in his luggage. He found his beta-blockers and Zoloft, amber prescription bottles hidden in a sock. He wasn't supposed to eat. He'd lied about his medications on the release form, too.

With his bucket and a handful of dried leaves Julio had handed him, he followed the muddy path to the river. It was cool that morning. It felt like he was walking through a cloud.

Through the mosquito net on his pith hat, he spotted a naked woman, his fellow traveler, the ageless one, Ingrid, bathing in the river. She squatted by the bank, her back to him, crushing the *chakruna* leaves, dunking them in her bucket, and using them to scrub her body. Her towel and clothes were draped over the roots of a tree. The roots extended from the trunk, tented around like the teepees he set up in his backyard when he was a boy, when Cowboys and Indians was a harmless game. She shivered from the cold river bath, a torturous luxury. Then she arched back until the top of her forehead was submerged and her hair fanned around her face and the white of her breasts shimmered above the water, orbs of light. She floated like a beautiful corpse. And then, she jolted up. Covering herself with her arms, she scrambled for her towel.

There had to be some sort of graceful way of dealing with this sort of situation, for stumbling upon a bathing woman in the shallow rim of a muddy river. If there was, Raymond didn't know it. When she turned towards him, he backed away.

"Sorry. I didn't see you." He held his free hand up and yanked at the edge of his mosquito net, which pressed into his throat. He tripped on a root as he backed away.

"Jesus," she said, "you fucking scared me." Wrapped in her towel, she glared at him from the edge of the river.

His stomach cramped and he worried that he might vomit. He felt his pills, one flat and round, the other oblong, circling each other in close orbit. He was afraid he might vomit them up. He labored up the hill and back to his *tombo*.

Eventually, the woman walked up the path, humming a vague memory of an *icaros*. Raymond's feet dangled above the floor; the fabric of the hammock cut into the backs of his thighs. She followed the song in her sundress, wellies, and tangled hair.

"I'm sorry about that," he called.

She frowned. Blots of sunshine broke though the canopy and dotted the side of her face. He could see her fine wrinkles. Her eyes looked clear, as Julio predicted. Glassy. Raymond wondered if his looked clear, too. There were no mirrors in his *tombo*, none in the camp. There was no way to know.

"I guess we're all a little new at this."

She'd weathered the *yawa panga* with an unearthly serenity. He watched her through the candlelight. When his head bobbed up from his bucket, he landed in her stillness. Her skirt knotted between her knees, her legs crossed, she remained erect through the ordeal. Her boyfriend knelt beside her, panting like a sick dog, his toes gripping the wooden slats. Between each purge, her lips moved. Raymond wished he knew what she was whispering.

"Is this your first time working with the medicine?"

He nodded. "Yeah. I mean. I guess."

"You guess? I think you'd remember. Maybe. You know the mosquitoes only come out at night, right? And only, really, in the rainy season." She gestured towards his hat and the black mosquito net that muted the colors of the world. "I mean, do what you want, but you don't need it."

His face flushed as she continued along the path. Tears welled in his eyes. He was embarrassed, though no one could see. He slammed the hat on the floor of his *tombo* and kicked it to the ground. He was mad at Mayung for making him bring it. He curled his fists and shook a post until, winded, he started to laugh. He thought of the boy, five years old, who behaved better than he did.

The boy liked bugs. He collected bloated worms from the sidewalks on rainy days and carried them like kings or corpses to the softened ground. He offered ants crumbs from his cookies. The boy would never consider burning them, as Raymond had, with a magnifying glass. The boy was everything like his mother. Nothing like him.

The day wore on. He drank the pink tea. He scrubbed himself in the river with his crumbled leaves. As the lethargic warmth of the jungle rose, Raymond waited. He watched the butterflies and hummingbirds. He wished for the fairy bug to appear.

He dozed. The ink of his uncapped pen bled onto the page of his journal, leaving a series of blurred, black dots. The heartbeat of the forest swelled; the sonorous laughter of the others carried. Smells shifted from sweet, to earthy, to floral, to the smell of luminous rain. He thought he heard himself blink. He wondered what Mayung was doing, if she reveled in the simplicity of having only the boy to consider. He decided that he harbored great affection for her and possibly for the boy, too. He supposed he married her because he didn't want to grow old alone. The prison of boredom loomed, along with the disintegration of virility, the insidiously slow, seeping loss of life force.

Did he love her, though? Did he love the boy? There were things he loved about her: her easy way with strangers, her calm, her soft humor, her devotion to their son. At night, she tucked the boy in and read to him in Mandarin first, and then English. He like listening to her voice from the other room. Her tongue was clumsy around American vowels and consonants and yet, she treated long words like hand-cut sapphires, taken out and admired when the light was right. In bed, she pressed her taut skin against Raymond's. Some nights, she rubbed his back and shoulders. When she sensed he was annoyed by the boy's rambunctiousness, she yanked Raymond's ears in a teasing way and reminded him that he'd been young, too. Only once had she raised her voice at Raymond, when he'd lifted his hand to strike the wailing child. "Boys don't cry," he spat. Mayung whisked the child into her arms and spat back, "Sometimes they do." But he wasn't sure that this was love or what love even felt like or what love was.

He thought he'd been in love once, when he met his first wife, but that love turned sour, and very quickly, too; their relationship devolved into the opposite of love, a slobbering and cruel monster who mocked its victims as they shored up their hearts.

Julio's assistants collected the group just before dusk. They made their way to the maloca in pairs. After a day of solitude, people were chatty. Save for Ingrid, who trailed behind, alone. Raymond hesitated and then decided to disrupt her calm. He slowed his pace until he was at the back of the group, walking next to her.

"Why did you come?" The back of Raymond's rolled up mosquito net scratched at his neck.

"Well, that's a question! Who knows?"

But he thought that of anyone, she did know. Even if she wouldn't tell him. She sighed.

"I lied to my wife to be here," he said. "I told her I was collecting butterflies."

"I'm an artist afraid I'm running out of things to say."

Raymond nodded as if he understood. "I ran out of things to say a long time ago. When people stopped listening."

"My art. Adam. My half-sister. My nephew. I love my nephew. I don't want him to grow up in a family where no one ever says 'I love you.' It shouldn't be that precious, love. It shouldn't be that hard. But it is. It's scary." She pulled back. "I'm sorry. That's too much. Much too much. It always feels like I'm falling."

She kicked off her sandals at the stairs of the maloca. Raymond sat on a rock to take off his mud boots. When he looked up, he was alone. The group was seated inside.

If Ingrid was at twelve o'clock, Raymond sat at six. Her boyfriend Adam –- Raymond had finally picked up his name—sat next to her, legs bent at the knee, leaning against the rounded wall. All in the group watched Julio apprehensively as he set down a beaten three-liter Inca Soda bottle filled with the *yage*. It resembled sludge. Surrounding the *maloca*, the leaves and vines rustled in the breeze. "The wind carries information." Julio lit his *mapacho*, thick as a small cigar. "And the leaves collect it."

"Tell me the things that can kill me here," the boyfriend said. This was a man, Raymond thought, who was afraid of silence.

"There's a tree in the forest, if you touch the bark, you'll die in fifteen seconds. There's a tree that grows rocks inside and when the clear-cutter comes, it breaks the blades. Maybe tomorrow we'll walk. I'll show you some plants." He arranged his mat, laying out a leaf bundle, a crystal, rattles, and a set of wooden chimes. He plucked a bit of tobacco from his tongue. "There's a snake that's very territorial and will chase you. You can't get away. It climbs trees."

"Are they here?"

"I seen one."

"What do you do if you piss one off?"

"You run side to side down the road and drop your shirt—any piece of clothing to attack instead. Very territorial. Very dangerous."

"God."

The jungle tobacco smoke was thicker than the whiny, parched brittleness of Raymond's father's Lucky Strikes. He'd smoked everywhere. You could those days. In the car, in restaurants, on the plane when they flew to visit Raymond's aunt in Florida. Raymond's childhood was hazy with smoke, but the jungle tobacco called to mind something different—the bitter earth his father once forced him to eat. Funny that Raymond remembered the punishment, but not the lesson.

"There's a black spider. It looks like a tarantula, but its sting is much worse. Its poison kills you in moments, but moments so painful they seem like forever. I've seen a snake so fat that it's two feet up from the ground. They sit still for days, months. Moss grows on them. A tree. Rabbits wander into their mouths. Sometimes a baby deer."

Ingrid shivered. Raymond closed his eyes.

"Snakes reside between spirit world and here."

"What else?"

"Stop," Ingrid said.

"What's the Fairy Bug," Raymond blurted. It was the best he could do to give her something.

Julio focused his eyes on Raymond. Blew smoke. Shook his head. "A fairy, I guess."

Again, Raymond's cheeks burned. He was thankful for the dark.

"Well, well, brothers and sisters, let's begin our ceremony." Julio blew smoke into a shot glass, poured the *yage* and drank. "*Salud*."

One by one, the tourists approached him and downed the brew.

The medicine was thicker than Raymond remembered, and bitter. He spat in his bucket. Julio blew out the candle and Raymond closed his eyes.

There was black at first, the dark of the jungle at night, protected from the moon. Raymond's limbs grew heavy. He focused on the grasshoppers' and beetles' harmonized crescendos. White dots floated inside his eyelids and the weave of the sounds of the jungle tightened as if the trees and vines and bats, beetles, and fireflies were singing the universe into being. Through the fabric of the bug song, a single voice rose, ducking and skipping across the aural landscape. It might've been seconds, or hours, Raymond wasn't sure, before he realized that Julio was singing with the insects.

And then, Raymond was sitting in the powder-green Chevy, his father at the wheel. As a boy, he loved sliding across the bench seats when they took a fast turn. Raymond felt the stickiness of the stitched vinyl seats, the sun magnified by the front window, the thrilling moment of silence after his father sped up and before his own body was set into motion. From that same silence, he witnessed his boy sprout from his mother's arms, first as a squalid, weak infant, a jaundiced thing, grabbing its soul in its fists, then as an indestructible toddler holding his mother hostage with his wails. Mayung scooped her body around him and wiped a tear almost before Raymond noticed it. As patterns spun, hospital gowns and spinning wheels and the intricate designs of the scarves Mayung imported, he realized that she understood that the ghost of his father still lingered within him.

And then, Raymond was gone.

He came to hours later. Dawn was breaking and the roundness of the *maloka* spun like a calliope as the leaves, trembling with dew, picked up the morning light. Raymond woke, curled into a fetal position, as Julio shook his leaf rattle above him. The sound permeated his consciousness. It became him. He couldn't talk. He didn't want to. He wanted silence, but he heard an elephantine moaning. He tried to locate it; he was making the noise. His throat was soft. His eyes felt new. He'd seen an angel. He was sure of it. The angel's impossible beauty overwhelmed him; a coat of vines crept around the angel's arms and through its fingertips. He'd seen death, too: a darkness so comforting, so seductive, so *full* that he'd tried to crawl inside. It tickled his ears and brushed the back of his neck, not in the simple, honest way that Mayung touched him, but more like the absentminded caress of a child's fingers.

Like the boy's.

His son's.

Michael.

His son.

He wept.

Julio and his helpers pushed Raymond's drunk body upright and leaned him against the wall to blow smoke on his crown, down his shirt, into his hands. He pressed the center of Raymond's heart.

There stood silence between them, weighted like warm sand. An absence of thought. An understanding that defied human language. Raymond bowed his head, humbled. The feeling had no name, but he may as well call it love.

It took two of Julio's men to help Raymond to his hut. He was limp, his feet, the roots of a wilted weed. They laid him in his hammock. Gently rocking, he longed for the velvet touch of death, but he imagined the boy's perfect skin and how his hands curled around Raymond's fingers when Mayung finally cast him into his arms, insisting that he hold his infant son.

First, he was too old to have a baby, then too old to care for a child. Now, he might be too old to watch his son, to watch Michael, graduate high school. Or college. Or to see him get married. He was hopefully too old to see his son die.

In the noisy stillness of the rain forest, Raymond listened again for the silence. He tried to hear himself blink. Life, he thought, was as seductive as death. He missed Mayung and the boy. He didn't need to know any more. He decided to go home.

In the morning, he packed his things. Julio's men carried his bag to the riverbank, where they waited to flag a dugout boat to take him to the port town. Raymond waited in his *tombo*. He sketched butterflies. Tried to find words that described their oily purples and blues.

Later, Julio would tell the group that Raymond had gone. That the medicine was not for him. That he'd lied about his medications. The journey was too harrowing for someone with his lackluster health. The group would solemnly nod and then easily forget him.

Aside from Ingrid, Raymond hoped. Pensive and wistful, weak

from the *dieta*, her skin smelling like flowers, her collarbone pushing against her skin. She'd pause at his hut when walking up the hill from the river to catch her breath. The butterflies would fly around but not through the *tombo*.

The thatch roof would've fallen in by then, the wooden platform warped by a sudden downpour. The hibiscus would be wilted, and the brush turned black, as if death had walked through.

On the slat bed, the strangest bug would stare at her, a grasshopper with striped legs and small feathers sprouting from its elbows. It would hop when she got close and then . . . float.

FORTY-SIX

Waiting to turn forty-six is like standing in the unrelenting sunshine. Everything green is wilted. Beauty is parched into nothingness.

Forty-six travels on the nose of a bee. It falls to the ground like the stinking fruit of a ginkgo tree. It sprouts legs and a tail and teeth. It snarls behind trash cans and car wheels, barely hidden from view. A feral cat. A stray dog. A cornered rat. Crooked teeth. Bloodshot eyes. Patchy fur and raw skin.

When Kate jogs, forty-six nips at her heels. Her lungs cramp as she loops the park. The walls of her heart buckle. She skips over maps of cracks and dried gum on the last leg of her run to the carousel. Leaning on her knees, she catches her breath. The painted horses, frozen in a fevered race, pull at their bits.

Forty-six grows bolder. When Kate cooks dinner, it drools, ravenous, under the kitchen table. It tears at the hem of her scrubs as she walks to the subway. When Brad kisses her goodbye and good morning and goodnight, its forty-six's copper penny breath she tastes.

On the flight back from New York, after dropping Pierre off at college in California for his first semester, forty-six drapes over her shoulders like a rotting mink stole. Like rigor mortis. Like death. Filling the holes Pierre's absence has created.

"What do you want to do for your birthday?" Brad asks.

Kate simply shakes her head 'no.'

"It happens to the best of us."

※

When Brad turned forty-six, Kate changed their diet. They cut down on red meat. They started going to yoga. When he slept, she listened for his breath. She held her cheek above his mouth and felt for the gentle breeze. When he was away on business or with friends, she waited for the phone to ring. Especially at times when it shouldn't.

"You know what else happens?" She stares out the window. The plane rides just above the clouds, a view, she's sure, humans were never meant to see. "Death. Divorce. Infidelity."

"You sound like your sister."

When Ingrid turned forty-six, eight years ago, Kate called her almost every day. She stopped by her apartment unannounced. If Ingrid didn't answer the door, Kate let herself in to make sure she hadn't suffered a stroke on her living room floor. She waited for the phone to ring. Especially at times when it shouldn't.

When her father turned forty-six, thirty-four years ago, he died while he was visiting his family. Twelve-year old Kate wasn't waiting for the phone to ring, but it did.

"You know what else happens," Brad says, "grandchildren."

"Not yet, please."

"The expansion of time. Inner peace. The sense of a life well lived. It's going to be okay."

"Promise?"

He nods. He looks tired. The flight attendant walks the aisle, her finger brushing the tips of the headrests, tapping each tilted seat. The pilot directs the crew to prepare for landing.

Brad frowns and closes his tray. Without looking, he reaches for Kate's hand. He always knows where it is. His knuckles are wider than they used to be. The hair on his forearm is flecked with white.

She doesn't remember much about her father, not his voice, nor his walk, nor the jokes he told, though she remembers he told them. She does remember his dark hair. Hers is the same color. He had a wave over his forehead that Pierre now has, though his hair is dirty blonde. Pierre has Brad's eyes, a crash of ocean blue. He has his father's height, his smile, and soon, when he grows into manhood, he'll have Brad's way in the world. He was born with a shock of black hair and an old man's features. For a few months, Kate wondered if she'd get to know her father through her son. But more and more it becomes clear that he is Brad's boy. Kind, shy, thoughtful. Uncomplicated.

For the party she doesn't want, they decorate the backyard of their Brooklyn home with streamers in discontinued Target colors—wine, mulberry, and iris. Brad mixes violet-infused cocktails garnished with brandied cherries. They serve banana pudding and empanadas on joyfully tacky children's party plates left over from a decade of Pierre's birthdays. For most of the gathering, Kate heats hors d'oeuvres in the kitchen and then loops the patio to clear plates. Ingrid, well on the other side of forty-six, has fallen into a joyful exuberance. Success, or age, or both have changed her. They've dulled her sharp edges. She's released her hawkish concern. She no longer reads the secret language of sisters. Kate's downward glances and forced smile and jagged shrugs go unnoticed. The last few years, Ingrid's turned her attention to her nephew Pierre, watching him chip through the eggshell of his youth. She took his hand and led him into his soft darkness and he brought her out, pulled her with two hands, and wouldn't let go. There are days when Kate is almost jealous of them. Because Pierre's not there and Ingrid has a flight in the morning, London, and she always leaves parties early anyway, she says goodbye an hour after she arrives. Kate walks Ingrid outside.

"I'll call when I'm back," Ingrid says.

God how Kate wishes she'd stay.

Three long blocks away, a train squeals to a stop. The sound bounces down the avenue to Kate's doorstep, chirping like the Japanese beetles that infested the lawns of her childhood every summer. Their carcasses, empty shells, piled up in the forks of the willow tree roots where Kate once held a funeral for her lucky rabbit's foot.

Kate says, "Okay."

Instead of returning to the party, Kate slips into Pierre's bedroom, climbs the ladder of his loft bed, and lays her head on his pillow. It's two weeks since he's left and she still hasn't washed the sheets. They smell like him. When he was a baby, the back of his ears smelled of sweet powder. The blonde hair that replaced his matte of black was so fine, she could barely feel it when she kissed the top of his head. He slept on Brad's chest, fat cheeks falling into the grace of gravity. Every mother carries her child one last time. An unmarked moment. A forgotten event. When was the last time he fell asleep with his head on her lap? When was the last time he ran into her belly and hugged her hips and cried over a wasp circling or a dog growling at him or missing a catch in the little league game? The last time she carried him drunk with sleep into the house? The last time she pushed him on a swing? She doesn't remember any of those moments and she wishes she did.

"I was looking for you." Brad leans in the doorway. "People are leaving."

"Here I am." She climbs down the ladder and brushes past him.

"They want to say goodbye."

"I'm saying goodbye."

Their backyard is mostly brick and dirt. Flowers and vegetables huddle in ports and beds along the perimeter already preparing for a retreat into fallow winter. When the last guest is gone, Brad holds open the rapacious mouth of a black garbage bag. Kate tosses in spent paper plates and plastic forks.

"I think people were happy," he says.

"I think so."

"Are you happy?"

She nods. Clears another plate. Pulls down a strip of streamers.

"I don't believe you." He sits on the bench by the picnic table.

The cats dig their claws into the screen door, one gray, one mittened black. Brad shrinks in the tired twilight. She traces her finger along his forehead, where his hair used to be before it receded, then the shadows of his creases and wrinkles.

The corners of his lips pull down. "I don't know how to make you happy anymore. Is it me? Are you unhappy with us?"

She sits on his lap and rests her head in the well of his neck. "God, no," she says. "It's the night shift." She's agreed to six weeks of night at the hospital, starting in the first hours of forty-six. Living at night, sleeping during the day. "It always throws me." How can she explain to Brad or Ingrid or anyone what living at night is like? The molasses of midnight? The dream day becomes? The ghost of her father, forever forty-six, humming in the corners? How can she explain how nothing at night is real, though it is truer than that which is blinded by the sun? How can she describe the naked truth of night?

His arms fold around her and they fit, just like that.

"I love you," he says. He's crying now.

She curls deeper into the bowl of his stomach, her ear pressed to the outside of his heart. Forty-six purrs from the firepit. Beyond the fence, the traffic sounds like waves, a cycle of lazy tide pulling sand to shore. "Are you drunk?"

"No." He rocks her in his lap. The cats sit behind the screen door, side by side, sisters, and watch.

Sleep is different during the day. Dreams are different, too. They're a confusion of waking life and morbid imagination. Stilted and paper-thin. They can't help but let the light in. She sweats beneath the covers, clammy and restless. She hears everything. The cats scratching litter. The mailman slipping mail into the mail box. The school bus brakes, children running down the street. Forty-six's drowsy sighs as it sleeps, one eye open, on the corner of the bed.

Toothpaste tastes different in the middle of the day. The artificial sweetness lingers through two cups of coffee. Jogging is harder. Forty-six stumbles along, tripping over its own feet. When Kate catches her breath at the curve of the carousel, forty-six wheezes. Sometimes she sits on a park bench and waits for the frozen, breathless horses to whinny and scream. Then, she and forty-six jog back home. For a few weeks, forty-six settles in and Kate almost forgets that it's there.

The night forty-six builds up the courage to bite, Kate rides the subway to work. Across from where she's sitting, a fifteen-year-old girl, maybe older, sucks her thumb. She leans into her mother. The two figures melt around each other; their flesh bulges—pockets of water separated by a thin fabric called skin. They sit still as sculptures aside from the girl's suckling cheeks and her mother's running nose. At the far end of the car, a homeless busker pounds a lifeless children's drum with pencil wrapped in packing tape. A man applies foundation, blue eye shadow, false eyelashes and mascara. By the end of the tunnel, he's become a she, slips off her work shoes and steps into platform pumps. A woman in a business suit huffs Sharpie markers, uncapping them one at a time from a box stolen from her office's supply cabinet. She drops the spent markers on the subway floor. Night is all these things. It's when people peel away their masks of conformity, peel away the lies, peel back their skin and grief and pain and allow their essence to emerge. Essence becomes presence. No more pretending.

As the subway car jostles on into the station, Kate thinks about a woman yesterday who gave birth to a dying baby during the hazy hours between night and morning. The child had doll's feet, clenched and frozen. Seizures marked his birth. The doctors forced his lips apart with their gloved hands, got him to breathe. The mother wailed and reached for the child, but they didn't give him to her. The regulators beeped, the child-sized pads for the monitors covered the infant's chest. The child screamed, the weak cry of being dragged back from the grasp of death into the painfully lit world of life. The falling faces of nurses and doctors, Kate's included, admitted that they knew the baby's breath would stop again, if not that night, then the next. The baby wouldn't make it more than a day or two in the world.

A crush of doctors, administrators, social workers descended into the room to beg the mother for the baby's organs. At their hospital, a baby is waiting for a heart. In Denver, another needs a liver. Somewhere in New Mexico, a newborn is hooked up to dialysis. A baby born with damaged eyes in Utah could see. There's more good news than bad in the maternity ward, but Kate is used to death. They all are. Maybe they've become numb to the searing pain of other people's loss. Even the social worker's nasal voice and the bend in his spine, his sugary smile and reflexive sighs seem milky and fake.

As Kate walks past the bodega by the hospital, she remembers the shadows in the room, the baby's father and the mother's mother. The doctors promised them they'd try to keep the baby alive and also promised that he'd die. They gave the mother an hour, as if an hour with a dying newborn is a gift to be given, to decide. Papers needed to be signed. Hospitals alerted. Transport of the baby's precious organs arranged.

While Kate sleeps at home the following afternoon, forty-six nestled like a pup in her hollowed stomach, the baby is whisked to surgery. There, bereft of his vital organs, he dies.

By the time Kate jogs to and from the carousel the next afternoon, the mourning mother has checked out of the hospital, her belly still swollen with memory of birth.

While she drinks coffee, showers, and dresses for her shift, the mourning mother lies in her own bed and tries to sleep.

Working third shift is like living in someone else's dream.

She'll soon lose night forever. She'll watch it slip away. She'll feel her skin being stitched to the daylight, to asphalt and concrete, to the raging painted horses at the carousel. There's only so far day will let some people wander.

*

Sounds of the hospital at night: fluorescents hum like wasps, the orderly's cart confesses its sticking wheel, the machines gossip, sleep murmurs, televisions whisper, sometimes outside a siren whines. The night orderlies have permanent purple circles around their eyes. And the lips of the physician assistants are always cracked. The night shift cleaner, a benevolent giant, rides his floor polisher while chewing the cap of a ballpoint pen. Rebecca, the nighttime Natal ICU nurse, has button lips, wide-set eyes, a heartshaped face with a narrow chin. Her knees barely bend when she walks and her fingers are knotted lengths of twine. There are reasons she prefers the company of the tented, sleeping babies of the NICU.

All the while, new mothers fall into dreamless sleep; newborns straddle two worlds. They suck at the air and discover their hands, their feet, their muzzled limbs. In the NICU, the smallest ones, the dark horses, born sick, decide whether to stay or return home. Their mothers, if they're still in the hospital, weep, their sobs tamed by tiredness.

Dr. Evans is also on nights. He fades under the strain of trading day for evening. The thinning circle on the top of his head reflects stripes of the overhead lights and his lashes brush his glass frames. He is a daisy of a person, plainness personified in its most striking form. He's why she agreed to work nights, too.

The coffee in the cafeteria comes in paper cups with playing cards printed on the sides and bottom. Kate drinks from the Jack of Spades. The Queen of Hearts lurks below. Dr. Evans has the Nine of Hearts, two rows of red kisses separated by a single, lonely kiss. There are a few others, pairs at round tables, hiding behind plastic flowers in glass vases. They are the relatives of the ill and dying, hospital employees ragged from lack of sleep, or, sometimes, a drunk who's wandered in to sober up, all characters in the dream. Dr. Evans bites the rim of the cup. He's stuck in last night's dream when one mother wept with sorrow and another with joy because her baby would get the heart it needed to live.

"I held his little heart in my hand." He turns his cupped palm over and stares into it, as if he's still holding the baby's heart. "A beating walnut. It was that small." His eyes well with tears, magnified by his thick glasses. Kate feels like she can feel it, too, the bud of a flower, the seed of a soul. The fragile beauty of a spider web that holds everything to the beating heart. "I was so tired. I am so tired. But I can't sleep." He rubs his eyes, then the stubble on his chin. "I'll never be the same."

Over space, over time, she wonders what Pierre is doing. If, in his sleep, he feels the draw of his connection to her and to her father who exists and doesn't, who lives and die and lives and dies over and over again, etched in the fragile glass of memory. She searches for Ingrid, too, all the way in London. And Brad. He's always last in her thoughts, but he's always there. She looks at Dr. Evan's hand, palm open on the table, and for a flash imagines what life would've been like with someone else. How easy it is to destroy a good thing with one bad decision. Brad needs her, she thinks. You'd never know it from how he walks in the world, the confidence he exudes, his good looks. He's hardly had a bad thing happen to him. He's the most fragile of them all.

"Life is crazy," Dr. Evans says. "You know?"

If forty-six claims her, she decides she'll haunt Pierre like her father haunts her.

Thinking back on the moment, she did see the father of the dead baby in the cafeteria. He didn't stand out among the sunken faces and shadows. How was she supposed to recognize one face amongst the blur? Faces blend together. Chins bow. Stubble softens hard angles. Eyes recede. She was deep in conversation. She was on break.

Kate wanders the rows of babies in the NICU sleeping in tents and incubators. The premature are at one end, vulnerable to everything including their mother's touch. At the far end are the growing survivors, almost ready to go home. Webs of wire and tubes of oxygen are taped to the babies' faces and bodies. Fighting for their lives before they even know what living is. The baby with her new heart is among them, swaddled in a pink blanket that protects her bandaged chest. She rests in a foam nest, held firm, unable to turn or fuss. Kate reads her chart. Chloe. Chloe's lips suckle the air. She's dreaming. Kate wants to see the scar.

What if Pierre had been among the struggling babies? What if he'd been born sick? What if he'd died? Who would she be having never known him? She calls to mind the feel of his new skin the first time they touched. He flattened onto her chest and latched on and learned to breathe all at once. His crown radiated warmth and smelled like light. The first time she picked him up she knew she'd never drop him. She misses her son. Misses waiting for him to reveal the secrets of her father. Misses wondering if, when his voice finally settles, she'll hear her father speak again.

Maybe there was a sound, a rustle. A whoosh against the chirps of the monitors. The scuffle of her soft soled shoes. The beat of a boot. His eyes are bloodshot. His hair, tangled. His breath smells like burning plastic. In the light, with her tired eyes, she mistakes him for forty-six, reared on its hind legs, grown into the size of a man. She recedes between the rows of babies.

"I'm here for my son." His voice is tender and low, like a lullaby. He's drunk. He steps deeper into the NICU, past the first sleeping baby, three months premature, the size of a man's hand. "My son."

She doesn't trust what she's heard and points past him, towards the hallway and the hospital pharmacy, but he bounds forward and grabs Kate by her ponytail. Her hands reach back to stave off the pain. "I want what's left of my son."

Her neck twist, her hands shoved beneath his, she remembers his dog eyes, his stained flannel shirt, how he hid his head in his hands the night before. He shoves her and she stumbles, nearly upsetting an incubator. She sees the glint of a gun. No need to point it. Its presence is threat enough.

"Which one has him?"

"He's in the morgue." She tries to pull against him. There's no give.

"His heart is here. I want it. It's mine."

"I don't know."

He pushes her further inside. She pulls up a chart. The letters jumble. She can't read. She drops it, moves to the next bed, the next chart. Her hands shake. Her eyes focus on the names on printed cards outside the cribs, stickers of stars and teddy bears on the corners.

Now he raises the gun. Now he clicks off the safety. Now he points it at her. If she can find one, one she knows will not survive—won't make it through the night—but they surprise you. The weakest become strong. The strongest sometimes fade. And only one has stitches across her chest. Kate's knees give.

"You're not even looking," he yells. He cracks the butt of his pistol across her cheek.

Her hands reflexively cradle her face. It burns, but it doesn't yet hurt. She sees Brad sitting across from her at the kitchen counter, his look of surrender as she says goodbye. She feels the fading heat of coffee through cheap paper cups and the heaviness of the blanket on Pierre's unmade bed. She hears herself breathe. The air becomes oil. Chloe gurgles in her sleep and Kate doesn't know who to betray.

"I'll kill all of them if I have to." He waves his pistol over a sleeping child.

"I miss him."

"I want my fucking heart."

Rebecca walks by the window of the NICU. Her mouth drops when Kate catches her eye. He notices. He turns. He shoots towards the wide window. The glass shatters. Kate hurls herself, all ninety-eight pounds, into his back. He stumbles. His elbow catches her cheek. He throws her to the floor.

A few years ago, she tells the interviewing police officer, during Christmas, she was walking down Broadway to meet her sister for coffee. A man a block away was running through the crowd towards her. She stepped aside. He changed course, plowed into her and knocked her to the ground. She scrambled for her purse. He leapt over her and ran. The thing that impressed Kate most was that she hadn't had the chance to finish her thought before she felt the sting of the sidewalk. She managed to walk ten blocks and only discovered she'd been crying the whole way when Ingrid jumped up from the table at the café and folded her in her arms.

The bullet is the same way. He turns towards her, a gray metal barrel at the end of his reach. Before she can finish her thought, there's a blinding burst of noise and her shoulder is locked to the ground. Her head throbs. Her neck aches. The warmth of her blood is serene as it spreads. Her body curls into a fetal position, her good arm wrapped around her head. She hears sobbing, but doesn't know where the sobbing is coming from. Later, she realizes it's her. Running footsteps, too many of them, and the bruised blue of a police uniform, pass through the low hum of screaming voices. She blacks out, into a dreamless sleep.

There was nothing brave about it. There are no heroes. As far as she knows, she hasn't saved any lives. And it isn't lucky that she's only been shot in the shoulder. Luck would've been none of it happening. Luck would've been one baby born healthy and the other baby born the same. Luck would've been any number of happy endings.

Even so, when she finally wakes from surgery, Pierre's by her side. Ingrid sits cross-legged in a chair at the foot of the bed. Brad paces the hallway. Her shoulder hurts. Everything hurts. And she feels lucky.

"Dad. Dad. Dad. She's awake."

Kate's groggy and stiff. The contusions on her cheeks smart. Her lips are dry and she's thirsty as hell. The shades are open. She doesn't know what time it is, but she knows it's day.

I KNOW YOU LOVE ME, TOO

It'd been a year since Kate was shot, the muscles of her shoulder torn through. Though a nerve in her arm had been stretched from surgery, slightly beyond repair, Kate seemed fine. Happy, even. Relieved of the pressures of perfection. On the year of her convalescence, she painted the rooms in her house. She bought new furniture. Took up cooking Indian food. Brad bought her a piano. She learned to chop, write, and cut paper with her left hand, all with a giddy joy.

Watching her made Ingrid apprehensive. Her back froze. Her paintings took on hues of darkness she didn't understand. None sold the year after the shooting. For the first time in years, Ingrid applied for retail jobs. There'd been headaches. Pinches in her abdomen. The removal of abnormalities. Where Kate's scars were sloppy stars that had risen and fallen and hardened into aching pink, Ingrid's were divots of a laparoscopic invasion. When in thought, Kate's ran the fingers of her left hand along the ridges and bumps of her scars. Ingrid did her best to avoid hers, those little points of poison. She pulled away when Adam brushed against them in bed. The surgery left Kate's right hand weaker than the left, unable to learn new tasks, but it remembered all it had previously known. Ingrid's hand bore the subtle brunt, a dull throb on numbness. She forgot how to mix her paints. She forgot how to paint.

It was a common occurrence, the shaman said, as common as stubbing a toe. As common as cutting oneself with a kitchen knife while slicing tomatoes. As common as doubling over from the pain of tapping your funny bone. Souls signed contracts. One person's pain was taken on by another, kept holy and safe until owner of the trauma was ready to take it back.

The shaman wore blue jeans and a button-down shirt. Her hair fell past her waist. Ingrid sat cross legged on a woven tapestry. The shaman laid a feather between them. *Hawk? Eagle? Owl?* Ingrid didn't ask. She wanted to touch it, to run it through her fisted hand. Angled, rugged vanes, pointed and brittle spine. Outside, on 28th Street, plants lined the sidewalk from the subway to the beat down building door. Ficas and office palms, dwarfed and braided trees in plastic pots formed a low canopy and dripped with the city's version of dew. Wild dandelions flourished in the cracks of the sidewalks in the flower district. Potted plants wistfully sent their roots downward, wishing to be a part of the earth.

"How long does it usually last—this transference of pain?"

The shaman shrugged. "Depends on the contract. Depends on the souls. Depends on the need."

Ingrid sighed and laid back on the carpet, hands resting on her belly, eyes on the flimsy panels of the drop ceiling. The shaman brushed strands of hair from Ingrid's cheek and dropped a dot of oil, sweet scent, on her forehead.

"Depends how long it takes for the lessons to be learned."

"We're not even that close." Ingrid closed her eyes.

"You're closer than you think."

Kate called while Ingrid was with the shaman. She left a message on Ingrid's phone. Ingrid listened to it in her studio, hand on brick, looking out the window at Riker's Island and cloudy blue of the river, the low sky. She locked a canvas in an easel, butt up against the wall. She chose a big one and swept gesso in broad strokes across its cover, white on white, white on her jeans. White on the bird tattoo on the inside of her forearm. A wash of white. The maps she'd drawn no longer led towards home. With a dull pencil, she etched two squares, corners barely touching into the wet paint. *Who are souls to one another? How do they speak? Are souls formless? Can a formless thing shatter?*

The telephone message:
    I'm cleared to go back to work.
    Brad thinks I should take a trip.
    I need this.
    Please come.
    That's how Iceland happened.

Brad paid for everything. Hotels, airfare, the cab to JFK. Coffees and water as they waited for their flight. He paid for the car rental. After a moment's panic, Ingrid in the passenger seat, the GPS cradled in her lap, Kate taught herself to drive stick shift in the Keflavik airport parking lot. Ingrid neatened the stack of tourist brochures Kate tossed on her lap as Kate's weaker hand grappled with the gear stick and the car lurched and stalled. Ingrid sat silent as Kate cackled with flat laughter. Two souls trapped in a red Subaru, tethered to each other, knotted souls, a chain dropped into the corner of a jewelry box. The grinding gears called forth a future stagnant and still. Kate shifted back to neutral and forced a smile.

"I'll get this beast on the road."

"Okay."

Nodding towards the GPS, Kate said, "Plug that sucker in."

Ingrid's arm throbbed for no reason, her heart punched her chest. But Kate . . . she was always fine.

They drove on the Ring Road, out of the city. Through golden fields and into mountains. There were hairline scars where lava had suddenly stopped its flow. One side of the road bulbous with rounded rocks, the creep of green moss made the hard lava seem soft, on the other side, grass—a mix of gold and green. It was misty and the road, wet. They drove through a sprinkling of rain and then a swathe of sunlight. Past water and through clouds that kissed the horizon. The GPS was quiet most of the ride. Kate and Ingrid were mostly quiet as well. There were no other cars.

"You've never driven stick before?"

"Once. One summer in college. My friend taught me on her Karman Ghia. Her father died that summer." Kate stretched her right hand opened and closed, rest her right wrist on the edge of the steering wheel. Kate's lips pursed, eyes forward, hands gripping the wheel, the road endless before them. "Look through those brochures. Tell me what you want to do."

"I thought Brad planned everything."

"He's paying. It's our trip."

"I don't care," Ingrid said. "Whatever you want."

"You never do. Care. Much."

Outside, a heard of small horses beyond a wire fence stared at the car. Each and every one of them looking up from their grazing to watch it pass by.

Ingrid tried to count the times she'd seen Kate cry. As kids—there was the time she skinned her knee roller skating and Ingrid carried her home. The time a boy kicked a rock in her face and gave her a black eye. She didn't cry at their father's funeral. Neither did Ingrid. They'd done that before and after, in private. She'd cried on 9/11. Everyone had. Ingrid cried on the plane ride back to New York when all she knew was that Kate'd been shot. Did Kate cry over it. Maybe. Ingrid didn't know. Maybe Ingrid had cried for her.

Why don't you cry?

Even thinking of tears burned Ingrid's eyes. She closed them until the moment passed. *I'll come back for you later,* she promised, *when I'm finally alone.*

Hedda was a friend of a friend of a gallery owner Ingrid knew. She ran a bed and breakfast outside of Akureyi. They'd stay the night in the field in a covered flatbed truck she'd converted into a small bedroom. When they arrived, she showed them her studio. She knew how to trap smoke in glass. Shelves of jars, bell jars and bulbous enclosures, jelly jars, old peanut butter jars, test tubes and beakers held the moving and ethereal, fragile and formless movement.

"Is it real?" Kate bent towards a rounded glass urn, the upward journey of its neck, a blue marble connected the urn's stem to its body.

"Everything's real," Hedda said. Her hair choppy and short, dyed red. Spikes of bangs against her worried forehead.

Ingrid leaned in, examined the sculptures at the back of the studio, her hands tucked safely in her pockets. She had the urge to leave fingerprints on the spotless glass, to scar the ethereal bodies with evidence of sloppy humanity. It wasn't really smoke in the jars, she saw. It was the illusion of smoke. The eyes and the mind created creating movement where there was none. Frozen souls. Trapped souls. *I want my soul back. Intact.* Ingrid's neck tightened. Kate laughed. Hedda nodded. They could be mistaken for lovers, Ingrid thought, but then Kate's left hand shot up and under her collar, to the scars on her right shoulder and a coldness and a strength overtook her. That's what Ingrid saw, anyway.

Hedda turned. "We could teach her to drive in my field."

"I'm good," Ingrid said. "Don't need a car in the city."

"Still. A good skill to have."

"Ingrid's only willing to go so far," Kate said. "She likes being a little outside of life. On the fringe."

A beat-up pickup truck kicked up dirt as it rolled up the drive.

"My husband. You'll join us for dinner."

"Of course," Kate said. "Can I help you in the kitchen?"

"Do you mind," Ingrid said, "I'd like to take a walk."

They split company at the barn door. Hedda and Kate went inside the house, Ingrid, into the field.

*

The shaman had searched for fragments of Ingrid's soul and found them on the shore of a rocky beach. Shards of it were lodged between stones at the edge of a shore. Broken, bloated and heavy with salt water, unable to find their way home. She showed them the way.

"Have you ever almost drowned?"

"No."

"Maybe you were pulled under? An undertow?"

Ingrid knew the rocky beaches of New England. The brackish water. Balancing on jags of rock to reach the sand bar at low tide. The jetty, crooked and wet, wood fading into water.

"Of course I lost my balance. I cut myself on barnacles. There were sunburns, too. The rocks were covered in algae. So slick and slippery. I'm sure."

"Something happened. A shift of paradigm. You learned you were no longer safe or immune to pain."

Walking back to the subway, through the canopy of office plants, past the wig stores on Sixth Avenue, she thought back to days at the beach. She looked for her father in those memories. He wasn't there. She looked for her mother, too. The only one she imagined on the beach with her, in the water, balancing on rock, was Kate. Kate playing *hide*. Ingrid never *seeking*. Kate throwing herself against Ingrid, yelling, howl-like laughter covering her frustration. Ingrid was eleven, twelve, thirteen and Kate, four, five, six years old. Did she once attack Ingrid in the water? Fling herself at Ingrid's legs with all her weight? Did Ingrid once fall? Did she turn her ankle and limp across the sand? Perhaps, perhaps, and perhaps.

"I met the weeping soul of your mother. I carried it to more fertile ground." The shaman sat back, hands folded in her lap.

"And my father?"

The shaman shook her head. "No. I didn't see him at all."

∗

She should've asked the shaman if the soul of an artist looked different than the soul of a nurse. Or what a soul even looked like. Could one soul be mistaken for another? Did they bear a family resemblance? Were the families of souls different than the families of humans? And where did missing pieces of a soul travel too? How far could a piece go before gravity tugged at the edges? And what happened when you found it? And what happened if the shard had been softened and rounded by gravity and force? If it no longer fit into its mother. Was there a cosmic surgical glue or suture to stitch it back into place? Would it leave the faintest line of a scar?

The only witnesses to the shooting were twenty-two ailing babies in the NICU, most of whom were sleeping until the scream, the percussive beat of the bullets, the flash of people, security guards, doctors, nurses, orderlies, storming the room. At which point they woke and added to the chaos, a chorus of crying. That's how Ingrid imagined it, anyway. She imagined the gunman, lean and tall, all legs and arms, a smoking gun backlit in the doorway, frozen by his own temerity. She imagined Kate on the floor, curled into the fetal position, her scrubs wicking blood, knees pressed into her chest. Shaking from shock. Ingrid couldn't help it - imagining herself into the moment. Watching, then kneeling, then curled around Kate, whispering the parts of prayers she'd learned in Sunday school—the bits she could recall.

Of the babies who were there, none would remember Kate or that night. Many would never know. None would be able to pinpoint the crash of violence and love they'd been born into, save for one who will insist that she remembers that night in a hazy, dreamlike, underwater way. She'll grow up hearing bits of the story during litanies of details spilled at doctors visits, of praise and sad glances and finally through following up on her strange dreams.

Ingrid saw her. She sought the baby out through the window at the NICU, counted down the row. Traded the memory of holding newborn Pierre in her arms for the mirage of holding the child, a fine raised line over a heart that would grow with her, a heart given to her. A heart that was not originally her own. Ingrid wondered if one day that baby would grow up to ask: *Where is my broken heart? Where did it go? With what other body parts from what other people? With what other stories and how many other lives? How many souls?* She'll want to know: *how much of me is him? And who are we?*

Ingrid wandered away from the trucks and vans that'd been converted into guest rooms. Away from the barn and the house and the jars of smoke. Away from Kate and the Hedda and the mountains. She waked through tall grass and onto a gravel path and found a stream. A duck lay on its side. Perfectly still. Perfectly dead. In avoiding it, she stepped off the path, and rolled her ankle. Her hands caught her fall, but there it was, her volatile soul possibly slipping away—shattered upon impact. If she could see where the pieces had gone, she'd crawl through the grass to collect them. She'd hold the broken pieces in the palm of her hand but she wouldn't know how to piece them back together. She didn't know how to paint. She didn't know how to drive. She didn't know how to love the people she was supposed to love. She sat beneath the stubborn sun, the heavy clouds, the far shadows of the mountain. The ghosts of memory in her muscles. Not only hers, but her mother's and grandmother's, and great grandmother's and grandfather's, and her father's. And she cried—not because of them, but for them. She let them cry through her until the sun finally winked and color of blood beneath skin faded. She limped back to the house.

The ache in her ankle subsided by the time Ingrid reached the kitchen door. She knocked. Kate answered, a napkin wrapped around her bad hand. Spots of blood.

"Cut it cutting carrots." She pulled the weave of the napkin tighter. "I was showing Hedda how well I slice with my left hand."

"We'll wrap it in gauze after it breathes a bit longer," Hedda called from the kitchen. Kate led Ingrid into the house.

Later in the bed of the truck, beneath the heavy blankets and comforter, Kate crawled onto her stomach and watched the mountains through the back window of the truck shell.

"Do you remember the ocean? When we kayaked?"

"Yeah. I guess."

"You were so angry."

"I wasn't."

"Yeah. You were."

"No. I wasn't."

"Okay." Kate laid back under the covers. She slept on her side, her good arm wrapped around her bad, her good hand resting lightly on the opposite shoulder. Ingrid couldn't sleep and slipped out from under the blankets, down to the edge mattress where she found her shoes and coat. She opened the back of the truck bed and stepped into the twilit field.

Though the stars were shy, the moon shone, defiant. A bright crescent hugged its darker half. Its light rivaled the softness of the sun. The tips of the tall grass were golden and reminded Ingrid of the bioluminescence she'd seen in a bay off the ocean, her hand stirring the light, the light following her hand. She brushed the tops of the grass as she walked further into the field.

She'd been at a dinner meeting in London when Brad left a message that Kate'd been shot, details unknown, his voice a forced calm. But even the message she'd felt a dizziness and a tightness in her heart. Pressure behind her eyes. A fragile panic. Which is why she slipped away from the table and checked her phone messages in the restaurant.

"We don't know yet. But she'll be fine," Brad said in an unconvincing way. "She's always fine." His voice broke. "Pierre's on his way home."

Ingrid returned to the dinner table pale and precariously

balanced on a tipping point, the moment before falling. Adam stood up, alarmed by the changes that phone message had wrought.

"I have to go," she said. Adam had embraced her before she even told him the news. Rafael laid down his fork and stared. "I'll call you later," she whispered in Adams ear. She left the restaurant and hailed a cab outside a fancy watch shop, its windows done up for Easter. The not knowing pulled her through London, through Heathrow, through the air, and to Kate's hospital bedside. Later, Ingrid would remember that there was no question, not even a moment of hesitation, no choice. In the hours of transit: visions of her sister, a spreading pool of blood, and Ingrid pressing her hand into Kate's wounds, curling around her, calling for help. She inserted herself into a false memory; a weave of roots knotted them together. The agreement, the dreams, the transference of pain.

All the dreams she used to have of her father gave way. Darkness replaced them. Simple darkness. Rich darkness. Darkness as the absence and presence of things she could not understand.

They drove east, Kate's wrapped right hand gingerly maneuvering the gear stick. Rain sprayed the windshield and the road peeled forward, empty aside from them.

"Good thing there's no traffic," was all Kate said for a while.

Ingrid switched on the radio and they listened to static, mostly, as she searched for music. Kate kept her eyes on the road.

They drove past the lava fields, some black, some softened by moss, the violence reclaimed. There were places where a line had been drawn, where the lava stopped and the grass grew and the miniature forests, trees an inch tall. A microcosm of the forests that'd been decimated by the Vikings and never grew back.

"Hedda told me that the landscape in her hometown changed in her lifetime. The pond moved a mile east and the mountain cracked up. They built greenhouses over the steam plumes. Weird living in a place that changes so drastically."

"New York changes. Everything changes."

"But not in ways you can see. Not with such immediacy. You don't see the scars."

Rain soaked through Ingrid's sweater as they ran from the car to a hotel that sat on the hill, huge windows facing the northern mountains. Ingrid shivered over coffee. Kate, unscathed, pulled her hat over her ears.

"Let's buy sweaters before the ice cave," she said.

"I'm not going to buy a sweater," Ingrid stated. She didn't understand her own stubbornness.

"Brad's buying it."

"I don't want Brad to buy me a sweater."

"I'll buy it then." Kate's hand found her scars.

"No."

"Fine," Kate said, with a withering voice.

Ingrid surrendered. Kate won.

The sweaters at shop set up in the shadow of a church. A white-haired woman, rugged and strong-jawed, barely looked up from her knitting as Kate plowed through the piles of sweaters, searching for the most garish she could find, burnt orange, white collar, yarn so thick that the sweater stood on its own.

"You look like a piece of candy," Ingrid said. She'd chosen grey.

"I know! Now I can go anywhere." Her cut hand reached for her scars. Then she said, "I guess it'll be good. Going back to work."

"I think so."

"I mean, what else am I going do?" She dropped her left hand and looked at the bandage, the edges of the tape curling away from her skin. "Right?"

The van picked them up outside the church, the tour guide, charmingly gruff, flirtatious. He joked as the van lurched over the pitted lava field, black on black, a desert of bulbous stone.

"Look out for trolls," the tour guide said.

"I think I saw one!" Kate gleefully pressed her hands against the van windows.

A little girl in the front seat looked back. "I saw one, too."

In the blue light, Kate's eyes were crossed with fine wrinkles. Uneven blotches of pink on her cheek, her nostrils glowing red with cold even though the van was warm. Rarely had Ingrid seen her sister in morning light, this close up, this early in the day. Rarely had she looked at her for this long.

The groups crawled into the tight chamber on their bellies, the walls and floor tiny teeth bit at the knit of Ingrid's new sweater. There was a tourist behind her and one in front and the floor of the cave seemed farther than it was. The tour guide told her to slide down head first. He held out his arms to catch her, to guide her to the ground.

"I can't do this," Ingrid whispered to herself, but the sound echoed in the cave and Kate smiled brightly, her teeth the thing that Ingrid saw most vividly.

"You can," Kate called from the cave's floor.

Ingrid let go and slid into the cave and crawled to the cave wall and helped herself up. The light from her headlamp illuminated shadows and wrinkles folded into the rock as the tour guide led them across a slick of ice, and then down, down, down.

In the ice cave, with spikes and spirals reaching from cave ceiling to its floor.

"Like the Hedda's sculpture," Kate said, one gloved hand to the ice.

The little girl asked, "Does it drip down, or up?"

They entered a chamber where the ice had formed ledges and the group was invited to sit, or stand, whichever they preferred. They turned off their headlamps until the tour guide's was the only one encased in ghostly light. He looked each tourist in the eyes, and then nodded, his hand slowly, dramatically, reaching towards his own headlamp. He switched his light off.

Ingrid breathed in the overwhelming darkness, listened to the sound of blood spinning through veins and the drips of ice turning back into water. It was as dark when eyes were opens as it was when they were shut. The same darkness encased her insides, her heart, and maybe her soul. Lungs, brain, bones, the body a perfect puzzle.

It was the same darkness Kate saw. It had to be.

In the space between breaths, a moment of grace swelled and softened. She listened for Kate, and realized she didn't know where she was. Or if she existed in the darkness, or if, bereft of light, both of them ceased to exist, stripped down to their very essence. Two souls stitched together with black thread. A suture, the slightest scar, a fault line between them. A rough embrace, an apologetic bow, the jockeying for position, crying quietly, crying privately, crying from the force of their collision.

She heard: the rustle of a windbreaker; a cough; a sigh. Then a moan. A sob. The freedom to rip open a wound. Silent tears streamed down Ingrid's own face. She'd been crying, too.

They reached Husavik around six, a seaside town buffeted by mountains, lakes, the ocean. The steeple of a white church cut the green of the landscape and they walked the town in the spitting rain. Gulls and crows screamed at one another.

"They say that crows the most intelligent bird," Kate said. "But—intelligent compared to what? Seems stupid to compare animals to humans." She kicked a rock. The birds scattered.

"Do you think dad would've liked this?" Ingrid paused by a pair of Santa boots bolted to the sidewalk. A post office box with North Pole Only painted in white script on the front.

"Don't know." Kate paused for a minute. "I don't even know if I remember my memories of him."

"My mom gave me a DVD of old family films. I didn't recognize his voice. I thought, at least, I'd remember the sound of his voice."

They turned down and alley. Kate stopped. "Say that again."

"What."

She closed her eyes. "The thing you just said."

"I thought, at least I'd remember the sound of his voice. What are you doing?"

"Trying to memorize yours."

In the morning, they waited in line on the docks with the other tourists, the collars of their tourist sweater, thick wool, peaking from under their windbreakers. It was warmer on the coast and Kate pulled off her hat. In the overcast morning light, Ingrid saw for the first time, strands of gray in Kate's walnut hair. Around the ears, across her part. An hour later, they boarded the boar. From the deck, the water looked choppy. The smell of diesel, the gentle rock of the ship. Ingrid grabbed the railing as they pulled out of the mooring and sped into the endless ocean.

"You okay? " Kate yelled over the noise of the engine, the breaking water, the chatter of the captain over the speakers. Where the boat cut the water, it churned a frothy white. Blue water tapped the edge of the boat. It looked like breaking glass.

Ingrid nodded.

"You always are," Kate said. Or at least Ingrid thought that was what she said. She stood for a moment, staring at Ingrid, as if expecting something. Ingrid wiped her nose, dripping from wind. She said something else, but Ingrid couldn't hear.

Kate turned away and pushed herself through the crowd.

The boat drove into the ocean. Blue. White. Gray. In the far distance, rain clouds let loose. Water color strokes of rain. Way, way off was a glacier, edges softened by the distance. Soon, the engine cut and the boat bobbed gently and the passengers stood silent, tracking the water for movement.

Ingrid searched the crowd.

Someone yelled, "I see one," but it was only a wave. Everyone held their breath.

Ingrid looked towards the ocean, then back through the crowd.

She didn't want to miss the whale. She didn't want to miss watching her sister see the whale. She stood at an angle, flanked by strangers and waited.

Finally, Kate elbowed through the swollen crowd, her bad arm stitched to her side. Ingrid had a flash of an image, a memory she couldn't place, the two of them diving off the far end of the jetty, dripping with seaweed in the brackish New England Sound. Maybe they were even holding hands. pretending that they were ever bit of the water and the water was every bit of them. Two bodies separated by skin.

Ingrid waved and reached for Kate. She made room at the railing. Kate pressed against Ingrid.

"If I could stay here forever, I would," Kate said.

"You like it that much?"

"No."

Ingrid hesitated to speak. The things she knew had no language. She settled for the most honest words she could find, an act of bravery. "I don't know what I'm supposed to say."

"It's like a beautiful nowhere. Like maybe we don't really exist." Kate's gaze flickered towards Ingrid, then to back to the water. "I'm scared."

Ingrid answered, "I am, too."

Someone yelled "Blowhole, nine o'clock" and the crowd rushed that side of the boat.

Out in the ocean, water spouted. A flock of gulls cut low across the horizon. Kate's injured arm forgot itself and pointed, her good hand rested on her scars. Ingrid couldn't hear Kate's wonder, didn't dare look away from the water, but she already knew what it sounded like. Vulnerability wrapped in exquisite pleasure. They breathed in. They breathed out.

Then the whale was upon them.

It was bigger than anything Ingrid had ever seen.

She wept for the beauty of it.

ACKNOWLEDGMENTS

I'm deeply thankful for all the characters who have supported this endeavor, from vague idea to the first sentences to the last scrub through, with thoughtful feedback and question . . . There are so many people who've contributed to this project.

I owe a particular debt of gratitude to Kelly Dalke for her good notes and close reads and beers and story-talk through many late evenings. I also am deeply thankful to Tom Paine for seeing a larger story in my work and teasing it out. Joslin Williams gave the best, most specific notes, which helped me fill in worlds with words of authenticity. Special thanks to Mekeel McBride and Christina Ortmeier-Hooper who were the first readers of my earliest draft. And many thanks to my University of New Hampshire cohort, including, but not limited to: Beth Ann Miller, Kaely Horton, Emily Pavick, Brittany Smith, Shannon Slocum, Mike Bjork, and Alexandra Grimm.

I'm especially grateful to Patricia O'Donnell for her close reads and cheerleading and Pat and Jeff Thomson for the gig at University of Maine, Farmington where I was gifted stability, time, and support to finish the collection.

I also want to thank those friends and family who unwittingly gave me fodder for these stories. Mark Lotito, for saving a little bird, and Mary and Curtis Rutherford for saving me in one of my darkest moments. Andrew Garman for his apple trees on the roof, Dan Rogers for his sideways-growing beard, my father for leaving me with the biggest mysteries to unravel and questions to confront, and to the backstage doormen and artists of the Broadway theater who taught me how to tell stories by sharing their own.

There's a deep well of gratitude to David Bowen and Judith Claire Mitchell for pulling my stories from a pile of brilliant pages by brilliant writers and seeing some magic in them. And to New American Press for making those pages into a book.

And lastly, of course, my sisters. Without them, I wouldn't know what the complex, nuanced, and strange word *sister* means.

AMY NESWALD is a fiction writer and screenwriter. Her work has appeared in *The Rumpus*, *The Normal School*, *Bat City Review*, and *Green Mountain Review*, among others. She is recent recipient of the New American Fiction prize with her debut novel-in-stories *I Know You Love Me, Too,* will be released in the autumn of 2021. Her screenplay *The Placeholder* was awarded a Best Screenplay award at the Rhode Island Film Festival in 2008. When she is not writing, she teaches creative writing at the University of Maine in Farmington and continues plugging away at her animated short films about monster children.

CPSIA information can be obtained
at www.ICGtesting.com
Printed in the USA
LVHW041336170623
750060LV00002B/266